FIERCE QUEEN

LA RUTHLESS: BOOK 2

SADIE KINCAID

RED HOUSE PRESS

For every single reader who has made my dreams come true!
Love Sadie x

LA RUTHLESS

Fierce Queen is a Dark Mafia, forced marriage romance that deals with mature themes which may be triggering for some.

It is Book 2 in the LA Ruthless Series, featuring Alejandro and Alana Montoya and follows on directly from Book 1 which should be read first.

Click here to read Fierce King or visit Amazon.com

CHAPTER 1

ALANA

$\mathcal{M}$y pulse throbbed in my temples as I stood there with my mouth half open, staring at my husband. I had no idea what the hell was going on here. Alejandro Montoya was the King of LA, and I was supposed to be his queen. I was the woman he was supposed to share everything with, even his secrets. So, what the hell was I missing here? Why had he taken such an aversion to a pregnant sixteen year old girl?

I had first met Lucy Gallagher a few months earlier at the women's shelter I worked at. She had lied about her age to the shelter manager to get herself a bed. But when the truth had eventually come out, she had been taken into the care of the authorities. I had been the one Lucy had confided in and I've felt a sense of responsibility toward her since. Alejandro had asked his lawyer to work on the case and they had assured me that Lucy would be placed with a good, caring family. But now, she had turned up at our house — late at night and in obvious distress. So why was my husband turning her away?

'What is it?' I asked him. 'Why won't you let Lucy in here?'

He turned to me and frowned. His tongue darted out of his mouth as he licked his lower lip before running a hand through

1

his thick, dark hair in exasperation. 'Because her name isn't Lucy for a start. She is not who you think she is, Alana.'

I stared at him, blinking in shock. 'Then who is she?'

Alejandro pushed his hands into his trouser pockets and glared at me.

My heart was hammering in my chest as possible scenarios ran through my head, none of them good, and I felt anxiety churning in my stomach. 'Alejandro, who is she?' I asked again, the tremor in my voice audible now.

He sighed loudly before looking to his driver, Jacob, who had burst in on us a few moments earlier to tell us of Lucy's arrival. 'Let her in then,' Alejandro snapped before he turned back to me. 'She can tell you herself.'

Alejandro and I stood in silence in for what felt like an eternity while we waited for Lucy to be shown into the den of our house.

I glanced over at him as a multitude of questions and assumptions raced around my head, hoping for at least some hint of what I was about to discover. He stood tall and fierce, glaring at the open doorway. With his hands still in his pockets and his feet planted wide apart, he looked as though he was preparing to go into battle and I swallowed the knot of anxiety that was lodged in my throat.

Was he nervous? Maybe.

Angry? Most definitely. I could feel it coming from him in waves as he stood there. It was hard to believe that just a few moments earlier, I had been lying beneath him on the sofa, giggling and waiting for him to tear my panties off.

I wanted to ask him again who Lucy was. I wanted to shake him and demand answers, but he looked so intense standing there, and a part of me was too afraid to find out why a sixteen year old pregnant girl had made him react this way.

Lucy walked into the room and Alejandro sat on the sofa, his eyes remaining fixed on her. She ignored him and looked straight at me, her eyes brimming with tears.

'Lucy! Are you okay?' I asked as I crossed the room to her.

'Yes,' she said as she wiped the tears from her cheeks with her sleeve.

'Come on in. Have a seat,' Alejandro snarled as he signaled the armchair. 'And then you can tell us all why you're really here, can't you, Lucia?'

As he spoke his last word, her face paled and she visibly started to tremble as she stood there looking at him. Then, in a few seconds, it was as though she regained her composure and she transformed in front of my eyes, her jaw tilted in defiance as she tossed her long dark hair over her shoulder.

'So you know who I am?' she said as she crossed her arms over her chest.

Alejandro scowled at her. 'Of course I do. Did you honestly think I wouldn't find out? I take a particular interest in anyone who gets close to my wife, and you of all people should know that.'

She glared at him.

'What's going on? Lucy? Or is it Lucia?' I said as I looked between the two of them.

'Tell her,' Alejandro snapped.

Lucy looked at me and my heart started to hammer so violently in my chest, I thought that everyone in the room must have been able to hear it too.

'My name is Lucia Ramos. I am the only surviving member of the Ramos family.'

'Ramos?' I repeated. The name sounded familiar to me.

'Yes,' she said softly.

'Why do I recognize that name?' I asked.

'Because they were one of the biggest firms in Chicago. At least until two years ago when the entire family was wiped out. All except Lucia here,' Alejandro answered.

I stared at Lucia. I recalled the story vividly. It had been all over the news at the time. A father and two sons were slaughtered in a gangland style execution in their own home. The body of his teenage daughter had never been recovered and she was assumed to have been kidnapped and murdered. Or worse.

I swallowed as I remembered how often I had wondered about the fate of that poor girl and how many times I had prayed that she had escaped.

'Please, have a seat, Lucia,' Alejandro said again as he indicated the armchair. 'And tell us what really brought you to LA, and why the hell you have dragged me and my wife into your fucked up life.'

I shot him a look of annoyance. She might have lied, but she was still just a child. Did he have no compassion at all?

Lucia walked further into the room and sat down and I followed her back toward the sofa. Alejandro reached for me and took my hand, pulling me to sit beside him. I was thankful to have something solid beneath me as my knees trembled.

She stared at us both and then she took a deep breath. 'I watched my father and my brothers slaughtered and when they came for me, I ran.'

'And that's it? You just ran and they never caught up with you? You expect me to believe that?' Alejandro asked, his handsome face pulled into a frown.

Lucia glared at him defiantly. 'I used to run track for my high school. I was the best in the district. I also knew my neighborhood better than any of those goons. So I ran, and then I hid. I lived on the streets for a few weeks until the heat died down a little. But I knew I needed a long-term plan. It was only a matter of time before my father's enemies came looking for me, or the state found me and put me into care. So I went to see one of my brother's friends, Blake. I thought that he'd be able to look out for me. And at first he did. He got me false papers. He told me he loved me. We were planning to move to Boston and get married, but it seemed he was just after the kudos that marrying a Ramos would give him. He was still seeing his ex-girlfriend behind my back. I caught them fucking and laughing about what a sucker I was. So, I ran. Again. I caught the first bus I could find and I ended up here in LA.'

I sat in stunned silence, wondering how the hell this poor kid had coped with all of the tragedy in her life. But Alejandro didn't seem to share my concern and he narrowed his eyes at her. 'So it was just a coincidence that you ended up in the shelter where my wife works?' he snapped.

I frowned at him and was about to tell him to back off, but Lucia was already answering his question.

'Believe it or not, it was. A very fortunate and happy coincidence, but I didn't seek Alana or you out, Mr. Montoya.'

Alejandro snorted and shook his head in apparent disbelief.

'But why would Lucy seek me out? Or you?' I asked. I was completely bewildered by this whole thing.

Lucia's lip trembled and I heard Alejandro sigh deeply. 'Because, Alana, the family believed to have murdered Lucia's family are... I mean, were our biggest rivals in Chicago. Our family is very well known in Chicago. And, as Lucia well knows, sometimes our enemy's enemy can be our greatest ally.'

'They *were* your biggest rivals?' I asked, wondering at the meaning behind his deliberate use of the past tense.

Lucia laughed. 'Before their boss and his second had their heads chopped off and put on spikes.'

Alejandro flashed her a look and she stopped laughing and clamped her mouth shut in a dramatic, teenage fashion.

'What?' I looked at Lucia and then Alejandro. 'Did you have anything to do with that?'

'Alana!' he snapped. I should have known better than to ask such a question in front of Lucia, and I looked down at my hands. I felt completely out of my depth here.

Alejandro reached for my hand and squeezed it before he

carried on addressing our guest. 'Let's pretend that I believe you ended up in LA and at the shelter by chance, what brings you here to our door tonight, *young runaway?*'

'Oh, that,' she said with a sniff. 'I hate that foster home. They hate me too. They tried to make me go to church to confess my sins. They think me being pregnant means I'm this complete lost cause and that I need to repent. They made me read the bible after dinner! And the guy is a creep!'

'Lucy,' I said, still unused to her real name. 'You can't just run away. Did you even tell them you were leaving?'

She shook her head.

'They'll be worried about you. You're going to have to call them,' I insisted.

'Okay. But can't I stay here with you guys tonight?' she asked, her eyes wide and imploring.

'No!' Alejandro barked.

I put my hand on his knee and squeezed. 'Maybe just for tonight? It's late.'

Alejandro shook his head.

'Please?' Lucia pleaded.

He rolled his eyes. 'Fine. One night. Then you're out of here and back to your foster family.'

She nodded eagerly. 'Thank you.'

'You'll still need to call them,' I reminded her.

'Of course. Can I borrow your cell?'

'Where is yours?' I asked her. No teenager that I knew would be without their cell phone for more than five minutes.

'The Bakers took it off me. They said it was too much temptation. In case I spoke to any boys.' She pulled a face and looked down at her rounded belly. 'Like, I'd want anything to do with any boys!'

CHAPTER 2

ALANA

I handed Lucia a pair of my pajamas and sat on the bed in the spare room she had chosen to sleep in. It was the same one I'd chosen on my first day here, before Alejandro had come storming in, in a rage, demanding that I sleep in the master bedroom. It was hard to believe that had been just six months earlier. It felt like a lifetime ago.

'Thank you so much for this, Alana,' she said softly as she sat on the bed beside me. 'I truly didn't know who you were when I first met you. And then when I found out, well, I already liked you, and well...' She shrugged and wiped a tear from her eye. 'I suppose there was an element of self-preservation involved when I realized you were Alejandro Montoya's wife. I should have told you. I wanted to. But I also want to leave Lucia Ramos behind. I want to be Lucy Callaghan,' she sniffed.

I squeezed her hand. 'I understand why you didn't tell me.'

She blinked at me. 'You do?'

'Of course. You've had no-one to rely on but yourself. You did what you needed to do. You are an incredibly brave young woman,' I said, and I meant it. I could hardly even begin to imagine what she'd been through, seeing her own family murdered, then living the past two years in fear.

I watched as the tears rolled down her cheeks. 'You remind me so much of my mom,' she sniffed loudly.

I wrapped my arms around her shoulders and she rested her head on my chest until her tears were soaking my shirt. 'I wish she was here,' she sobbed.

I held her while she cried. There had been no reports about her mom in the shooting at her house and I wondered what had happened to her. I had so many questions about this young girl beside me, but they would have to wait for another time. Right now, all that mattered was that she was safe here.

When Lucia stopped crying, she sat up straight and wiped her eyes again. 'I haven't cried this much in two years,' she said with a faint laugh. 'Thank you again for letting me stay here tonight.'

I nodded. 'You're welcome.'

She smiled at me and something about the way she looked at me made me anxious. 'Promise me you won't run away, Lucia. I know you don't like the Bakers, but I will speak to Alejandro and see what we can do.'

'I hate it there, Alana,' she whispered. 'They hate me.'

'Just give me time, sweetheart. I promise I am on your side, but there is red tape involved. I'd let you stay here if it was up to me.'

'Thanks. But I'm pretty sure Alejandro won't want me here. My family weren't exactly...' She shook her head. 'It doesn't matter anyway.'

'I wish it were as simple as me convincing Alejandro to let you stay here. That's the easy part,' I said as I chewed on my lip.

For some reason that made Lucia laugh out loud.

I smiled at her as I saw a glimpse of the carefree teenager she should be. 'What?'

'The fact that you have so much control over the King of LA is funny, but so is the fact that you have absolutely no idea just how powerful he is, Alana. Red tape does not exist for a man like your husband.'

I frowned at her. 'We can't just take you in and keep you here, even if we wanted to.'

Lucia stood up and took a deep breath. 'Alejandro Montoya can do whatever the hell he pleases, Alana, and you're his wife, so that means you can too.'

CHAPTER 3

ALANA

I walked through the house with Lucia's words still in my head. Was it true that Alejandro had such influence that we could just become her legal guardians? Just like that?

I knew that Lucia had lied to me, but I completely understood why. Despite who her family were, she was still a scared, sixteen year old girl with no-one to turn to. I had come to care for her a great deal in the short time I'd known her and I was certain that we had come into each other's lives for a reason.

I closed the bedroom door behind me and walked toward the bed, my feet sinking into the plush carpet. Alejandro was lying with his hands behind his head staring at the TV. He glanced at me as I crossed the room but then turned back to the screen. He was still angry and I knew he was annoyed with me for suggesting that Lucia spend the night, but fortunately I also knew the perfect way to cure him of any bad mood.

I pulled my dress over my head and tossed it onto the floor before removing my bra and doing the same. Slipping under the covers, I pressed my body against his, placing my hand on his chest.

He grunted in response and I couldn't help but smile. He was so hot when he was angry.

'Thank you for letting Lucia stay,' I purred.

'She goes back to that family tomorrow,' he snapped.

I resisted the urge to tell him that I wanted her to stay with us for the foreseeable future, or how much she hated her foster placement and how worried I was that she would run away again if we sent her back there. That could wait until he was in a better mood.

'She's just a child, Alex,' I said instead.

He turned to me with a scowl on his face. 'She's dangerous, Alana!'

'Her enemies might be, but she's not.'

'Same thing,' he snorted.

I felt the anger flickering in my chest. 'I can't believe you have so little compassion for her. She's a kid and she is terrified. She has no-one. I thought the cold hearted bastard routine was just an act you put on, but clearly I was mistaken.'

He moved before I could even finish my thought. Rolling on top of me, grabbing my wrists and pinning them flat to the pillow beside my head. 'You think I'm a cold hearted cabrón?'

I looked into his dark eyes, full of fire and passion, and I shook my head. 'I know that you're not,' I whispered. 'So why won't you help Lucia?'

'I have helped her. I will. But that doesn't include her staying here.'

'But-'

'I feel bad for her, Alana. I know she's been through hell and she deserves to be safe and protected, but you are my priority,' he interrupted me. 'Keeping you and the rest of my family safe are the only things that matter to me. And inviting Lucia into our home is a risk.'

'I know,' I nodded my agreement. I knew there was no use

arguing with him right now, so I tried a completely different tactic. 'Do you want to comer tu coño?'

He blinked at me before laughing softly and I was happy to relieve the tension.

'What?' I asked.

'What do you think you just said?'

'I asked you if you wanted to eat my pussy, didn't I?'

'Not quite, princesa,' he chuckled.

'Well, do you?' I flashed an eyebrow at him.

'Always,' he growled.

I watched as his dark head disappeared beneath the covers and I arched my back in pleasure as he trailed soft kisses down my body toward the apex of my thighs.

He pressed his nose against my panties and inhaled deeply. 'You smell fucking delicious,' he growled before hooking his fingers into the top of them and peeling them down my legs. He sat back on his knees so the covers fell away and tossed my panties onto the floor.

Then his head bent low again, parting my folds with his thumbs before blowing a cool stream of air over them.

I wriggled beneath him and he grinned wickedly. 'Now, voy a comer tu coño,' he growled as he hooked his forearms around my thighs and pulled me closer to his face. He licked the length of my folds before pushing his tongue into my wet opening as his nose rubbed against my clit. I moaned out loud as I felt the familiar fluttering and pulling in my abdomen.

He sucked and licked and I felt a rush of wet release which made him groan against me. Then he continued exploring every inch of my pussy with his expert mouth and tongue until I was coming apart around him.

'I love making you come in my mouth, princesa,' he growled against me. Then he was moving up the bed, nudging his rock hard length at my opening. 'But not as much as I love to feel you come on my cock. Burying myself in your tight little coño is my favorite thing to do in the world.'

I wrapped my arms around his neck and drew him closer to me, until I could clearly see my arousal glistening on his lips and his stubble. 'Good, because it's my favorite thing for you to do too.'

'Spread those legs wide, princesa, I want all the way inside you.'

I did as he instructed and then he slammed into me, making me gasp. 'Alex,' I groaned loudly as shockwaves rocketed through my body.

'You on the edge again already, princesa?' he chuckled.

I bit my lip as I tried to stop myself from coming for a second time so quickly, but his relentless pounding was hitting right at that sweet spot inside. I felt the pressure building in my abdomen as my thighs started to tremble. My walls tightened around him, pulling him deeper inside me until he was groaning in Spanish in my ear.

I screamed his name when my orgasm hit and he increased his efforts until his eyes rolled into the back of his head as he came, cursing loudly in Spanish as he did.

He continued holding himself up on his forearms as we both let the aftermath wash over us. 'Not bad for a heartless bastard?' he said with a cock of his eyebrow.

I blushed. 'I didn't mean that,' I whispered. 'I'm sorry.'

'How do you always manage to bend me to your will, mi reina?' he asked softly.

'I don't. You're always the one in control, you know that.'

'Hmm?' He shook his head and laughed. 'I think maybe you like to give me the illusion of control, but you have it all really, don't you?'

I swallowed. I didn't think that was true at all. My body responded to him of its own volition. Even when I'd hated him, he'd had a power over me that I couldn't comprehend. 'I'm not sure about that,' I whispered. 'You make all of the rules, and I obey them. Well, at least most of the time.'

'But you have my heart in a vice, mi amor,' he breathed. 'There is nothing in this world I wouldn't do to keep you safe and make you happy. And you know it.'

I felt my breath catch in my throat. 'I love you so much,' I whispered. 'Your heart isn't in a vice, Alex, it's in a safe, and I will never let anyone else anywhere near it. I promise you.'

CHAPTER 4

ALEJANDRO

I opened my eyes and groaned in pleasure. Looking down to see the most beautiful dark head of curls bouncing up and down on my cock was one of my favorite ways to wake up. I ran my fingers through her hair and she looked up at me, her huge brown eyes sparkling through long lashes.

'Buenos días, princesa.'

'Morning,' she mumbled as she took me to the back of her throat.

'Fuck!' I hissed as my stomach muscles contracted and my cock throbbed against her tongue. 'Bring that beautiful mouth up here,' I growled as I tugged on her hair.

She released me and looked up, licking her lips as she crawled up the bed toward me. 'You weren't enjoying that?' she grinned.

'Very much, but I don't want to come in your mouth, princesa.'

She pressed her soft body against mine, her nipples hard against my chest. 'Oh. Where would you like to come?' she purred.

'In your sweet, hot coño. So, why don't you slide yourself

onto me right now and show me how wet sucking my cock has made you?'

She grinned at me before pushing herself up so she was straddling me. Then she rubbed her folds over my cock, coating me with her juices, as my dick twitched beneath her. She ran her hands over her breasts, squeezing them as she continued grinding herself on me. Her tits were far too big for her delicate hands and they spilled out as she kneaded the soft flesh. I resisted the urge to reach up and grab them myself and show her how it was done. Instead, I rested my hands on her hips, allowing her to continue her little show as she tugged at her hard nipples and closed her eyes.

'Eyes on me, princess,' I growled. 'If you're going to tease me, then you're going to look at me while you do it.'

She did as she was told, opening her eyes so they were locked on mine as she kept on rubbing herself on my cock and playing with her nipples. I sucked in a breath as she slid one hand down her stomach and between her thighs. She bit on her bottom lip as she started to rub her clit slowly and my cock jerked violently against her in protest.

'If you want to come this morning, you'd better slide yourself onto my cock right now,' I ordered.

She giggled, but she reached between us, squeezing my thick length and guiding it into her soaking wet heat.

'Jesus, Alana!' I hissed. 'You're dripping wet, princesa.'

'I know,' she purred as she sank deeper onto me, taking every last inch. 'Alex,' she groaned as she started to roll her hips over mine.

'Show me how much you love my cock,' I growled as I struggled to maintain any control. She lifted herself up and slammed back down onto me.

I looked up at her, her perfect mouth open as she moaned my name, her incredible tits bouncing as she impaled herself on my shaft, her skin pink and flushed because she was so close to the edge. She was so fucking beautiful.

My fingertips dug into her hips as I tried to hold myself back, but it was impossible. I pulled her hips down onto mine, holding her in place, and I felt a rush of her cum as she allowed me to take control. Taking hold of her arms, I pulled her toward me until she was lying flat against my chest. Wrapping one arm around her waist and placing my other hand between her shoulder blades, I pressed her to me as I fucked her hard.

She whimpered against my neck as her walls clenched around me, milking me until my balls drew up into my stomach and I shot my load into her.

I cupped her chin in my hand as I ground out the last of my orgasm, making sure she took every last drop of my cum as I tilted her face to mine, kissing her as the last shockwaves of her orgasm trembled through her body.

When she had stopped shaking, I pulled back from her. 'Lucia still has to go,' I said with a flash of my eyebrows.

She closed her eyes and rested her head on my chest, and I ran my fingers through her hair. 'You're an asshole,' she murmured as she wrapped her arms tighter around me.

I smiled as I looked down at her. My feisty little princess. I knew this conversation wasn't over. I hadn't been lying the night before. She allowed me to be in control, but the truth was that she held all of the power in our relationship. With a single word, she could bring me to my knees, and she knew it.

I WALKED into the kitchen to see Alana and Lucia at the breakfast bar. Lucia was eating a bowl of cereal while Alana leaned against the counter with a mug of coffee in her hand. They both looked at me and my heart sank in my chest.

Fuck!

'Why does it feel like there is an air of conspiracy in here this morning?' I asked as I poured myself a mug of coffee.

Alana and Lucia looked at each other, all wide eyed and innocent.

I leaned against the counter opposite them. 'As soon as you've finished your breakfast, Jacob will take you back to the Bakers' house,' I said before taking a swig of my coffee.

'About that...' Alana started.

'No,' I shook my head. 'One night. That's it. We agreed.'

'But, Alejandro...'

'Alana!'

'Alex!' she snapped and I glared at her. She only ever called me Alex when we were alone and it felt like she had shared an intimate part of our relationship with this stranger sitting in our kitchen.

I narrowed my eyes at her, and then at Lucia, who was staring at me with her mouth half open and a spoonful of cereal suspended halfway between her face and the bowl.

'Just what the fuck are you suggesting we do? Take her in? Just like that? You don't know her, Alana.'

'And you do?' she snapped.

'I know her family,' I snarled and that seemed to snap Lucia from her daze.

'Don't talk about me like I'm not here,' she yelled, causing Alana and me to turn our attention to her. 'And I am *nothing* like my family,' she spat.

I put my coffee mug onto the counter. 'You still haven't told me exactly what it is you two want.'

Lucia shoveled a spoonful of cereal into her mouth so I looked at my wife instead.

'Lucia doesn't want to go back to the Bakers,' she said.

'That is not my fucking problem,' I snapped.

'I want her to stay with us, Alejandro,' she added. 'Lucia wants to apply for emancipation, but until she does, she'd like to stay here.'

'What? That could take months.'

'I know. But where else can she go?' Alana pleaded.

I took a deep breath. Back to the Bakers. Anywhere but here! That was what I wanted to say, but I couldn't look at Alana and say those things because she was doing that big brown eyes thing that made me weak at the knees.

I looked at Lucia instead. 'Come with me,' I snapped.

Lucia stood up obediently.

'What? Where are you going?' Alana asked as she took a step toward me.

'I only want to talk to her. You want me to think about letting her stay here, then there are things I need to know.'

I walked out of the kitchen toward my office, with Lucia following close behind me.

A FEW MOMENTS LATER, I was sitting at my desk and Lucia was sitting opposite me. She glared at me defiantly. She was different around Alana – vulnerable and relaxed, and I wondered which one of those personas was an act. Perhaps they both were? Or maybe they were both real? I considered myself a good judge of character. I was skilled in the many ways of making people tell the truth, but often, I didn't need to employ them. I could tell when someone was lying to me — at least I usually could.

'My office is sound proof. Anything you say in here will be between you and me,' I told her.

She nodded. 'Okay.'

'Why did you come to LA?'

'I already told you the truth. I wanted away from my rotten ex-boyfriend and far away from Chicago. LA was the first bus leaving the station.'

'Why did you target my wife?'

She frowned at me. 'I didn't target her. In case you hadn't

noticed, your wife is kind of a good person. She was nice to me. Seemed like she cared about me and I hadn't felt like that in a long time. I liked her before I even found out who she was.'

'And when you did find out?' I snapped.

Lucia shrugged. 'I know I should have backed off. I knew there was a chance you'd figure out who I was...'

'So, why didn't you?'

'Because I also know that if I'm important to her, then by default maybe I'm important to you. And that keeps me, and my baby, safe.'

I sat back in my chair and rubbed a hand across my jaw. I hadn't been expecting that level of honesty.

'Hey, don't judge me. It's self-preservation. I've had to survive on my own for the past eight years.'

'No judgment from me. We all do what we have to, kid. Tell me what happened the night your father and brothers were murdered.'

She swallowed and I saw a slight trembling in her lip before she regained her composure. I didn't enjoy making her relive the experience, but it seemed like she was going to become my houseguest for the foreseeable future and I had to know what I was letting myself in for.

'Eight men came into my house while we were sleeping. Four of them were my father's own men. They knew the alarm codes. They knew where he kept his guns. They dragged all of us into the kitchen. Luca and Sammy put up a fight. My father did too. But there were too many of them. They shot them all in the head while I watched. When they shot my father, his brains exploded all over the kitchen. As they were laughing and wiping them-selves down, I ran out of the back door. They chased me of course, but I had been running through those streets since I was eight years old. They were never going to catch me,' she said as she wiped a tear from her eye.

'Did you see the men who killed them?'

She nodded. 'You took care of all of them, Mr Montoya, don't worry about that,' she said with a half-smile. 'I suppose I should thank you.'

I ignored her last remark. The truth was we had taken out the firm responsible, but it had been nothing to do with Lucia and her family, and I wasn't stupid enough to admit anything to this kid.

'You said you've been surviving on your own for eight years? Why?'

She looked at me, her frown turning to a scowl as though she was annoyed at herself for revealing too much. 'You heard the rumors about my father,' she said with a shrug. 'He was every bit the evil bastard people believed him to be. You think because I was his child, I was spared any of that? And my brothers weren't much better. Pigs!' she spat.

She shifted in her seat and suddenly looked like a frightened little girl again. Her father was a snake. He double crossed almost everyone he worked with and it made him many enemies. I'd also heard the rumors about his cruel streak too, and now I wondered just how far that went. I wasn't about to ask her though. That was her business. 'Your mom died when you were eight?' I asked instead. I already knew that but I wanted to hear it from her.

'Yep. He killed her. The only person in my life who ever gave a shit about me.'

It was my turn to frown now. Her mom had died from an overdose. 'He killed her?'

'Yep. He might not have forced those pills down her neck himself, but he was the reason she took them.'

I nodded and we sat there in silence for a few moments.

'Does anyone but Blake know you're in LA?' I asked her.

'I don't think so. He probably told his cousin, Calvin, but he's just a pot-head, and he doesn't know anyone worth telling.'

I nodded. Little did she know, Calvin had already been taken care of a few weeks earlier when my men had been looking for Blake.

'If anyone is still looking for you, it's only a matter of time before they find you. You know that? And I can't put my family in danger, Lucia.'

'I know,' she sniffed. 'If I could just stay here until I figure out my next move? I could apply for emancipation, but you're right, that could take months. Maybe you could get me some new papers instead? I could move on to somewhere new and start afresh — again!'

I couldn't help but smile at her. We both knew that she was always going to be a target. She would always need protecting until she was capable of protecting herself.

I ran my hands through my hair. I knew that I would live to regret this, but what choice did I have? 'You can stay here until we can figure out a more permanent solution.'

She looked up at me, her eyes wide with surprise. 'Really?'

'Yes. Really. I'll have my lawyer sort out the paperwork to make Alana and me your legal guardians for now.'

'Thank you so much. You won't regret it, I promise,' she said with a huge smile.

'I'd better not. But before you go running to tell Alana, I need you to know that if you are under this roof, you will do whatever I ask you to do, Lucia.'

She blinked at me and suddenly her smile was gone, and her eyes were full of fear. She visibly trembled in her seat, her knuckles white as her hands gripped the armrests on the chair. I felt bile rising in my throat. What the fuck had this girl been through?

'Like what exactly?' she asked quietly.

'Like clean up after yourself. Don't get in my way. Respect my privacy. Don't leave the house without one of my guards.'

'Oh?' she said as her arms and hands relaxed and she sat up straighter in her chair.

'You can prove what a good houseguest you are tonight. Alana and I have a dinner at my hotel. We'll be staying over. You won't be here on your own though. The staff and the guards will be here to keep an eye on you and my housekeeper, Magda, will make you dinner.'

'Okay,' she nodded. She still seemed a little uncertain and I wondered if any man in this young girl's life had ever protected her the way they should have, or at least not taken advantage of her. It made me want to prove to her that wasn't what she should expect in life. It made me want to protect her.

'I can promise you that no harm will ever come to you in this house, Lucia. You're safe here. And, while you're my responsibility, I will do everything in my power to protect you.'

She rewarded me with what seemed to be one of her genuine smiles then. 'Thank you, Alejandro.'

I nodded. 'You'd better go and tell Alana the good news.'

'I will. And thank you, again.' She blushed slightly as she stood up and walked out of my office and I couldn't help but wonder if I had just been completely played.

I'D GONE to take a shower to get ready for work after my talk with Lucia. Walking out of the bathroom, I saw Alana walking through the door to our bedroom. She ran over to me and threw her arms around my neck, pressing herself against my body which was still wet from my shower.

'Thank you,' she whispered in my ear. 'I promise you won't regret it.'

'I already do,' I said with a sigh as my hands dropped to her ass.

She looked up at me. 'Why?'

'Because now I'm going to have to relax the no panty rule. I can't have you walking around here with no panties when we have an impressionable teenager in the house, can I?'

She giggled against my neck. 'Oops. I suppose not. But, maybe we could change it to no panties in the bedroom.'

'Ever?' I flashed my eyebrows at her.

'Ever,' she grinned.

I ran my hands over her incredible, round ass and squeezed. 'You're wearing panties right now, princess,' I whispered against her ear.

'Then you'd better rectify this situation immediately,' she purred against my neck making my cock harden. 'Because I wouldn't want to break the rules and have you spank me, would I?'

I reached for the hem of her dress and pulled it up to her waist before fisting my hands into her panties and tearing them over her soft skin. I smiled as her body shivered in anticipation and she groaned out loud.

I dropped my hands back to her naked ass. Her skin was so soft, it was begging to be spanked. 'I just remembered, I still owe you a spanking from last night,' I growled in her ear, recalling how we'd been disturbed on the sofa by Lucia's arrival the night before.

'Oh, yes, that's right. You do.' She unwrapped herself from my embrace and stepped back with a wicked grin on her face. 'Where would you like me?'

I narrowed my eyes at her. 'Unfortunately, I have a meeting I need to get to, princess. Your spanking will have to wait until tonight. Don't forget we have a dinner with the mayor and we're staying at the hotel.'

'I know. I'm looking forward to it. I didn't realize you had to leave so soon though. So you're just going to leave me all wet and needy for you? Am I going to have to take care of myself?' She pretended to pout but the mischief in her eyes gave her away.

'No.' I pulled my towel from my waist and tossed it aside. 'I've always got time to fuck you, princess.'

I watched as a flush crept over her neck and smiled. 'Come here,' I ordered and she stepped back toward me.

I reached for her hair, wrapping it around my fist before tilting her head to give me better access to her neck. The expanse of creamy soft skin made me want to bite her — hard. Instead, I licked from her collarbone up to her ear and she shivered. 'You taste so fucking good, Alana,' I growled. 'I wish I had time to eat your pussy too.'

'So do I,' she groaned.

I placed my hands on her ass cheeks and lifted her so she could wrap her legs around my waist. I pressed her against the wall and sealed my lips over hers, pushing my tongue inside her mouth and wishing it was her pussy I was exploring instead. But I had ten minutes to spare. A quick fuck was all I could afford. It wasn't enough, but then ten hours wasn't enough when it came to her. I could fuck Alana for every minute of every day and I would still want more.

With that thought in my head, I pushed my cock deep inside her soaking wet heat and she groaned into my mouth.

CHAPTER 5

ALANA

We were on our way to the shelter and I had asked Hugo to make a pit stop on the way. I was bringing Lucia with me for the day. She had spent a few weeks at the shelter when she'd first arrived in LA. It was where the two of us had first met after she had turned up there with papers stating she was eighteen year old Lucy Gallagher. She had settled in well there, but hadn't been able to stay once we discovered she was actually only sixteen — and pregnant. She was looking forward to coming back there with me for the day and catching up with some of the residents. It would save her sitting at home all alone, especially as Alejandro and I were going out later in the evening too.

Lucia had called her foster family, the Bakers, the previous evening and told them she was staying with us for the night, but now that we were making it a more permanent arrangement, I felt the Bakers deserved an explanation.

'Here we are,' Hugo said as we pulled up outside their house.

I stepped out of the car and straightened my shoulders.

'You sure you don't want me to come with you?' he asked through the open driver's window.

'No. I'll be fine. I'm sure I can handle the Bakers. You keep an eye on Lucia,' I said, glancing back at the teenager in the back seat who was fidgeting nervously.

I walked up the path and took a breath as I knocked on the front door. A few moments later, a woman with short blonde hair and bright orange lipstick answered. She looked me up and down, giving my high heels a withering glance before she smiled sweetly.

'Can I help you?' she asked.

'Are you Melody Baker?'

'I sure am. Who wants to know?'

'My name is Alana. I've come to speak to you about Lucy.'

Her smile immediately turned to a scowl. 'If that girl has stolen from you, or been causing trouble, it ain't no fault of mine. She can't be controlled. She stayed out all night last night. Little tramp,' she hissed.

I took a half a step back as her words washed over me. 'What?' I stammered. I'd heard that the Bakers were a good family. Sure, they were a little too God-fearing for my liking, but they were supposed to be caring. That was what Alejandro's lawyer had promised me. That Lucia would go to a good, caring family.

'I said she's a tramp. She hasn't been sniffing around your husband or something, has she?' she sneered. 'I saw the way she looked at my Gary and he saw it too. Girls like that don't know when to keep their legs closed.'

I sucked in a lungful of air as I willed my heart to stop hammering in my chest. I couldn't believe the level of hatred and nastiness directed toward Lucia, who was still just a kid. I took a step forward again, and brought my face close to Melody's. 'If you *ever* speak about Lucy or any other young girl like that again, I will slap you so hard you'll be brushing your teeth through your ass for the rest of your life,' I hissed.

She took a step back and blinked at me.

'And as for your husband, Gary, is it? If I find out he has had even one impure thought about that little girl, I will hunt him down and castrate him myself.'

Melody kept blinking at me in shock, her mouth hanging open for a few seconds before she regained her composure. 'How dare you come to my house and speak to me like that,' she snapped, puffing her chest out. 'Just who the hell do you think you are!'

I pointed my finger in her face. 'I am Alana fucking Montoya. I am the fucking Queen of LA, and I am also Lucy's new guardian. Now, you can call the cops, or your church, or your momma for all I care, but I can assure you it will do you absolutely no good, because my husband owns this goddamn city. Now, crawl back into your hole and go think about why you're such a nasty bitch and why your husband thinks that a sixteen year old child has been looking at him,' I snarled and then I turned on my heel and marched down her path, my six inch heels clicking all the way.

I looked at the car and saw Hugo and Lucia, the windows rolled down, and both of them with huge grins on their faces. I bit my lip and flashed my eyebrows at them. I had never spoken to anyone like that before in my life, but hearing her talk about Lucia like that had woken the tiger in me.

I climbed into the back seat of the car and Lucia threw her arms around me while Hugo gave me a round of applause. 'Wow, Alana!' Lucia said as she sat back and started to laugh. 'You just handed Melody Baker her ass!'

'You sure did, Boss,' Hugo added as he started the engine of the car.

'I did, didn't I?' I said as my cheeks flushed with heat. 'I didn't go too far, did I? I just… God, what a horrible woman.'

'You definitely didn't go too far,' Hugo replied.

'No way,' Lucia added.

I sat back against the seat and made a mental note to have another word with Alejandro's lawyer. I didn't think the Bakers were the right kind of family to be fostering any kids. What Melody had said about her husband had made my skin crawl.

WE'D DONE a full day at the shelter and Lucia had loved catching up with some of the women and children she'd met there while she'd been a resident herself. She had been put to good use entertaining some of the younger kids for the day and was proving herself to be a natural. I was just thinking it was almost time to go home when Hugo popped his head into my office.

'Evening, Boss. I'm going to take Lucia home now. I'll see you tomorrow.'

I blinked at him. 'You're leaving without me?'

'Yup. Your chariot awaits outside, Ma'am,' he said and laughed to himself. 'Have a great evening.' Then he walked out of my office leaving me staring after him.

I closed down my computer and made sure I had all of the paperwork I needed for home before grabbing my purse and locking up my office. I shouted goodbye to the shelter manager, Kristen, and then walked out of the doors.

My breath caught in my throat at the sight of the sexiest man in the world sitting outside waiting for me in the sexiest car I had ever seen. He revved the engine of the Bugatti Veyron and grinned at me as I approached.

I opened the door and climbed inside, sinking into the luxurious leather seat and inhaling the new car smell. 'This is like a million dollar car, Alex. When did you get it?'

'More like two million, princess, and I'm test driving it for now,' he said with a shrug. 'I'm going to see if it makes this hot chick I'm into put out before I make a decision.'

'Well, if she doesn't, let me know, because I will so put out for this car.' I grinned at him and he started to laugh as he pulled the car away from the curbside.

'You like it then?'

'Hell, yes.'

'Then it's all yours, princess,' he said. 'As long as you don't mind me breaking it in for you first.' He pressed his foot down on the gas and the engine roared as he sped off down the freeway.

'What?' I shrieked above the noise. 'I can't take this. It's too much.'

He slowed down and turned to me. 'Too much? You're my wife, princesa. Besides, it's not a gift. My money is yours too. You know that.'

'I'm not quite sure it works like that,' I laughed.

He lifted my hand to his lips and kissed my fingertips. 'It does where I come from.'

I shook my head in amazement. This life felt like a fairytale sometimes. 'Anyway, where are we going? And what have I done to deserve this?' I asked.

'I just told you the car isn't a gift,' he replied.

'I didn't mean the car,' I smiled at him. 'I mean you coming to pick me up from work. I thought I was meeting you at the hotel later?'

'Well, I heard what a badass you were today at the Bakers' house, and I couldn't wait any longer to tell you how proud I am of you.'

'You heard?' I put my hands over my face, recalling how rude I was to Melody Baker earlier. 'Does Hugo tell you everything about my day?'

'Yes. Ever since the whole Amelia Grant lunch incident, he tells me *everything*.'

'Oh yes, the lunch incident,' I said as I recalled the time Alejandro had thought that Hugo and I were having an affair because I hadn't been going to the charity ladies' lunches he'd set me up with. After I'd discovered they were a bunch of stuck-up bitches who were more interested in champagne and gossip than charity, I'd found charity work at the shelter instead.

'So I cancelled my late meeting, and I thought we could both get ready at the hotel. I've had some dresses sent over for you.'

'Thank you. That sounds perfect,' I said as I sat back in the seat with a sigh. He had great taste in clothes and I loved knowing that I was wearing something he had helped to choose for me.

'I'm proud of you, princess. Standing up to that Baker woman like that.'

'Well, you know I don't usually like conflict, but she said such horrible things about Lucia and I just saw red. It was like something inside me snapped and I couldn't help myself from telling her what I really thought of her.'

'You're going to be an amazing mom to our kids, Alana,' he said, his tone serious all of a sudden.

'You think so?' I asked. My mom had never really been there for me and I wondered if I'd inherited her selfish streak. I was mostly raised by my grandma, and she was one of the kindest and toughest women I had ever known. I liked to think that when Alejandro and I had children, I'd be just like her, but who knew?

'I know so. Mi reina feroz,' he said as he kissed my fingertips again.

'What does that mean?' I asked him.

'My fierce queen,' he replied, squeezing my hand tightly. 'Our kids are going to be amazing, you know that right?'

I smiled at him. 'Yes.'

'I can't wait to have some little Montoyas running around,' he smiled and then he turned to me. 'You are ready for that, aren't you?'

I nodded. 'Yes. With you, I'm ready for anything,' I said and I meant it. I couldn't wait to spend every day of the rest of my life with him and fill our house with children and grandchildren.

'You ready for me to open this baby up?' he grinned.

'Hell, yes!' I laughed. 'What are you waiting for?'

CHAPTER 6

ALANA

*A*lejandro and I walked into the bar at his hotel. He had his hand on my lower back, dangerously close to my ass. I looked up at him and smiled and he responded with a cheeky wink. We had finished our dinner with the mayor and had decided to have a quick nightcap before heading up to our suite, because Alejandro had someone he needed to speak with.

I liked the mayor and his wife, Bree, and we'd had a great evening together. They knew that I volunteered at a women's shelter, and they'd been keen to hear about the plans the manager, Kristen, and I had for the place in the future, but all I wanted to do now was have some time alone with my incredibly sexy husband, and thank him again for agreeing to let Lucia stay with us for a while. Sometimes I could hardly believe that I was married to him, and given the unusual and tense start to our marriage, that we were both so happy.

We approached the bar and the bartender smiled a greeting to us. 'Good evening Mr and Mrs Montoya. Your usual, sir?'

'Yes, two,' Alejandro replied as he guided me to a bar stool.

I was about to sit down when I heard a familiar voice behind me. 'Alana Carmichael! Is that really you?'

I turned around. 'Bobby Conroy!' I said with a huge smile on my face. 'What the hell are you doing here?'

'I'm here for the convention,' he said as he took a step toward me. The hotel hosted dozens of conventions every year and I knew that the current one was something to do with tech giants and app developments.

Alejandro slipped an arm around my waist possessively before Bobby could pull me into the hug he was clearly gunning for and I felt a thrill of unexpected pleasure shoot through me. I was used to constantly bumping into Alejandro's insanely beautiful ex-girlfriends. It was about time we ran into one of my exes. 'Bobby, this is my husband, Alejandro,' I said as I leaned into him, full of pride and contentment.

'Wow! You're married?' he asked with a flash of his eyebrows, and then he extended his hand to Alejandro, who shook it firmly.

'And Bobby is?' Alejandro growled.

I bit my lower lip. Who was Bobby? My first crush. My first kiss. The boy who I'd thought would be my first everything. I decided not to lead with any of those things though.

'Bobby was my high school boyfriend,' I said quietly.

Bobby's eyes darted to mine as if to remind me that we had been so much more than that. I took a second to drink him in. I hadn't seen him for almost seven years, not since the time he'd come home for his first Christmas break after he'd left for college. He'd been a major jock in high school and the girls had always loved him. But, for some reason, he had chosen me. He'd always been attractive as a boy, but as a man, he was swoon-worthy. His sandy blonde hair was short on the sides and longer at the top. His blue eyes still twinkled like the ocean. He was tall and his muscular frame filled out his suit perfectly.

He wasn't a patch on the sex god standing beside me, but still, he was fine. And given my numerous brushes with Alejandro's ex-girlfriends, who were all beyond gorgeous, I was secretly pleased that he had turned up here looking so good. Maybe

Alejandro would learn how it felt to stand there with a hundred questions buzzing through his head. Not that he had anything at all to be jealous about.

I sensed that Bobby was about to say something when another man walked up and stood beside him. 'There you are, buddy,' he said with a lop-sided smile. He was dressed in a suit too, but looked like he'd enjoyed one too many drinks.

'Hey, Justin,' Bobby turned to him. 'This is my old friend, Alana, and her husband, Alejandro.'

'Alana?' Justin said with his eyes wide and his mouth hanging open. 'You mean the one that got away, Alana?'

Bobby sucked in a breath before laughing softly and I felt Alejandro tense beside me, his grip on me tightening.

'The one that got away, huh?' I laughed too. 'I think you must be mistaking me for someone else, Justin.'

'Just how long did you two date?' Alejandro said. His voice was calm and controlled, but I could feel the rumble of anger coursing through his body.

'Not that long,' I replied.

'A little over two years,' Bobby said immediately after.

Just then the bartender placed our drinks onto the bar. At the same time, one of Alejandro's security guards walked up beside him and spoke quietly in his ear.

'Joder!' he cursed before turning to me. 'I have to deal with something. I won't be long.' He looked at Bobby and back at me and I saw the vein bulging in his neck. He leaned down and kissed me softly. 'Behave,' he murmured against my skin and then he walked away with his employee.

ALEJANDRO HAD BEEN GONE for over twenty minutes and I was already onto my second glass of Scotch. His expensive tastes in whisky had rubbed off on me, and I had come to enjoy the taste of the expensive liquor and the way it warmed my throat when I sipped it. I sat between Bobby and Justin and learned that they had become overnight millionaires after developing a piece of security tech. They were the keynote speakers at the convention in the hotel.

After ordering another round of drinks, Justin excused himself to use the restroom, leaving Bobby and me alone.

'I'm really glad I bumped into you, Alana,' he said softly as he looked into my eyes. 'I've always regretted the way things ended between us.'

'It was a long time ago, Bobby,' I said, recalling the Christmas he had come home from college and told me he had slept with someone. I supposed I couldn't blame him. I had made him wait for two years and when he'd gone off to college in another state, halfway across the country, I could hardly blame him for giving into temptation. How ironic that the night he told me was the night I was planning to have sex with him and lose my virginity. It had hurt more than anything at the time though, but it wasn't something that bothered me any longer. 'We were just kids. Besides, everything has turned out for the best.'

'Are you happy?' he asked me, his eyes full of concern.

'Yes. Deliriously so,' I said with a smile.

He smiled back at me. 'Then I'm happy for you,' he said as he placed his warm hand on my shoulder and squeezed gently. I was suddenly aware of someone behind me and Bobby's hand was removed.

'Touch my wife again and I will break every bone in your arm,' Alejandro snarled.

Bobby stood up from his stool and no doubt fueled by one too many whiskies, he squared up to Alejandro. 'What the hell, man? Get your hands off me!' he snarled.

I swallowed as I jumped off my stool. This was not going to end well for Bobby. I placed my hand on Alejandro's arm and squeezed gently. 'We were just catching up. Come on. Let's go up to the suite.'

He turned and blinked at me, searching my face for a few seconds before he let go of Bobby's arm. 'Stay the fuck away from her,' he snarled at Bobby before grabbing hold of my elbow. 'Let's go, princess.'

'Bye, Bobby. Enjoy the convention,' I said with an apologetic smile before Alejandro practically frog-marched me out of the bar.

'What the hell is your problem?' I hissed through clenched teeth as we approached the elevator.

He turned and glared at me. 'We'll talk upstairs,' he snarled.

The elevator ride to Alejandro's suite was torturous. I was on one side and he stood on the other, looking as hot and as angry as I had ever seen him. I kept stealing glances at him but his eyes were firmly fixed on the doors. I could feel fury radiating from him in waves and I swallowed. I hadn't done anything wrong, but despite that, I was anxious about what was going to happen. I was already due a spanking.

Dear God, was I going to be able to sit down tomorrow?

After what felt like an eternity, the doors opened and we walked across the hall to his suite. As soon as we were inside, he went to the small bar and poured himself a Scotch.

I walked over to the sofa and took off my heels, waiting for some explanation from him, but he sipped his whisky in stony silence and stared out of the window.

'Alejandro!' I asked. 'What the hell has gotten into you?'

He slammed his glass down onto the small table and stalked toward me. 'Are you fucking kidding me? I find you sitting at the bar, flirting with your ex-boyfriend, who has his hands all over you, and you dare to ask me what has got into me? Really, Alana?' he shouted.

'I was not flirting!' I snapped. 'I was talking to him. And he put his hand on my shoulder for, like two seconds. That is not the same thing as having his hands all over me.'

He glared at me, his eyes full of fire and fury. 'You were sitting in my hotel, in my bar, with some fucking asshole draped all over you. How the hell do you think that makes me look, Alana?'

I couldn't help but laugh. 'So, this is all about your fragile ego, is it?'

He snarled at me, his teeth bared as though he was about to reply, but I didn't let him. 'Shall I tell you how it looked? It looked exactly like what it was. Two people talking. There was nothing untoward going on. We talked. Just like you talk to all of your ex-girlfriends in that same bar at least once a week! It also looked like you are a man who trusts that his wife loves him, so much so he is happy to leave her in the company of another man while he deals with some business. *That* was how it looked — at least until you went all alpha-male and threatened to break Bobby's arm, and then you just looked like a jealous, insecure asshole!'

He glared at me, his nostrils flaring.

Oh shit! I'd gone too far. Nobody ever spoke to him like that. He looked like he might explode as he stepped toward me. I took a step back from him. That little voice in my head told me to stop talking now, because he was already beyond pissed and I was just going to make him madder. But I ignored that little voice — because I was beyond pissed too, and I had done nothing wrong.

'You have screwed half of the women in LA, and I have to deal with bumping into them on a regular basis and watch them fawning all over you. But *one* time we bump into someone from my past and you act like a jealous jackass!'

He took another step closer and I edged back toward the window. 'That is completely fucking different,' he growled.

'Different how?'

'Because none of those women meant anything to me. But, him! He meant something to you. The one that got away?' he sneered.

'He said that, not me!'

'Tell me who he is to you!' he barked as he advanced closer toward me.

I took another step back from him. I had never seen him so angry and with each step he took closer, I took one further away from him until my back was pressed against the floor to ceiling window and I had nowhere left to go. 'I told you, he was my high school boyfriend,' I stammered.

'Yes, you did tell me that, but that's not all, is it? I'm obviously missing something. Now who, or what else, is he to you?'

I swallowed as I looked up into his eyes. 'I don't know what you want from me, Alex,' I said quietly as blood started to pound in my ears.

He banged his fists on the glass either side of my head so fiercely that the window rattled and my heart almost leapt out of my chest. I knew there was no chance of the reinforced glass breaking, but we were forty floors up.

'I want your obedience!' he snarled.

I blinked at him. 'My obedience? Seriously?' There was something much more going on here than him having a problem with me talking to my ex.

He continued to glare into my eyes. 'I asked you a fucking question, Alana.'

I glared back at him. 'He was my first crush and my first kiss. I thought he would be my first everything else too,' I said with a slight shake of my head.

'So you were in love with him?' he frowned.

'No. I suppose I loved him once, but just like I loved my best friend. He was comfortable and... I don't know. I told you I've never been in love before and that's true. I did love Bobby, but not in the way that I love you.'

He continued to glare at me. 'Go on,' he growled.

'He went away to college and we agreed to try and make it work.

He came home for the Christmas break and I knew he was going to ask me to marry him because his sister told me so. I didn't want to marry him, but I didn't want to break his heart, either, so I planned on giving him my virginity instead, hoping that having sex would make things better between us. Like, maybe it would make me fall in love with him?' I shrugged and looked for any sign of understanding from Alejandro, but he continued glaring at me, as fierce as ever. 'Anyway, before any of that happened, he told me that he'd cheated on me. And as much as it was a relief, it hurt like hell too. His betrayal cut me deep. I never really trusted anyone again after that.'

I felt some of the anger leaving Alejandro's body as he pinned me against the glass with the weight of his large frame. He brushed my hair behind my ear. 'I hate that he got your first kiss,' he growled.

I lifted my hand, stroking his jawline as he pressed his cheek into my palm. 'You got my first everything else though.'

'But I want it all.'

'You might not have got my first kiss, but you will get every other one for the rest of my life. Isn't that enough for you?' I smiled at him.

He bent his head lower and kissed me softly and I melted into him. He kept his hands beside my head, caging me in as he pressed his hard body against mine. I pulled back from him and he groaned out loud.

'Besides, I don't have *any* firsts with you,' I said softly.

He narrowed his eyes at me as he reached behind me and pulled down the long zipper at the back of my dress, causing it to fall to the floor in a pool of fabric at my feet. Then his hands slid to my ass and he lifted me, wrapping my legs around his waist. 'You're so very wrong about that, princess,' he growled as he sealed his mouth over mine and carried me across the hotel suite and into his office.

Once we were inside, he set me down on his desk. 'You are

the first woman I have ever fucked in my office,' he said with a wicked grin.

'You can't count things like that,' I said with a laugh.

'Why not?' he frowned as he slid his arms around my waist, pulling me closer to him until I could feel his erection pressing between my thighs.

'Because this is just a room. It doesn't really mean anything.'

'That's where you're wrong, princess,' he said as he started to trail delicious soft kisses up my neck. 'I've never fucked a woman in my office because I have never trusted one enough to allow them in here before. This office is full of my secrets, Alana, and I only share them with you.'

My insides melted like warm chocolate at his words and I felt pride swelling in my chest. 'But you've never actually fucked me in here,' I purred in his ear.

'I'm about to change that fact in around ten seconds,' he said as he tore my panties off.

I PRESSED my head back against the pillow and closed my eyes in pleasure as Alejandro's expert hands roamed over my body. He had fucked me mercilessly on his desk in his office, with one arm around my waist and one hand around my throat as he had ground out the last of his rage and fury brought on by our inter-action with Bobby earlier. What happened in there had been all about him, and my reward was that right now, it got to be all about me.

He sucked one of my nipples into his mouth as he toyed with my clit.

'Who was the first man to touch this hot little coño, princess?' he growled.

'You,' I panted.

He moved his fingers from my clit and slid two of them inside me and I felt a sudden rush of wet heat at the intrusion. 'Who was the first to finger fuck your tight cunt?'

'You were,' I groaned as I bucked my hips to take more of him.

'Hmm.' He lifted his head and looked directly into my eyes as he moved his fingers in and out of me, while he brushed my clit with his thumb. 'Did he ever make you this wet? Because you are fucking dripping all over me, princess?'

'You know that he didn't,' I groaned.

He continued finger fucking me slowly as he swept the pad of his thumb back and forth over my clit. I felt my walls squeezing him, desperate for more but he continued teasing me relentlessly, until I was desperate to come.

'Alex! Please?' I begged him.

'Oh, princess, you know how much I love to hear you beg,' he growled as he took pity on me and pushed his fingers and his thumb hard against those sweet spots that had me falling apart around him.

When he had rubbed the last of my orgasm from my trembling body, he shifted his weight until he was nestled between my thighs and his cock was nudging at my opening. He lifted his two fingers to his mouth and sucked them clean as he stared into my eyes. 'Your cum is fucking addictive, do you know that? Now, tell me, who was the first man to taste you, Alana?'

'You,' I panted as the last waves of my climax washed over me.

'And who was the first to fuck you? Your pussy, your mouth and your sweet, juicy ass?'

I bit my lip as I looked up at him. His eyes were still full of fire, but it was lust fueled now rather than anger. 'You,' I breathed.

'That's right, princess. And I am the only man who is ever going to do any of those things to you ever again. Every single inch of your body belongs to me. You got that?'

I nodded. His possessiveness was so hot. I wrapped my arms around his neck. 'Yes.'

He sucked in a breath and I heard a low growl in his throat. Then he pushed his huge cock into me and fucked me so hard, I forgot all about Bobby Conroy and every other man I had ever even so much as glanced at.

There was only Alejandro and me, and the rest of the world fell away.

CHAPTER 7

ALANA

I woke in the night to Alejandro softly kissing my neck and his warm hand sliding between my legs.

'Alex,' I groaned in pleasure as the tingling in my thighs started already.

'Hey, princess,' he growled.

'Hey.' I pushed back, pressing my ass against him and feeling his cock, which was rock-hard and ready to go, as usual. 'What's up?' I giggled. 'Apart from you, that is?'

'I couldn't sleep.'

'Is everything okay?'

He stopped kissing my neck and pulled his hand from between my legs, resting it on my hip before he sighed deeply. 'It's just work stuff. Nothing you need to worry about.'

'You can talk to me though, you know that? Anything that concerns you is important to me too. If you're worried about something...'

'I told you it's nothing for you to be concerned about, princess,' he interrupted me.

'But-' I started to say.

'It's my job to protect you, Alana, not the other way around,' he snapped and suddenly the atmosphere in the room changed.

I swallowed. 'Just a few hours ago, you said that you trusted me enough to share all of your secrets with me.'

He sighed deeply, his breath warm against my neck. 'This isn't about me not trusting you, princess. I just don't want you in that part of my world. It's dark and dangerous and... everything you're not.'

'I'm not sure the world works like that, Alex. If it's a part of your life, then it's mine too, whether you like it or not. Sooner or later, you're going to have to trust that I can handle it.'

'I know you can handle it, princess, but I'd prefer that you don't have to.'

I opened my mouth to reply as his hand squeezed my hip and he moved his body closer to mine. I sensed that was the end of our conversation and if I kept pressing him, we'd only end up in the midst of another argument. I wished that he would open up to me more about his work. I didn't need, or want, the details of what he did, but I felt so helpless when he was so obviously distracted and worried by something that I couldn't help him with.

'I just remembered that I still haven't given you your spanking from the other night,' he said softly against my ear.

I pushed back against him and he groaned, his breath warming the skin of my neck. This was the way I helped him deal with whatever was going on in his life, wasn't it? It wasn't perfect, but it was what we had for now. I shivered in anticipation at his words. 'You want to do that right now?'

He nipped at my earlobe. 'Yes.'

'When I'm all warm and snuggly and you could just slide your cock in me and fuck me back to sleep instead?'

His cock jerked against me as though it had a mind of its own and was signaling it preferred the latter option.

'Yes,' he hissed.

'But I've been a good girl tonight. I'm not sure I deserve a spanking,' I purred. 'You were the naughty one who threatened to break someone's arm.'

'Hmm. Well, you know I'm an only child. I don't play well with others. And I definitely do not share my favorite toys.'

I groaned as his fingers slid through my folds, nudging at my opening. 'So, I'm just a toy, am I?'

'Hmm,' he mumbled against my neck and the vibration sent shivers down my spine. 'But not just any toy. My favorite one,' he teased me as he started to slide a finger inside me.

'You're a very bad man,' I purred.

'Yes, we both know that, princess,' he said as he pulled his hand from between my thighs and sat up, swinging his legs off the end of the bed. 'So get your ass over here. Now.'

I groaned loudly, feigning a protest as I shuffled over him, until I was lying across him with my bare ass over his lap. A nervous energy thrummed around my entire body. I lived for his spankings. He slid his warm hands over my ass cheeks and chuckled softly. 'This ass is fucking incredible, princess. I'm going to turn it a beautiful shade of pink and then I'm going to fuck it.'

I clenched my thighs together at the thought. This man was a devil, and I loved him so much. Sometimes I felt like I could hardly breathe from the intensity of the feelings he stirred in me. As if reading my mind, he cupped my chin with his hand and turned my head, bending his head low before kissing me softly.

'Te quiero, princess.'

'I love you too, Alex.'

A few seconds later, his hand landed sharply on the fleshy part of my ass cheek, sending a jolt of heat and pleasure shooting through me. Alejandro gave two types of spankings — one for punishment and one for pleasure. Both of them made him hard, and me hot, wet and needy. But this was most definitely the latter. He landed three more strokes before he slid two of his thick fingers inside me and the sound of my arousal filled the room as he pumped them in and out. A few moments later, he pulled his hand back and I heard him sucking his fingers clean.

'Your cream tastes so much sweeter after a spanking, princess,' he growled before he slapped my ass again, making me groan out loud. 'I think I should put you over my knee every single day. What do you think?'

'Yes,' I panted out loud and he chuckled softly.

'Good girl.'

CHAPTER 8

ALEJANDRO

The following day, Alana and I arrived back at the house, and I was relieved to see it was still standing and our young runaway was sitting cross-legged on the sofa in the den, eating a bowl of cereal.

'Hey guys. Did you have a good night?' Lucia asked as we walked into the room.

'Yes, it was great,' Alana replied as she sat down beside her on the sofa.

'Hmm, and we ran into an old friend of Alana's too,' I added.

Lucia looked between us both with a grin and I saw Alana roll her eyes. She obviously thought that having Lucia around meant that she could get away with acting like a spoiled brat.

She was wrong.

I leaned over the sofa and planted a kiss on her head before pressing my lips against her ear. 'Roll those eyes at me again, princess and I will take my belt to your ass,' I whispered.

She tilted her head to look at me, a flush creeping over her cheeks and a smile on her lips.

'How was your evening, Lucia?' I asked as I straightened up.

'It was okay. Your friend, Jax, stopped by to see you. He

47

thought you weren't leaving until seven. He's nice. He ordered me a pizza.'

'Oh?' I frowned. I hadn't been expecting him, but then I hadn't been seeing as much of him lately. Since Alana had come back from New York a week earlier, I had spent almost every moment with her.

'Yeah. He came back this morning too. He's waiting in your office.'

'Thanks. I'd better go see what he needs. I'll join you both for lunch later,' I said as I squeezed Alana's shoulder.

'Okay. And then I was going to pop to the shelter for a few hours. I need to catch up with Kristen. Lucia can come with me,' Alana replied.

'Great,' Lucia said with a smile. 'It will be good to see everyone again.'

Leaning back in my chair, I studied Jax as he sat opposite my desk.

'So, you think the Ortegas are making a move?' I asked him.

He nodded. 'They've done nothing yet. But it looks to me like they're getting their ducks in a row, amigo.'

'Fuck! I told you Joey was a snake. I knew it was only a matter of time before he started trying to muscle in on our territory.'

'Seems you were right about him. But we've got men watching him. If he makes a move, we'll know about it.'

'I fucking hope so, amigo. I want extra men here at the house until the problem is dealt with.'

'Of course. On that note, the Ramos girl?'

I shook my head and sighed loudly. 'I know, but what could I do? She turned up here the night before last. She's on her own. She's pregnant.'

'But she's Miguel Ramos's kid. You'd better hope the apple fell far from that tree, Alejandro.'

'I know. Did you ever hear about him and his kids? Any rumors about the way he... I don't know, the way he treated them?'

Jax narrowed his eyes at me. 'He was a cruel bastard. He used to make his sons fight each other until only one of them was left standing. But, beyond that, I've not heard anything. Why do you ask?'

I shrugged. 'Just wondering. I don't think Lucia had a particularly good relationship with him.'

'Wouldn't surprise me. But, still, you are harboring the last surviving members of the Ramos family — two generations of them. I hope you know what you're doing, is all. Don't get me wrong, she seems like a real nice kid, but she's a Ramos.'

'It's a short-term arrangement, believe me. As soon as I can figure out a way to get her out of here while keeping her safe, she'll be gone.'

Jax nodded.

'In the meantime, I want you to speak to her. See if there's anything she can tell us that we might find useful.'

'You want me to interrogate a pregnant sixteen year old girl?' he frowned.

'No,' I laughed. 'Just talk to her. You have a unique way of getting information from people that they don't even know is important.'

We were interrupted by a knock at the door. 'Come in,' I said.

The door opened and Lucia popped her head inside. 'Magda wants to know if Jax is joining us for dinner.'

'I'd love to,' Jax answered. 'I haven't had any of Magda's cooking since you got married, amigo,' he winked at me.

'Great. I'll let her know,' Lucia said with a smile.

'Actually, Lucia, we were just talking about you. Come on in.'

She stepped inside my office and closed the door behind her before taking a seat next to Jax.

'If you're okay with it,' I said, 'I'd like you to talk to Jax about what happened the night your father and brothers were murdered.'

'Okay?' she frowned at me.

'Jax has a talent when it comes to interpreting information. I want to make sure there is nothing you or I have missed. The more information we have, the better we'll be able to keep you safe. That's why I want you to speak to him, but I won't lie, any information about our competitors or our enemies, is always useful to us.'

She looked at me for a few seconds and then she nodded. 'Okay, but I'm not sure what else I can tell him that I haven't told you.'

'Thank you, Lucia. And I need you to know that you can trust him. If ever you need anything and me or Alana aren't around, then you contact Jax okay?'

She nodded. 'Okay.'

I pulled open my desk drawer and took out a new smart-phone. 'I suppose you'll be needing one of these?'

Her eyes lit up. 'Yes, thanks. Not that I have anyone to call. But I like to play games and search the net and stuff. And they have this app that tells you all about how your baby is growing.'

'And you can order pizza on them too,' Jax added.

Lucia started to laugh, the sound filling my office, and I couldn't help but smile.

CHAPTER 9

ALANA

*A*lejandro stood by the front door and glanced at his watch and I bit back a smile. He hated to be kept waiting and he was barely able to hide his frustration.

'Lucia!' he shouted. 'If you're not down here in two minutes we're going without you.'

There was no reply and he shook his head in annoyance. I slipped on my heels and walked over to him. 'She's just nervous about what to wear,' I said with a smile, placing my hand on his cheek. 'She's been excited about this all day. She'll be down soon.'

'She'd better be,' he growled.

It had been two weeks since Lucia had first arrived at our house and we had discovered that tomorrow was her seventeenth birthday. Alejandro had arranged for us to have dinner at a very exclusive restaurant and Lucia had been beside herself all day deciding what to wear. The two of us had gone shopping earlier and she had ended up being so torn between five different outfits that I'd insisted on buying her them all. She needed some new clothes anyway.

Alejandro sighed as he continued looking at the stairs. Then he turned his attention to me, sliding a hand over my hips and onto my ass. 'You look beautiful by the way. Red really suits you.'

I looked down at my new dress. It was cut just below the knee but it was tight and accentuated my slim waist and curvy thighs. 'You think?' I said as I bit on my lip and placed my hand on his chest. 'I'm really glad you like the color because it's exactly the same shade as my panties.'

'Fuck!' he said as he sucked in a long breath.

I leaned closer to him, my lips brushing his ear. 'They're see-through too.'

He squeezed my ass possessively. 'Don't tease me, princess or we won't make it to the restaurant.'

'You can't disappoint Lucia. I just told you, she's been excited about this all day,' I grinned at him.

'She'll forgive me when she sees her birthday present,' he growled as he moved his head and ran his teeth along my jawline before nipping and tugging on my earlobe sending a shiver of pleasure through my entire body.

I laughed as I wrapped my arms around his neck. 'Actually, she probably will.'

We had only found out yesterday that it was Lucia's birthday. As well as arranging this birthday meal, Alejandro had ordered her a brand new car and it was being delivered the following morning. I had been surprised by his generosity, not that he couldn't easily afford such a lavish gift, and he was usually generous with his money, but he had been so resistant to Lucia staying with us. It seemed she was working her way into his affections despite his insistence that she would be out of our lives as soon as possible. I looked up at him and smiled.

He smiled back at me and I felt a rush of wet heat as he pressed his body against mine. 'I'm going to tear those panties off you as soon as we get back home then,' he growled in my ear before he sealed his lips against mine, licking along the seam until I opened my mouth, allowing his tongue to swirl against mine. I leaned against him as my legs started to tremble.

'Oh my God! Can't you guys keep your hands off each other for like two minutes?' Lucia sighed behind us.

Alejandro removed his hand from my ass and I turned to see her walking down the stairs in a beautiful aqua blue dress which was the perfect tone for her skin.

'You look beautiful,' I said to her with a smile as she walked toward us. She stopped at the bottom of the stairs and gave us a twirl.

'You certainly do, chica,' Alejandro agreed.

She blushed slightly and walked toward us. 'Gracias,' she said quietly.

AN HOUR LATER, we were sitting on the terrace of the restaurant. I looked out over the ocean and gave a contented sigh.

'I think this is the most beautiful view I have ever seen in my life,' I said.

'I couldn't agree more, princess,' Alejandro said as he winked at me and I realized he wasn't talking about the ocean.

Lucia giggled as she looked at the two of us.

'What's so funny?' I asked.

'You two,' she replied. 'You're so sweet together.'

'Sweet?' Alejandro asked with a frown.

'Yeah. Like whenever you're near to each other, you're always touching.'

I almost choked on the mouthful of water I'd just taken. 'What?' I spat. Had she noticed Alejandro's hand squeezing my thigh a few minutes earlier? No. She'd been reading her menu and his hand had been under the table. It had been perfectly innocent compared to what he usually did when we were in a restaurant together.

She started to laugh louder. 'I don't mean like that. I mean look at you now. Your shoulders and hips are touching. Alejandro has brushed your hand or your arm at least half a dozen times. Most couples don't sit that close together at a restaurant, you know. At least most that I've ever known. I just think it's sweet how much you guys are into each other, that's all,' she said with a shrug.

'I don't think I've ever been called sweet before in my entire life,' Alejandro said as he picked up his glass and took a drink of his wine. Then he sat back against the seat and put his arm around me.

'I never said *you* were sweet,' Lucia said with a roll of her eyes. 'I've just never really seen a couple like you two before.'

'What about your mom and dad?' I asked and I felt Alejandro tense beside me.

'No way.' Lucia shook her head and picked up a bread roll. 'They... Well, they weren't like that at all.' She sniffed before taking a bite from her bread.

'Wait until you taste the lobster here, Lucia. It's incredible,' Alejandro said in an obvious attempt to change the subject.

WE HAD FINISHED our meal and were waiting for dessert when the waiter brought over a bottle of champagne to our table and placed three flutes down in front of us.

'Gracias,' Alejandro said as though he was expecting it and the waiter smiled and walked away.

'What's this for?' I asked.

'I have something to tell you both,' he grinned as he lifted the bottle from the bucket and popped the cork. 'And before you get too excited, Lucia, this is practically alcohol free,' he said with a flash of his eyebrows.

'Damn!' she said with a grin as Alejandro filled our glasses.

I watched him with a smile on my face. Whether he would

admit it or not, Lucia's presence in our lives was bringing out a softer side of him.

When our glasses were full, he handed each of us one. 'I got a call from my lawyer today. The paperwork making us Lucia's legal guardians has all been signed off. It's official. You're stuck with us for a few months yet, kid,' he said.

I opened my mouth in surprise and Lucia gave a squeal of delight.

'Wow! That was quick,' I said.

He shrugged. 'I pulled some strings.'

'Thank you,' Lucia said, her face shining with happiness.

I swallowed the lump in my throat as we raised a glass in a celebratory toast.

'I'm so excited, I think I'm going to pee,' Lucia said with a grin as she stood up from the table. 'Be right back.'

I watched as she walked to the restroom, with Hank keeping a close eye on her from his vantage point near the front of the restaurant. When she was out of our sight, I turned to Alejandro and placed my hand on his thigh. 'That was very sweet of you to rush those papers through.'

He scowled at me. 'That's the second time tonight I've been called sweet, princess. Don't go making a habit of it.'

'Well, it was,' I said as I leaned toward him. 'I love seeing the softer side of you.'

He edged his face closer to mine. 'Don't get used to it, Alana,' he growled. 'There is nothing soft about what I'll be giving you as soon as I get you alone.'

I opened my mouth in mock indignation. 'Is sex ever far from your mind?' I whispered.

'Not when you're sitting next to me in that dress and see-through panties, princess.' He leaned even closer until his lips were brushing my ear. 'If Lucia wasn't with us, I'd have fucked you in the car on the way here and taken those panties of yours hostage. Then you'd have had to sit here eating your meal with my cum dripping down your thighs,' he growled.

My insides turned to hot liquid as he planted a single, soft kiss beneath my ear.

'You're a devil,' I whispered and he laughed softly.

'That's better,' he said in his low, growly voice that reverberated through my body.

'But, seriously, thank you so much for what you did for Lucia. I would have hated her to go back to live with the Bakers.'

'I know.'

'Have I ever told you how much I love you?'

'Not often enough, princess,' he said as he lifted my hand from his thigh and kissed my fingertips. 'But I look forward to you showing me later, because our teenage runaway is on her way back over.'

LUCIA HAD EATEN SO much ice-cream for dessert that she had declared herself fit to burst and after another heartfelt thank you and a round of hugs, had taken herself off to bed as soon as we got home.

'Do you fancy a quick nightcap?' I asked Alejandro as we walked down the hallway.

He glared at me, those dark brown eyes almost black as he licked his lips. 'Okay. My office. Now.'

I swallowed. His office was soundproof. He did keep some of his finest Scotch in there, but we'd usually have a nightcap in the den or out on the patio. There had to be an ulterior motive for him wanting to go there instead. There was nothing soft or sweet about him right now. My fierce devil was back and I loved it.

I walked down the hallway to his office with him close behind me. I stopped at the door. It was locked. He stood behind me, so close that I could feel his hot breath on the back of my neck. He reached in front of me, his hand sliding between me and the door as he slowly keyed in the entry code, prolonging the contact between his wrist and my groin.

Pressing his body against mine, I felt the heat from his skin even through our clothes. Then his other hand snaked around my waist until I was completely caged in by him. He was wearing the cologne I loved and the scent of him was heady and intoxicating. It was a complete, overwhelming assault of the senses and I suspected he knew exactly what he was doing to me.

His breath skated over my neck and our bodies were pressed so tightly together it was hard to fathom where I ended and he began.

'Voy a follarte tan malditamente duro,' he growled in my ear and I felt a rush of wet heat between my thighs as my legs trembled. Even if I hadn't known what that phrase meant, I would have been a quivering mess, but I did know, because he had said it to me so many times before. *I'm going to fuck you so damn hard.*

Dear God, he was going to nail me into oblivion.

The lock opened with a loud click and Alejandro pushed the door ajar, allowing me to step inside. He followed me into the room, kicking the door closed behind us. Now nobody would hear a thing.

I turned around to face him and he stood there staring at me, his eyes roaming over my body as though he was a starving lion and I was his prey.

'Take everything off except the panties and the heels,' he ordered.

My hands trembled in anticipation as I reached for the zipper at the back of my dress and pulled it down. Then I shrugged the fabric off my shoulders and pulled the material down over my hips and legs until it was a pool of red at my feet. I unclasped my bra at the front and my heavy breasts sprung free — my nipples already hard under the heat of his gaze. I dropped that too and stepped out of the dress.

Alejandro licked his lips as his gaze travelled over my body and down to my sheer, red panties. 'They are fucking dangerous, princess,' he growled as he walked toward me.

'I'm not sure panties can be dangerous, Alex,' I breathed.

'Hmm. We'll see.' He grinned at me, then looked down at them. 'I can see they're already damp.' I felt the heat searing across my cheeks. 'I wonder how much wetter I can make you without even touching you?'

I bit my lip as he edged even closer until I could feel his warm breath skittering over my skin.

'What do you think, princess?'

'A lot more,' I whispered. I was sure he could make me come just from his dirty talk, but I'd much prefer he used other means.

'Shall we try?'

'I'd rather not,' I said as I stood there with my hands by my sides. I was desperate to reach out and touch him, but his office was his domain and he was in complete control here.

'No? Why's that?' he growled as he leaned his head closer, until his lips were dangerously close to the skin on my neck.

'Because I want you to touch me,' I gasped.

At my words, he placed his lips on the base of my throat, kissing me softly and making me groan out loud.

'Greedy, princess,' he chuckled. 'You remember how you told me about those panties just before we were leaving, so that I would spend the whole evening thinking about them and not being able to do anything about it? You knew I would be picturing your hot pussy and wishing I could bury myself in it, didn't you?'

'Yes,' I admitted.

'So maybe I should leave you all hot and wet and wanting me? Maybe I should make you stand here while I jerk off just looking at you?'

'You're not that cruel,' I panted as his lips dusted over the skin on my collarbone.

'Oh, I am. But I have a better idea,' he said as he stepped back.

'Up onto the desk.' He jerked his head upwards and I moved back and perched on the edge of the desk.

'Sit all the way back, princess. I want your feet on it too.'

I scooted back until I was sitting on his desk with my ass in the middle and my feet planted on the edge. I watched him as he pulled up his chair and sat down. Then he unzipped his suit pants and pulled out his cock. His eyes locked onto mine as he squeezed the shaft in his strong hand and I licked my lips in anticipation as I watched a bead of pre-cum run down the tip.

'Open your legs, slip your hand into those panties and play with that pretty pussy of yours. I want to watch you make yourself come.'

I felt my heart starting to hammer in my chest and heat flashed across my cheeks. 'What? Alex, I can't,' I gasped. I had never done that in front of him before. At least not like this, not when he wasn't involved in some way.

'You can and you will, princess. What is the point of wearing see-through panties if not to put on a show for me? Because that's what you wanted, isn't it?'

I swallowed as I looked at him. This hadn't been exactly what I'd had in mind.

'Don't make me ask again, Alana,' he warned. 'You make yourself come now or you won't be coming at all.'

I took a deep breath and slid my right hand into my panties, through my wet folds and onto my clit. I closed my eyes and started to draw slow circles around the swollen bud of flesh.

'Eyes on me, princess,' he barked.

Damn!

I opened my eyes and they locked with his as I kept on moving my fingers in slow, teasing circles. His eyes were full of fire and they burned into mine. Waves of pleasure started to build and I bit down on my lip to stop myself from moaning loudly. His eyes moved lower until they were fixed on my fingers between my thighs, and he kept on watching me intently, a wicked grin on his lips as he began to stroke his cock.

I arched my back and let out a groan. 'That's it, princess,' he growled. 'I can see your cum soaking those sexy little panties.'

I sucked in a breath and lay back on the desk so I could use my other hand too. I slid it inside my panties along with my other hand and pushed two fingers inside my wet channel.

'Fuck, Alana!' he hissed loudly as I started to work myself up to release, thrusting my fingers in and out while rubbing firm circles on my throbbing clit. I heard him growling in Spanish and it only spurred me on. I closed my eyes now that he couldn't see my face and imagined it was his strong fingers inside me rather than my own.

The pressure between my thighs intensified until my legs were trembling.

'I can see you're almost there, princess,' Alejandro growled from across the room. 'Your panties are soaked.'

It was as though his words tipped me over the edge and my orgasm washed over me slowly in long delicious waves. I lay back, panting for breath, my hands still inside my wet panties when I felt his hands on my wrists. He pulled my hands away and pinned my forearms to the desk at either side of my head.

'My turn.' He bent his head low, pressing his face against the damp fabric between my thighs and inhaling deeply. 'You smell fucking delicious, princess,' he growled and then his fingers were hooking under the band of my panties as he slowly started pulling them down my legs.

I leaned up on my elbows and watched him. 'Not tearing these ones, then?' I asked with a flash of my eyebrows.

He shook his head. 'Not these ones,' he grinned. 'I want to see that again.'

When I was naked, he dropped to his knees and wrapped his hands around the back of my thighs, pulling me closer to the edge of the desk. Then he ran his thick, hot tongue through the length of my folds. 'Your pussy is so fucking good, princesa,' he groaned.

I felt another rush of wet heat as his tongue started to swirl around my clit. The pressure started to build in my core, traveling up from my toes until every nerve ending in my body felt like it was on edge and ready to explode. My head tingled and my thighs trembled, and then he pulled me closer, sucking me hard as his tongue continued to swirl and my climax tore through me, ripping me open as I screamed his name.

He stood up and wiped his face with the back of his hand before grinning down at me. 'I do love to hear you scream, Alana,' he smiled at me before grabbing hold of my hips and reminding me what he'd said when we were standing outside his office thirty minutes earlier.

He slammed into me so hard I gasped for breath. I clenched my walls around him, drawing him in further, because I couldn't get enough of him. He looked down at me, holding me with the intensity of his gaze as he fucked us both to a shuddering climax.

When we were done, he wrapped his suit jacket around me and lifted me into his arms. I snaked my arms around his neck and melted into his body, feeling completely sated and spent.

'You are incredible, princesa,' he whispered in my ear as he carried me upstairs to bed.

'You're pretty incredible yourself,' I murmured.

HALF AN HOUR later we lay in the dark, listening to the sound of our breathing in the quiet stillness.

'What happened with Lucia's parents?' I asked Alejandro, remembering her reaction in the restaurant earlier when I had mentioned them.

'Her mother killed herself when Lucia was eight. She blames her father for her death.'

'Oh, that's awful. And was he responsible?'

Alejandro pulled me tighter to him. 'Maybe? She intended to kill herself. She left a note. I knew Miguel Ramos to be a double-crossing snake and a cruel and vicious cabrón. But then he was an enemy of my family, so why wouldn't he present like that to me? Only from what Lucia has told me, he wasn't any different with his own family.'

'Oh, that poor girl,' I whispered.

'Hmm. She said her brothers weren't much better. I don't know, Alana. Who knows what that kid has had to endure in her life? I hate to think about it.'

'Me too. Maybe now that she knows she's safe, she might get help if she ever needs it. You know, like therapy?'

'Maybe. We have to let her make her own choices though. She's still a kid, but she's not. You know what I mean?'

'Yes, I do. I'm just glad she has a safe home here for now though. Thank you for that.'

He kissed the top of my head. 'Anything for you, princess. You know that,' he said softly, but I knew that he was lying. Lucia Ramos was getting through the King of LA's titanium armor and there wasn't a thing he could do about it.

CHAPTER 10

ALANA

I turned on the shower, letting the hot water run over my face as I stepped beneath it. I flexed my neck and it pinched slightly. I'd been neglecting my daily yoga sessions since Lucia had moved in with us. I realized I would have to get back into some sort of routine with it; I'd never be able to keep up with my sex-crazed machine of a husband otherwise.

'Mind if I join you, princess?' I heard a low growl behind me.

I turned to face him. I definitely hadn't been neglecting marathon sex sessions with this devil walking toward me, but I still couldn't get enough of him. 'Of course not,' I smiled at him as he stepped under the water with me and slipped his hands around my hips and onto my ass, pressing me against his body.

'You look so fucking sexy when you're wet,' he growled against my neck.

'Well, I am always wet around you,' I giggled.

He bit down lightly against my skin and I yelped in pleasure, feeling a rush of heat between my thighs. 'I was only coming in here for a shower. You're fucking insatiable, princess.'

'Me?' I feigned my astonishment. 'You're the one with your

hands on my ass. And you were also the man who couldn't wait to get me naked as soon as we got home last night.'

'Well, I'd had to sit in a restaurant and keep my hands to myself all night because our teenage runaway was with us. It's very unfair of you to put me in such a difficult situation.'

'What? You mean expecting you to behave like a civilized gentleman and not feel me up in the middle of a restaurant in front of our seventeen year old houseguest? Oh, yes, so unfair,' I giggled.

'Yes. Unfair when you wear those sexy fucking panties and I have to sit with a hard on all night,' he growled.

'You're a devil,' I purred against his ear.

'You'd better believe it, princess,' he said as his hands shifted to my waist and he spun me around so I was facing away from him. Then he pushed me against the tiled wall and kicked my ankles apart. 'Open. I want inside you now.'

'You're going to be late for work,' I gasped.

He pressed his body against mine, pinning me to the wall with just the right amount of delicious pressure before taking hold of my hands and holding them above my head. 'I know, but I need to fuck you,' he breathed against my ear before bending his knees slightly and thrusting himself into me. 'Because I can't keep out of your sweet little coño.'

'Alex,' I whimpered as he pounded into me.

'Come on my cock, princess. Do you feel how hard you make me? Can you feel how much I love your tight pussy?'

I squeezed myself around him as I felt a rush of wet heat coating his cock. His filthy mouth never failed to turn me into a trembling mess.

'Fuck, princess!' he hissed as he increased his pace.

I pushed against him, trying to take as much of him as I could. When he sucked on the tender skin of my neck, I climaxed with a violent shudder just before he found his own release.

He pulled out of me and gave me a sharp slap on the ass. 'That's for making me late, princess.'

I turned around to see him grinning at me. He pulled me to him and kissed me softly.

'And what was that for?' I panted when he let me up for air.

'That was for making me late, too.'

'We have to give Lucia her present before you go,' I reminded him.

'You give it to her,' he said as he pulled the shampoo from the shelf and squeezed some into his hands.

'But you chose it for her. You paid for it. You should at least be there.'

'We both paid for it, Alana. It's our money.'

I smiled as he lathered the soap into his thick, dark hair. I loved that he genuinely meant that — not that I wanted his money. I also knew the real reason he didn't want to be there when we presented Lucia with her gift. He didn't want her to be grateful to him. I could already tell she was working her magic on him and he was starting to care about our little runaway just as much as I was.

'She'll only thank you later, anyway.'

He scowled at me. 'I don't have time this morning, princess. Just tell her it's from you. She won't care. She'll just be happy to have a car.'

'Okay,' I said. I knew there was no use arguing with him. 'Will you be home for dinner tonight?'

'No.' He wiped the water from his face. 'I have meetings all day and evening. I'll have something at the hotel.'

'Okay,' I said. He'd been working much more than normal lately and I wondered what it was about. That insecure part of me wondered if he was getting bored of me already.

He must have seen the disappointment in my eyes, as he took hold of my chin and tilted my face up to his. 'I have some work stuff going on, princess. I hope it's going to be sorted soon. I would rather be here eating dinner with you than at my hotel.'

'I know.'

'In fact, I'd rather just be eating you,' he said with a wicked grin that made me laugh.

'Te quiero,' I said as I wrapped my arms around his neck.

'I love you too, princess.'

AN HOUR LATER, Lucia and I were sitting in the doctor's office waiting for her check up. Hugo and Hank were sitting opposite us. Alejandro insisted that both of them accompany us everywhere for the time being, and while I enjoyed Hugo's company, Hank was still a miserable ass. I don't think he'd ever once smiled at me during the whole time I'd known him.

'Thank you again for my car, Alana,' Lucia said as she sat beside me. 'I can't believe you guys bought me a freaking car.'

'You're welcome, sweetheart. Alejandro said every girl should get a car for her sixteenth birthday, and as we didn't know you then, a car for your seventeenth is the next best thing.'

'Well, I love it. I can't wait to take it for a spin. You'll come driving with me later, won't you, Hugo?' she asked.

'I'm afraid I can't, got to take the boss lady to work this afternoon,' he said.

'I'm sure Jax said he would be calling round later. He loves driving. I'm sure he'll take you for a quick spin,' I told her.

She seemed satisfied with that response and sat back in her seat. Lucia had been beside herself earlier that morning when I'd presented her with the new Mercedes that Alejandro had chosen for her. She'd refused it at first, telling me that it was too much, but I'd reminded her that Alejandro had more money than he could spend in twenty lifetimes and that she deserved something nice after years of struggle. After a brief pause she had gratefully accepted, giving me a huge hug and promising that she would look after it like it was her own child.

'Miss Montoya,' the nurse called and Lucia looked at me, her beautiful face pulled into a frown.

'Alejandro had our name put on your records for now, I hope you don't mind. He didn't want to bring any attention to who you really are,' I whispered.

She smiled at me. 'Of course. That's fine. Actually, I like it. Will you come in with me?'

'Sure,' I said standing up.

'We'll be right here,' Hugo said as he watched us walk into the doctor's office.

THE DOCTOR HAD FINISHED CHECKING Lucia and the baby over and confirmed everything was as it should be. She was making her notes when she looked up at Lucia. 'It's never too early to think about contraception for the future, Lucia. There are plenty of options. I'll give you some information on them and you can decide when you're ready.'

Lucia shrugged. 'I'm sure Alana will help me decide. What contraception do you use?' she looked at me.

'What? Oh, I don't use any. I never have.'

Dr. Kelly looked up at me as I spoke. I didn't get a judgmental vibe from her at all, but I still felt like I had to explain myself. 'My husband and I would like a baby,' I said.

'Oh, I see,' Dr. Kelly smiled. 'You been trying long?'

'Uh, about six months. And we're not really trying, just more not, not trying, if you know what I mean?'

She nodded. 'Well, when you do get serious about starting a family, you need to make sure you're having sex in your ovulation window. You know how to work that out, don't you?'

'Not really. It's not something I've ever really thought about, to be honest.'

'Well, that might be why you've never fallen pregnant yet. Unless you're having sex every single day, you might be missing your window.'

Lucia burst out laughing at this point and despite being a grown woman talking to a medical professional, I blushed to the roots of my hair.

Dr. Kelly glanced between the two of us with a look of bewilderment on her face.

'Lucia, you and I are all done. Would you mind waiting outside for a few minutes please?' she said.

Lucia stood up with a dramatic roll of her eyes. 'Hey, all I know is that Alana and Alejandro are doing it way more than once a day,' she giggled.

'Lucia!' I blushed again. How the hell did she even know that?

Lucia winked at me as she walked out of the door.

'I'm sorry if I embarrassed you, Mrs. Montoya,' Dr. Kelly said.

I shook my head. 'It's fine. I don't know what she's talking about. It's not like we do anything in front of her.'

She laughed softly. 'I'm sure you don't. But if you are having sex every day and you haven't fallen pregnant yet, it might be worth us running some tests.'

'Oh. Why?'

She shrugged. 'Maybe you're not ovulating regularly? You have a window of about six days per month where you're fertile, so if you're having sex around those times and haven't fallen pregnant yet, it could be worth checking out, just so you know what's going on.'

I blinked at her. 'I didn't realize there could be a problem.'

'There probably isn't. Maybe you're just not having sex around those dates?'

I felt a sick feeling in my stomach as I realized what she was saying. 'We must have been having sex on my fertile days. We have sex twice a day, at least.'

'Every day?' she frowned.

I blushed again. 'Yes. Except for two nights last month when he had to go away on business.'

'Oh?' She sat back slightly.

'We're newlyweds,' I offered with a shrug, feeling the need to defend myself again.

'Hey, I didn't mean to make you feel uncomfortable. I'm just jealous,' she started to laugh. 'But I do think it would be worth us running a few tests. My next patient cancelled so we can make a start now if you like? And we should really test your husband, too.'

'Well, let's start with me, and take it from there,' I said, wondering how Alejandro would respond to fertility tests.

'It could be nothing. We usually advise couples to try for twelve months before having tests, but I'm a fertility specialist and Mr. Montoya's insurance covers everything I offer, so there's no harm in getting ahead of the curve, is there?'

'No, I suppose not,' I said with a forced smile.

I sat in her office for another half hour, answering questions and providing blood and urine samples. I had never even considered that I wouldn't be able to fall pregnant when I wanted to. Alejandro and I had decided as soon as we'd started having sex that we wouldn't use contraception. I didn't like the idea of putting hormones in my body and he didn't want to wear condoms. As we were both happy with the idea of having a baby, we decided we'd see what happened. I hadn't really thought about it since.

We were both young, healthy and happy, and I assumed there would be no problems at all in that department, but now I was faced with the possibility that there might be a medical reason for why I hadn't gotten pregnant yet. I kind of wished I hadn't accompanied Lucia to her doctor's appointment now. Perhaps ignorance was bliss.

CHAPTER 11

ALANA

*I*t was late by the time Alejandro finally arrived home that night. I wandered down the hallway so I was standing waiting for him as he walked through the door. I was still feeling anxious about my visit to the doctor's office earlier. What if there was something wrong with me? Would he still want me if I couldn't give him a child?

'Hola, princesa.' He smiled as he looked up and saw me standing there. He walked toward me and pulled me into his arms. 'Did you miss me?' he growled before sealing my mouth with a kiss.

I wrapped my hands around his neck and melted into him. 'I always miss you,' I replied when he let me up for air.

'Something wrong?' he frowned at me.

I shrugged. 'Maybe. I don't know.'

He took hold of my hand. 'Let's get a drink and you can tell me about it,' he said and we walked down the hallway to his office.

Alejandro poured us a small glass of Scotch each and I sat opposite him. I noticed how tired he looked. He had been working so hard and had been having trouble sleeping lately, and I felt guilty for bothering him with my problems when he obviously had much more important things on his mind.

'So, tell me what's on your mind, princess?'

'It's not important. It can wait. You look tired. Let's finish these and go to bed?' I suggested instead.

He arched his eyebrows as he stared at me with a look of concern. 'I'm not tired. I'm just busy. And I will most definitely be taking you to bed when we've finished our Scotch. But, first I want to know what's on your mind. Nothing about my work is more important than you, so talk to me, princess.'

I took a sip of the whisky and then I told him all about my visit to Dr. Kelly earlier and how worried I was that there might be something wrong with me.

He listened intently, sipping his whisky as he did.

When I'd finished talking, I sat there, fidgeting with the hem of my dress as I waited for him to respond.

'Come here,' he said, his voice a low rumble.

I walked around the desk to him and he pulled me onto his lap, wrapping his arms around my waist and burying his face in my neck. 'There is nothing wrong with you, princesa. Doctors like to run tests. They're always looking for problems. That's their thing.'

'I know, but what if...'

'Then we'll deal with it. Whatever comes our way. Anyway, it took my mom two years to get pregnant with me,' he brushed the hair back from my face and cupped my chin with his hand.

'Really?'

'Really. So I'm sure we have nothing to worry about. Besides,' he growled as he moved his hand from my face and slid it between my thighs, 'what's the rush when we're having so much fun trying?'

I gasped as his hand reached higher and his fingers brushed

over my panties. My legs parted for him of their own accord and he laughed softly as he pulled the lace fabric to one side.

Sliding through my folds, he hissed as he reached my hot opening. 'So. Fucking. Wet.' Then he pressed his lips against mine, pushing his tongue and his fingers inside me at the same time and causing me to shudder as jolts of pleasure coursed through me.

He tasted of whisky and fire. I ran my fingers through his thick dark hair as he devoured me with his tongue. 'Alex,' I groaned into his mouth.

He pressed his fingers in deeper, curling them until he hit that perfect spot inside me and I felt a rush of wet heat.

'Fuck! Alana!' he growled as my juices coated his fingers. He pressed further inside until my walls were squeezing around him, pulling him in further. 'I need you to come so I can fuck you on my desk, princess,' he groaned as he brushed my clit with his thumb, circling the nub of flesh with the perfect amount of pressure.

'Alex,' I shouted as my climax burst through me.

He kissed and rubbed me through it, and as soon as my legs had stopped trembling he stood, lifting me from his lap and bending me over his desk in one fluid movement. I lay there and listened to the familiar sound of his belt and zipper opening. He placed one of his strong hands between my shoulder blades, pressing me against the mahogany while he pulled my dress up to my waist with the other. I lay there, breathless with anticipation as he pulled my panties down to my knees.

'You ready to be fucked, princess?'

'Yes,' I breathed.

'Yes what?' he teased as he pressed the tip against my opening.

'Yes, please,' I begged.

'Buena chica,' he growled as he slammed into me.

He leaned over me. 'You have no idea how much I love

fucking you,' he growled in my ear and then he slipped into Spanish as he lost himself in me, nailing me to his desk until I forgot all of my worries and anxieties about my trip to the doctor earlier.

CHAPTER 12

ALEJANDRO

The sound of my cell phone ringing on the nightstand woke me from my sleep. I rolled to answer it and frowned when I saw it was only 5am. I knew that if someone called me at this time it would be for something important, but that didn't stop me cursing under my breath. I got so little time with Alana these days, I resented any intrusion into it.

Picking up my cell, I saw Anton DeLuca's name flashing on the screen. He and his team were still looking for Lucia's ex-boyfriend, Blake Fielding. He had been on the missing list since he'd assaulted Alana almost four weeks earlier and I was completely stumped as to how some punk from Chicago could evade some of my best soldiers. I could have got Jax onto the case, but we were both tied up dealing with the Ortegas.

'You'd better have something for me,' I hissed as I pressed the phone to my ear. Alana turned in her sleep and draped an arm over my stomach.

'Who is it?' she mumbled.

'Just work, princess,' I said softly as I covered the mouthpiece. 'Go back to sleep.'

'We've found him, Boss,' Anton said.

'About fucking time,' I replied as I slipped out of bed and pulled on my sweatpants. I walked out of the bedroom and closed the door behind me, waiting until I was out of Alana's earshot until I spoke again. 'Now, bring the motherfucker here to me so I can deal with him.'

'That's going to be pretty difficult, Boss. He's already dead. He's just been chiseled out of a cement block and is on his way to the morgue as we speak.'

'What?' I snapped as I walked down the stairs and headed to my office.

'That's the reason we haven't been able to find him. He was part of the foundations of a new apartment building in Chicago.'

I stepped into my office and sat at my desk. 'What the fuck? How long has he been there? And how the fuck did you find him?'

'The cement was poured two days after Blake was in LA, so he must have gone straight back to Chicago. He'd obviously upset someone else too, because he was supposed to be buried down there forever. It would have been the fucking perfect crime. Except that there was a problem with the way the foundation was laying, so they dug part of it out to reset it and found a little more than they bargained for. We've had feelers out all over Chicago looking for this prick, so as soon as they identified it was him, someone let us know.'

'And it's definitely him?'

'Yep.'

'Fuck! Any idea who wanted him dead?'

'Other than you, Boss? No. It seems he didn't have many friends, but he didn't have any real enemies either. Not that we've been made aware of, at least none that would have gone to these lengths.'

'Who are the construction company?'

'Lambert and Hall. They're a local Chicago firm. Completely legit. We've spoken to the foreman and we're meeting the CEO later, but there seems to be no connection to Fielding and the company.'

'But someone must have had access to that site when the concrete was being poured?'

'I know. It doesn't make any sense, Boss.'

'No.' I frowned as I held the phone to my ear with one hand and fired up my laptop with other. 'At least that cabrón is dead, anyway.'

'Yeah,' Anton agreed.

'Now get yourselves back to LA as soon as possible. We have plenty of trouble to deal with here that I could use you and your team's help with.'

'Will do, Boss. We'll be back as soon as we can.'

'Good. And nice work, Anton.'

'Thanks, Boss.'

Two hours later, I was frowning at my laptop screen when Alana walked into my office carrying a tray. The smell of coffee and freshly baked croissants filled the room and my stomach growled in appreciation.

She was dressed in one of my t-shirts, and from the outline of her hard nipples through the fabric, not much else.

'Buenos días, princesa,' I smiled at her. Despite spending the last two hours on the phone and computer, giving myself a headache and trying to juggle business and deal with the Ortega family, being around her always made me feel lighter. I knew that I'd been neglecting her these past few weeks. I'd spent far more time working than at home and I missed spending time with her.

'You were up super early this morning. I thought you might like some breakfast?' she said as she put the tray on my desk.

'Smells delicious. Gracias, princesa,' I replied as I pushed back my chair and stared at her while she poured two cups of hot coffee.

'Cream?' she asked, seemingly entirely innocently as she held up the small white jug.

'Really?' I grinned at her.

'What?'

'Come here.' I held out my hand and she put the jug back on the tray and walked around the desk to me. As soon as she was close enough I pulled her onto my lap. She wrapped her arms around my neck and I ran my nose along her collarbone and up her throat. Even the smell of her skin made my cock twitch to life. 'Why do you always smell so fucking incredible?'

'I smell of sex, and you,' she groaned as she tilted her head back for me, allowing me easier access to kiss her neck.

'Like I said, incredible!'

She laughed softly. 'I need a shower. And I didn't mean to distract you from your work. I know you're busy.'

'You didn't, huh?'

'No,' she smiled sweetly.

'But you do realize how dangerous it is to come into my office, half naked and offer me some cream, Alana?' I growled.

She gasped softly and then started to giggle. 'I didn't mean that. I meant for your coffee.'

'I know exactly what you meant, you sex-crazed nympho,' I said as I trailed kisses along her throat. I slid my hand up the outside of her thigh and squeezed her ass. For the first time ever, I was relieved she was wearing panties, because if she hadn't been, I wouldn't have been able to stop myself from lifting her onto my desk and fucking her.

'I'm expecting a call soon and I need to take it, so do you think you can sit and eat some breakfast with me without driving me to distraction?'

'I'll try my best,' she purred in my ear.

I had meant that she should go and sit on the other chair, but she remained on my lap as she leaned forward and pulled our coffees closer to us. I shut my eyes and groaned as I realized that I couldn't bear to ask her to move.

'Would you like some jelly on your croissant?' she asked.

'Please.' I licked my lips and she wriggled forward again as she took a croissant and split it open.

My cock twitched and throbbed every time she moved. Who was I kidding? There was no way she was leaving this office without my cum dripping out of her.

'Are you done?' I asked with a flash of one eyebrow as she moved on my lap, doing everything so damn slowly.

'Almost,' she giggled.

'Do you have to move your ass that much just to spread jelly?' I groaned.

'Yeah. You have to work the jelly in. So that all of the pastry is coated in its sweet, sticky goodness.'

'Jesus, princess,' I growled. I didn't know if she was doing this on purpose, or I was just so fucking turned on that everything she said and did looked like it belonged in a porn film.

'Done,' she said as she turned to face me and sucked her finger clean with a wet pop. I groaned out loud. I couldn't take any more.

'What?' she asked, all wide eyed, as though she couldn't feel my raging boner pressing into her ass.

'Take off the panties. Take out my cock and get yourself onto it. Now,' I hissed.

Her eyes darkened with desire. 'I thought we were just having breakfast?' she whispered.

Fuck! She really didn't have a clue what she did to me.

'I said now, Alana!'

She stood up and slid off her panties, placing them on my desk before she straddled me, pushing down my sweatpants and freeing my weeping cock before sliding herself onto it easily. Her pussy was slick and hot and I groaned as she sank deeper, until there was nowhere left for her to go. Her feet couldn't quite reach the floor so she had little leverage to work herself up and down. She clenched her walls around me instead as she rolled her hips over mine.

'If you weren't in here hoping for sex, why are you so wet, princess?' I growled.

'I never said I wasn't hoping for sex. But *you* said we were just having breakfast. Besides, I've spent the last five minutes with your cock twitching against my ass, so of course I'm wet,' she breathed as she stared into my eyes and squeezed me tighter.

'Fuck!' I hissed, pulling her t-shirt up and over her head before throwing it onto the floor. I grabbed her by the hips and shifted her closer to me so I could suck one of her hard nipples into my mouth while one hand slid down to her clit.

'Oh! Alex!' she groaned just as my cell started ringing on my desk.

'Fuck!' I snarled as I reached for it. I pressed the phone to my ear with one hand and wrapped my free arm around her waist to try to hold her still against me.

'Hey, Neo. I appreciate you calling me so early,' I said as Alana kept on rolling herself over me and grinding herself on my cock. Neo Lopez was the newly appointed head of our Chicago operations and I wanted to speak to him about reaching out to every contact he had to find out more about Blake Fielding and the Lambert Hall Construction Company.

I sucked in a breath as Alana squeezed her pussy around me and I shot her a warning look. Her cheeks flushed pink and she stopped rolling her hips at least.

'No problem at all, Boss. What do you need from me?'

'I've sent you a link to a newspaper article...' I hissed as Alana's pussy continued squeezing me hard. And then I watched with a mixture of surprise, horror and desire as she slid one of her hands between her thighs and started rubbing her clit. Fuck, she was going to come and she was going to take me with her.

I moved the phone away from my face. 'Don't you dare,' I whispered in her ear.

She bit her lip and nodded, but she kept on going anyway — driving me crazy.

'You okay, Boss?' Neo asked.

I cleared my throat. 'Yeah. Just dealing with something,' I stifled a groan. 'So…The article… Find out everything you can about the body that was found… and the construction company.' I sucked in another breath as I felt Alana's cream dripping down my cock. 'Okay? Nothing heavy handed. The company might be nothing to do with it.'

'Okay. I'll get on it. No problem. I wanted a quick word about something while I've got you. Is this a good time?'

No, it's fucking not, Neo. My wife is currently riding my cock and she's about to make me blow my load in her. 'If you can make it real quick,' I snapped instead.

I tried to concentrate as Neo told me about some problems he'd been having with some of our competitors and asking for the best way to handle it. I appreciated he was new, and I also appreciated that he kept me in the loop, but I paid him to handle these things himself — by any means necessary.

Alana was on the edge. I could feel her body trembling. She stopped rubbing her clit and sat completely still, but it was already too late. Her eyelids fluttered and her cheeks flushed bright pink. I put my free hand on the back of her head and pressed her face into my neck as I felt her orgasm rippling through her body. She moaned into me as she milked my cock with her hungry little squeezes, until I felt like I was going to get a nosebleed from trying to hold off coming inside her.

'I trust you to sort it any way you need to, Neo,' I managed to say.

'Thanks, Boss. It was good to…'

I ended the call and threw my phone onto my desk. Wrapping

Alana's hair around my fist, I pulled her head up and she moaned out loud as her body kept on trembling.

'Did you just come when I told you not to, princess?' I growled as I wrapped my other arm around her waist, standing up and planting her on my desk so she was lying on her back, allowing me the perfect angle to rail into her with everything I had.

'Alex,' she groaned as I fucked her and it wasn't long before I was filling her with my cum.

I pressed my forehead against hers and we both panted for breath. 'I can't believe you just did that. Now, Neo Lopez has heard you come and I'm going to have to kill him.'

'What?' she blinked at me. 'No! You can't do that. I was quiet. He didn't hear me.'

I started laughing as I pulled out of her and sat back on my chair, pulling her with me so she was sitting on my lap again. 'I'm kidding,' I said as I brushed her hair from her face and kissed her forehead. 'And you were very quiet.'

Her hands flew to her cheeks and she blushed. 'Oh, God. Do you think he did hear me?'

'No. I would have ended the call if you'd started screaming,' I smiled at her. 'I wouldn't let anyone hear you come, princess.'

'I'm sorry. I couldn't hold on,' she said as she bit her lip. 'I did try.'

'I know you did.' I grinned at her. 'That's why I'm not spanking that beautiful ass right now.'

'Well, I do enjoy your spankings.'

'I know.'

'Especially over your desk,' she shivered and I couldn't help laugh.

'Maybe later, princess. Right now I need to tell you something.'

'What? Is everything okay?' she stared at me.

'You know I've been looking for Blake Fielding?'

'Yes.'

'Well, my men found him this morning. He's dead.'

'Oh!' Her hand flew to her mouth. 'Who? How?'

'I don't know. But that's what my call was about. I'm going to find out.'

'Do you think Lucia is danger?'

'No more than we already knew about,' I said as I kissed her forehead. 'I'll speak to her when she gets out of bed later.'

'Poor Lucia. I wonder how she'll take it. I know she wasn't his biggest fan, but he is her baby's father.'

'Well, we'll find out when I tell her. Now how about we actually eat this breakfast you made us before we go take a shower.'

'Sounds good to me,' she said reaching for her panties.

I snatched them off my desk before she could take them and stuffed them into my pocket. 'I think I'll keep hold of these.'

'But I have to walk back through the house and your cum is dripping down my thighs,' she whispered.

'Well if you had done as you were told like a good girl and not made yourself come while I was on the phone to my associate, I'd have given you your panties back. But you didn't. So they're mine now.'

'You're the devil,' she hissed as she grabbed my t-shirt from the floor and slipped that on instead.

'You'd better believe it, princess.'

IT WAS another two hours before I was finally dressed and ready to leave to go to the hotel. I had fucked Alana in the shower and then again in our bed, promising her that I'd make more time for her as soon as work calmed down — for me that meant as soon as this shit with the Ortega firm was over with.

They'd been making small, stupid moves, trying to get us in trouble with the licensing board and sending their goons in to start fights in our clubs and hotel bars. Nothing that we hadn't stamped out immediately, but it made me wonder if they were just distracting us while they got ready to make their big move. My father and my uncles usually handled the dirtier side of our business, but they were all getting older now. The youngest of them was my Uncle Carlos, but at forty-eight, even he wasn't as on top of his game as he used to be.

So, everything was slowly being handed over to me. Not that I hadn't expected it. But I enjoyed the actual business side of things more than the bloodshed. Although I was used to both. Between the ages of eighteen to twenty-three, I had worked with my uncles as the family enforcer.

However, my father and I had soon realized that my head for business was much more valuable than my aptitude for violence. We had an army of guys who could dole out beatings and punishments, but there was only really me and my father who could see the bigger picture. That was when he'd made me the CEO of Montoya International and I'd become somewhat more legitimate, which suited me fine. I still had to use brute force and outright fear when the occasion called for it, but at least half of the time, I got to solve problems with my head.

I felt like that was slipping away from me now though and I was getting dragged more and more into the murkier side of our business. My family's money was made in the arms and drugs trade. It was a business that was dangerous and unpredictable and one I hoped to be rid of entirely one day. Montoya International was a billion dollar company. We no longer needed the trade from our illegitimate earnings, but that was the side of the business that was the hardest to break free from and it was the side which the Ortegas were trying to get a piece of.

I knew that it was only a matter of time before I needed to consider a pre-emptive strike, even as I dreaded dragging my family into any kind of turf war. Six months ago, I wouldn't have thought twice about making that choice, but now that I had Alana to think of, decisions like that weren't so easy. I used to feel like I was invincible, but perhaps I was just reckless? Because the thought of putting her in harm's way, of losing her, was unthinkable.

I suddenly saw what my father had meant about love being dangerous, because a man with something to lose always had a weak spot — and there was no doubt that she was mine.

CHAPTER 13

ALANA

*L*ucia and I were sitting in the den watching TV by the time Alejandro arrived home later that evening. I had thought about telling her about Blake myself, but decided it was better to come from him. I had no idea what had happened to Lucia's ex-boyfriend other than the fact he was dead, but I knew that she would have questions and they were ones that I couldn't answer.

Alejandro walked into the den and sat beside me on the sofa, slipping his arm around my shoulder and planting a soft kiss on my forehead.

'We saved you some dinner,' I said as I placed my hand on his thigh.

'I ate at the hotel,' he replied and then he looked over my shoulder at Lucia, who was laughing at the movie she was watching.

'Hey, Lucia, can we talk to you about something?' he said and she turned to look at him.

'Sure. Is everything okay?'

'I think we should turn off the TV,' I said to her and she paused the movie.

'It's about Blake,' Alejandro started to say and Lucia pulled a disgusted face.

'He's dead,' Alejandro finished.

She blinked at him for a few seconds before she spoke. 'What?' She reached out and fumbled for my hand. I squeezed her gently.

'Where did you find him?' she asked.

'He was in Chicago. He was found this morning.' Alejandro replied.

'Did you?' She started to ask the question but didn't finish it.

Alejandro shook his head. 'No.'

She swallowed before nodding her head gently and placing her free hand on her stomach.

'Are you okay?' I asked her.

'Yeah. It's just kind of a shock to know that he's gone.'

'I know. And it's okay to be sad,' I reminded her.

She looked up at me. 'I'm not sad. Not really. Does that make me a horrible person?'

'No,' Alejandro and I replied in unison.

'I mean, I thought he was my friend, but all he ever did was use me,' she said as tears formed in her eyes.

I squeezed her hand tighter.

'He was as bad as my father and brothers,' she sniffed and I felt Alejandro stiffen beside me and wondered what that was about. 'Is it bad that I feel kind of relieved that he'll never come after me or my baby again?'

'No, that's not bad at all, sweetheart. In fact, it's perfectly understandable,' I assured her.

She nodded and wiped the tears from her cheeks with the sleeve of her sweater. 'What happened to him?' She directed her question to Alejandro.

He looked at me first and then he sucked in a breath. 'He was buried alive in cement.'

I winced at the thought of such a horrible death, but Lucia simply frowned. 'Wow! Do you know who did it?'

'Not yet,' Alejandro replied. 'Any ideas?'

Lucia shook her head. 'He was an asshole. But he wasn't stupid. He didn't usually piss off the type of people who would be likely to bury him alive in cement.'

Alejandro raised an eyebrow at her and she snorted. 'I guarantee you that if Blake had realized Alana was your wife, he would never have laid a finger on her. He only goes for easy prey.'

The way she referred to herself as easy prey and how accepting she was of that fact broke my heart. I squeezed her hand tighter. I couldn't even comprehend what this young girl had gone through in her life and how she was still this sweet, lovable kid after all of it.

'Well, you're far from easy prey anymore,' Alejandro said with a wink and she rewarded him with a huge smile.

'Want to watch the rest of the movie with us?' Lucia asked. 'It's really funny.'

Alejandro looked at the screen, which was paused on a still of kids in a high school hallway. I knew that he hated these kinds of films. In fact, he barely watched TV at all. I was surprised when he sat back against the sofa and put his arm back around me. 'Why not? I could do with a distraction,' he said.

I sat back too and leaned against him, placing my hand on his thigh and keeping hold of Lucia's with the other. A few moments later, the three of us were laughing at the movie. I turned to Alejandro and he winked at me and I thought that I had never loved him quite as much as I did in that moment.

CHAPTER 14

ALANA

*I*t had been almost two weeks since my first trip to see Dr. Kelly. She had called me back in for more tests a few days later and now it was just a matter of waiting for the results. I'd kept busy at the shelter and spending time with Lucia. She was proving herself to be a completely problem free house-guest and was really good company, especially as Alejandro was so busy with work.

I was reading by the pool when I got the call from Dr. Kelly telling me my results were in and asking if Alejandro and I could come in later that morning. I'd told her that of course I could and I was looking forward to seeing her. And then I'd put the phone down and almost thrown up with nerves and anxiety. If she needed to see me straight away, it couldn't be good news, right? If everything was okay, she could have just put me out of my misery and told me over the phone. But maybe they gave all news face to face?

My fingers trembled as I picked my cell back up and dialed Alejandro.

'Hey, princesa,' he said, his voice low and gravelly today, and in any other circumstances, it would have had me panting with longing.

'Hey. So, Dr. Kelly called. She has my results and she'd like us to go in this morning if we can. Are you able to make it?'

'Of course. I'll move some things around.'

'Thank you,' I said, my voice wobbling.

'Everything will be okay, princesa. No matter what.'

'Okay,' I whispered.

'I'll pick you up at eleven. Is that okay?'

'Yes. I'll let her know.'

'Te quiero, Alana.'

'Love you too, Alex.'

ALEJANDRO SQUEEZED my hand tightly in his as we sat in Dr. Kelly's office and tried to digest what she had just told us. But, I was finding it difficult to focus on anything she said after hearing the words *it will be very difficult for you to conceive naturally, Alana.*

Alejandro asked lots of questions and Dr. Kelly explained all of our options and what fertility treatment would be available to us, but all I could think about were those words and the fact that I may never be able to give my husband a baby. The heir that he so desperately wanted. The heir that his family needed. The only reason he had married me in the first place.

Half an hour later we walked out of the doctor's office and I was still in a daze.

Alejandro held onto my hand and I saw the way he kept looking at me with his eyes full of concern and it only made me feel worse. This was my fault. My body was letting us down. Not his. Knowing he was worrying about me was just making me feel even more guilty.

'Come on, let's get home. We can do something nice together this afternoon? Maybe go for a hike? Or to a movie?' he said as he guided me to the car.

'No. You have meetings all day. You should go back to the hotel,' I insisted.

'Alana, I'm not going to work when you're this upset.'

'Aren't you upset?' I snapped at him.

He frowned at me. 'Of course I am. But, we've only just found out about this, princess. I don't want to start talking about our options right now, but we have plenty.'

'But there's no guarantee any of them will work,' I sniffed.

'Alana.' He put an arm around my shoulder and kissed the top of my head. 'There is no rush, princess. We don't even need to think about any of that yet. Just let me take you home.'

'No.' I shook my head. 'I need to go to the shelter anyway. We have a huge fundraising event I need to plan for.'

He looked at me, his eyes still full of concern.

'I want to go to work,' I insisted. 'It will be good for me to keep busy. You go back to the hotel, go to your meetings, and I'll see you tonight.'

He frowned at me but then he nodded. He signaled Hugo over to him who had been waiting outside in his car. We always went everywhere with extra security lately.

'Can you and Hank take Alana to the shelter?'

'Of course, Boss,' Hugo replied and walked back to the car.

Before I could follow him, Alejandro took hold of my arm. He looked like he was about to hug me, but then seemed to change his mind. 'I'll be home for dinner. Okay?'

'Okay. I'll see you later,' I said as I forced a smile.

I WAS SITTING at my desk a few hours later, still reeling from the news Dr. Kelly had given us earlier. I'd made some calls and organized as much as I could for the fundraiser, but I could hardly focus on anything. All I wanted was Alejandro. I wanted him to tell me that everything was going to be okay and that what we'd found out today didn't change anything between us. I shook my head in annoyance at my own stupidity. I should have taken him up on his offer to do something together.

Hugo stood up and stretched his legs and I realized the poor guy had been sitting in my office for the past two hours without so much as a drink.

'Hey. How do you fancy finishing work early today?' I asked him.

He flashed his eyebrows at me. 'What exactly do you have in mind?'

'Can you take me to the hotel? I'll wait in the suite until Alejandro has finished with his meetings and you can go visit your mom. I know she's still a little under the weather.'

He frowned. 'I'll have to take you up to the suite.'

'I wouldn't expect any less,' I smiled at him.

'Okay. Whenever you're ready then.'

I closed down my computer and picked up my purse. 'I'm ready now. Let's go.'

FORTY-FIVE MINUTES LATER, Hugo and I were standing outside Alejandro's hotel suite. Four armed guards stood in the hallway.

'Is the Boss in?' Hugo asked.

'Yeah. He's in his office with his father.'

'I'll just let Mrs. Montoya inside then,' Hugo said and they stepped aside to allow him to open the door.

'Of course. Good afternoon, Mrs. Montoya,' one of the guards said and I nodded in greeting.

'Thanks, Hugo. I'll see you tomorrow,' I said as I walked inside and the door closed behind me. I hadn't seen Alejandro's father, Mateo for a few weeks, and thought I'd just say a quick hello and let them know I was there, then leave them to their meeting and wait in the suite.

I walked toward Alejandro's office. The door was open and I could hear their voices drifting through into the room.

'So, you're telling me she can't even have children?' I heard Mateo say. 'I'm sorry, mi hijo. It seems I chose you a defective model.'

'Papa!' Alejandro said.

'What? I would never have chosen her for you if we'd known that. She tricked you, hijo. What good is she to you, to this family, if she can't even give you an heir?'

I stood frozen to the spot with shock and anger. I knew that I was eavesdropping on a private conversation and I should walk away, but I couldn't. I stood there, waiting for my husband to tell his father that he was wrong. To tell him that I wasn't *defective* and that my value to him and to this family was so much more than my ability to reproduce.

I waited for him to stand up for me. For us!

But, he didn't. Then I heard Mateo again. 'Your mama is going to be devastated. You should find yourself someone who can give her some grand-babies.'

I felt the tears pricking my eyes as I turned on my heel and ran from the room. I put my hand on the door and wiped the tears from my cheeks. Alejandro's guards would never let me leave if they saw me crying.

I took a deep breath, plastered on a fake smile and opened the door.

'Everything okay, Mrs. Montoya?' one of the guards asked me.

'Yes. Everything is great. But, Mr. Montoya asked me to wait in the bar downstairs for him until he's finished his meeting with his father.'

'I'll escort you downstairs, Ma'am,' he replied.

'There's no need. He's just asked Hugo and Hank to wait for me at the elevator. I think you should stay here and look out for Alejandro and Mateo, don't you?'

He looked at me, his eyes searching my face. It seemed I was still a good actress as he pressed the button for the elevator and let me step in alone.

. . .

As soon as I reached the lobby, I walked through the reception, trying to hold it together until I got outside. A security guard stopped me and I told him that my personal security was waiting for me outside.

I took a deep breath as I stepped outside into the sunshine. Looking around the street, I had no idea what I planned to do next. All I knew was that I had to get as far away from here as possible.

I saw a cab waiting and jumped into it. 'Where to, Miss?' the driver asked me.

I looked at him. Where did I want to go? As far away from my husband and his father, who thought I was defective and had no use to them anymore, as possible. Far away from this city and its insanely perfect people, and to someone who loved me despite all of my flaws.

'LAX please,' I said as I sat back against the seat.

CHAPTER 15

ALEJANDRO

I looked up at the man I had always respected more than anyone else in the world and wondered what the hell had gotten into him. I'd told him about the news Alana and I had received earlier, expecting some words of advice and support. Instead, he launched into a diatribe about how useless Alana was to me now.

I let him talk. That was his way. He talked at people, usually talking them into submission. When he finally stopped I stood up from my desk.

'Have you quite finished insulting my wife?' I snarled at him.

He glared at me. 'Watch your tone, mi hijo,' he warned.

'No, I will not fucking watch my tone, Papa! How dare you come into my office and talk about my wife like that? She is devastated that she might not be able to get pregnant and if you can't be anything but one hundred fucking percent supportive of her right now, then I don't want you anywhere near her, or me.'

'Alejandro!' he hissed. 'I am your father!'

'No. Right now, you're just some jackass who is standing in my office insulting me and the woman I love. So, if there's nothing else, get the hell out.'

His nostrils flared as he stared at me, no doubt wondering whether he should punch me in the face for daring to speak to him like that, but a few seconds later he turned around and stormed out of my office.

I WALKED out of my hotel suite and into the hallway. I'd cancelled my final meeting of the day because I wanted to get home to Alana. I needed to make sure she was okay. But more than that, I needed her to make me feel okay, too.

'Evening, Boss,' Lorenzo, one of my guards said. 'Are you heading to the bar?'

'No. Straight home,' I said as I reached the elevator.

'But Mrs. Montoya said you were meeting her in the bar.'

I frowned at him. 'What?'

'When she left earlier, she said that you'd told her to wait for you in the bar.' I saw his Adam's apple bob in his throat as he swallowed.

'My wife was here?' I snapped as my heart started to race.

'Yes, Boss.'

'When?'

'About two hours ago. She left shortly before your father.'

Shit!

'What? Where did she go? You just let her walk out of here on her own?' I snarled.

'She told me that you'd asked her to wait for her in the bar. She said Hugo and Hank were waiting there for her.'

'Call the bar now, and see if she's there,' I said as I pulled my cell from my pocket and dialed her number. My heart sank as it went straight to voicemail.

'Fuck!' I hissed as I called Hugo.

He answered after a few rings. 'Everything okay, Boss?'

'That depends. Is Alana with you?'

95

'No,' he said, just as Lorenzo shook his head to indicate that Alana wasn't in the bar either.

I took in a deep breath, sucking in a lungful of air as I tried to tell myself that she was safe. She was simply upset and she needed some space. She was probably just back at the house.

'I took her to your suite. I let her inside and I closed the door. I thought she was with you.'

I heard the panic in Hugo's voice and it did nothing to calm my bubbling anger.

'It is *your* fucking job to protect her. Unless you actually hand her over to me, or she is in the house, she is *your* fucking responsibility!' I snarled. 'How could you just fucking leave her like that?'

'I'm on my way back to the hotel, Boss. I'll find her.'

'No. Go check at the shelter. Or any other place she might be. And you'd better pray that we find her soon and that she's fucking okay!'

'Of course, Boss,' he said as he ended the call.

I turned my anger on Lorenzo then, grabbing him by the throat and pushing him against the wall. 'How the fuck could you let her just walk down to the lobby on her own? Especially with everything that's going on with the Ortegas! What the fuck do I pay you for?'

'I'm sorry, Boss. But she said...'

I squeezed his throat so hard, he couldn't finish the sentence.

'I don't care what she said. It is your fucking job to protect me and my family. She is my family. If anything has happened to her..!'

I let him go and he gasped for air as he rubbed his throat.

I stepped back and ran my hands through my hair. My heart raced. Adrenaline coursed around my body as though it was my lifeblood.

I was wondering what to do next when I felt a hand on my

shoulder. I spun around to see Jax. 'Hey, amigo. What the hell is going on?'

I PACED UP and down my office. Alana wasn't at the house or the hotel. She wasn't at the shelter. She wasn't answering her cell. Security cameras had recorded her leaving the hotel and getting into a cab. I couldn't get hold of anyone who knew where she might be. It seemed like even Lucia was avoiding me.

I had men out looking for Alana every place I thought she might be. Jax sat watching me. I was about to suggest we go and do something useful when my cell phone rang.

'It's Lucia,' I said. Thank fuck! She had to know something.

'Hey, Alejandro,' she said breezily. 'I was taking a nap and I left my cell on silent. Sorry. Is everything okay?'

'Have you seen Alana?'

'No. But she sent me a text a couple hours ago.'

'What did it say?'

'Hang on. I didn't read it. Let me check.'

There was a few seconds' silence as she checked her phone.

'It says. *Hey sweetie. I'm going away for a couple days. Alejandro and Magda will look after you. Take care of you and that baby. I'll call you tomorrow.*'

'That's all?' I snapped.

'Yes. What's going on, Alejandro? Where is she? Why has she gone away? What did you do?'

'She got some bad news this morning, that's all. She just needs some space.'

'So why hasn't she told you where she's gone?' she asked in a snarky tone that made me want to remind her who she was speaking to.

'Look, Lucia. She's pissed at me. She's pissed at everything. But I'll find her.'

'Well, there's only one place she would have gone if she's gone for a few days, isn't there?'

'Where?'

She sighed dramatically. 'Back to New York!' She never actually said *dumbass*, but I heard it anyway.

Fuck. Of course she'd go there. 'Listen, tell me if you hear from her again, okay?'

'Yes. And Alejandro?' she said, sounding like a child again instead of a snarky teenager.

'What?'

'Please bring her home soon.'

'I will. Bye, Lucia.'

I put the phone down and Jax stared at me. 'She might be in New York. Speak to our friends at LAX and see if she got on a plane.'

'Will do,' Jax replied. 'But where would she go? She wouldn't go and see her folks, would she?'

'No. I don't think so. But she has a friend there. Kelly?' I said as I tried to recall one of our many conversations about Alana's life in New York. 'No, Kelsey. She lived in the same apartment building in Manhattan.'

'I'm on it, amigo,' Jax said as he pulled his cell out of his pocket. 'We'll have her back home within the next twenty-four hours.'

CHAPTER 16

ALANA

I looked up and down the familiar hallway and couldn't help but feeling a pang of loneliness. I've missed this place so much, but now I kind of feel like I don't belong here anymore. Taking a deep breath, I rang the doorbell. A few seconds later the door was opened and I felt a rush of emotion at seeing that familiar face. I had missed those sparkling green eyes and that huge smile so much.

'Alana! What the hell are you doing here?' my best friend, Kelsey shrieked as she threw her arms around my neck and squeezed me tightly. 'Why didn't you tell me you were coming?'

Tears pricked my eyes at the thought of telling her why I was here. I sniffed as I pulled back from her. 'It was a spur of the moment thing,' I said with a shrug.

'Oh, honey.' Suddenly her face was full of concern. 'Come on in.'

I followed her into her tiny apartment, the one that was just like the one I used to live in too, and it made me realize that I missed my new home so much. I started to cry.

'Alana,' she said softly as she guided me to the sofa in her living room. 'What is it honey? What's happened?'

I wiped my cheeks with the back of my hand. 'So many things. It's such a long story, Kels.'

'Well, why don't I pour us a huge glass of wine and you can tell me all about it,' she said with a reassuring smile.

I smiled back. It felt so good to be here with her. I'd missed her so much, and I knew I hadn't been in touch as much as I should have, but my life in LA was so far removed from New York. At first I hadn't wanted her to know that my marriage was a business arrangement and then I'd been so wrapped up in Alejandro. I felt ashamed of the way I'd treated her.

'I'm sorry I haven't been in touch much, Kels.'

'Hey,' she admonished me. 'I haven't called you as much as I should have either. But we are home girls. We will always have each other's backs. Besides, you've just got married to that fine ass billionaire. I didn't expect to be invited for a visit any time soon,' she laughed. 'Now, sit your ass down and I'll fetch us some wine.'

HALF AN HOUR LATER, I had told Kelsey about Lucia and Alejandro, and my visit to the doctor's earlier that day. She listened intently, handing me a tissue and topping up my wine whenever I needed it.

'Wow!' she said with a shake of her head. 'Sounds like you've had some six months, honey!'

I laughed. 'You could say that.'

'And so you just jumped on a plane to New York and didn't tell anyone where you were going?'

I nodded. 'Kind of. I sent Lucia a text telling her I just needed a few days. She'll tell Alejandro, but I just couldn't face talking to him. I still can't,' I said as I thought about my cell phone in my purse which was still switched off. 'Do you think I did the wrong thing?'

Kelsey held her hands up. 'Only you know that, honey. You

were upset. You have every right to come here and visit your best friend.'

'But?'

She sucked in a breath. 'From what you've said about Alejandro, it sounds like he's not going to be satisfied with you sending a text to your houseguest. Maybe you should give him a call?'

I chewed my lip and looked at my purse. 'I don't know. I'm still so pissed at him.'

Kelsey nodded in agreement. 'And you should be, honey. Letting his daddy say those things about you is kinda fucked up.'

'But?' I said again. One of the things I usually loved most about Kelsey was that she was open and fair. She always tried to look at all of the angles before making a decision, but sometimes, like now, I kind of wanted her just to nod and agree with me.

'Well, maybe he did say something to his daddy after you left? Maybe he was just hurting too, honey? Not that that excuses his behavior, but it sounds like he adores you and I think you should at least hear him out.'

'And I will. After I've calmed down and don't feel so goddamn emotional.'

'And you've made him sweat for a while?' Kelsey added with a wicked grin and a flash of her eyebrows.

I lifted my wine glass to my lips. 'Well, that's just an added bonus,' I grinned back. I didn't know if it was the wine, or talking to my best friend, but I was feeling a whole lot better about the entire situation.

CHAPTER 17

ALEJANDRO

*J*ax looked at me with a smile on his face as he put his cell back into his pocket.

'Seems your girl boarded the 4:15 flight to JFK, amigo.'

'Fuck!' I hissed. I hoped she wasn't going to see her snake of a father. I didn't think she would, but there was always a possibility. I hated that man with a passion.

'Samuel!' I shouted to my employee who was waiting in the other room. He came running into my office.

'Yes, Boss?'

'Call the airport and have the jet ready to go to New York as soon as possible.'

He nodded. 'I'll get right on it.'

'And call Hugo too. Tell him to meet us there. He helped get us into this fucking mess; he can help me fix it.'

Samuel nodded before walking back out of the room.

I looked at Jax again. 'You think you can find out who Kelsey is and get me her address by the time we land?'

He frowned at me. 'Of course I can. This is me you're talking to.'

I chewed my lip in frustration and Jax stood up and put a reassuring hand on my shoulder. 'She's safe, amigo. She'll be back in your arms in about eight hours.'

I nodded at him but I wouldn't relax until she was back by my side where she belonged. She must have overheard my father and me talking earlier. There was no other explanation for why she'd just take off like that, at least none that I wanted to think about right now.

Fuck! She obviously hadn't stuck around to hear me throwing him out of my office. What the hell must she think of me now?

A pain shot through my jaw and I realized I was grinding my teeth. No matter what she had heard, nothing justified her flying off to the other side of the country without so much as a goodbye.

'Shall I get the car brought round out front?' Jax asked, interrupting my thoughts.

'Yeah,' I nodded absent-mindedly.

'Okay. Meet us out front in five,' he said before disappearing out of my office.

I took my cell out of my pocket and called Lucia.

'Have you found her?' she asked.

'Yes. She's gone to New York.'

'Told you.'

'I'm flying there myself soon. We'll be back tomorrow morning. Don't leave the house while I'm gone.'

'Can't I come with you?' she asked.

'No,' I said and she sighed on the other end of the phone. I knew she would be worried about Alana too, but I had no idea of the reception I'd get when I found her. She would need handling, one way or another, and I didn't need Lucia around while I did that.

'I'll bring her back before you even wake up tomorrow,' I said.

'Fine. But, you'd better not hurt her,' she snapped.

'What the fuck, Lucia! You honestly think I'd do that?'

'I mean her heart, dumbass! I didn't think you were going to beat her up!' she snapped.

God, this kid was infuriating. 'I won't do that either,' I said with a sigh.

'Good. Then I'll see you both tomorrow.'

CHAPTER 18

ALANA

It was almost 2am, and Kelsey and I had talked non stop since I'd arrived. My stomach growled noisily as she was telling me about her latest dating mishap and she burst out laughing.

'Shit! I completely forgot to feed you,' she said with a snort.

'You don't have to feed me. I'm not your house-pet,' I giggled.

'I know that, but you must be starving. I have literally no food in the place. Let's order a pizza.'

'It's 2am!'

'It's New York, baby!'

'Of course. I forgot about Tony's on the corner.'

'I'll order one now. Shall we go ham and pineapple?'

'Yes,' I groaned. 'And a side of fries.'

Twenty minutes later there was a knock at Kelsey's apartment door.

'Damn! Tony got way speedier since I left,' I giggled.

Kelsey jumped up from the sofa. 'Food!' she half groaned, half growled as she grabbed her wallet and headed out into the hallway.

A moment later, I heard the front door close and Kelsey padding back toward the room.

She popped her head through the open door. 'Uh, I don't mean to startle you, but I think your husband is here,' she said with a flash of her eyebrows.

'What?'

'There are three, very serious and very stacked, men in suits standing in the hallway asking to see you.'

My heart lurched into my throat. 'Did one of them look like he had steam coming from his ears?'

'Yup,' she nodded.

'Then it's him,' I said with a groan.

'I kinda got the impression he's not gonna leave till he talks to you, honey. Shall I let them in?'

I chewed my lip as I thought about whether it was better to go out into the hallway and talk to him instead. But, what was the point when I knew there was not a chance in hell Alejandro would leave this apartment building without me.

'I mean, I'm all for standing my ground and telling them to get lost, but I do like my front door. You know?' Kelsey grinned.

'Okay. Let them in,' I said with a sigh.

'It will be okay, I'm here,' she said with a reassuring smile.

A few seconds later, I heard the door opening again and the sound of muffled voices filled the hallway. I stood up, wiping my hands on my jeans nervously. I looked up and swallowed as I watched Hugo and Jax walk into the room.

Shit!

Alejandro had brought the big guns with him for this and suddenly I felt like a runaway teenager who was about to get the ass-whooping of my life. A second later, he walked into the room behind them, looking incredibly hot and incredibly angry in his tailored suit and his crisp white shirt. My heart almost pounded out of my chest with both fear and anticipation.

He glared at me, his eyes fierce and full of fire. 'Hello, Alana,' he growled.

'How the hell did you find me so quickly?' I asked. 'You haven't implanted a tracker in my ass, have you?'

He scowled at me but I saw Jax chuckling softly as he took a seat on Kelsey's sofa.

Alejandro didn't find it in the slightest bit amusing though and he continued to glare at me. 'Is there somewhere we could talk in private?'

'Sure! You can use my room,' Kelsey offered.

I frowned at her and she shrugged apologetically.

'Lead the way, princess,' Alejandro said as he stepped back out into the hallway.

I walked out of the room and into Kelsey's bedroom with him hot on my heels.

As soon as he had closed the door behind us, he grabbed hold of me, pushing me against the wall with the full weight of his body, one hand wrapping my hair around his fist and the other wrapped around my throat. He kissed me fiercely, full of passion and possessiveness, pushing his tongue inside my mouth and claiming me. I responded in kind. I couldn't help it. My body craved him.

He pressed his semi-hard cock against my stomach and I groaned into his mouth. Every single one of my nerve-endings was screaming for him. He rolled his hips against me as a growl vibrated through his entire body.

I ran my hands over his muscular back and down to his perfect ass and squeezed. His hand released its grip on my throat, sliding down my neck, over my breasts and stomach until he reached the waistband of my skinny jeans. He tugged the button open with one swift jerk of his hand before pulling the zipper down slowly and slipping his hand inside my panties. My legs trembled in anticipation and I felt a rush of wet heat as he slid his hand between my thighs.

I leaned into him. My body craved his touch, feeding on it like a fire consumes oxygen. He slid his fingers through my wet folds and onto my clit, rubbing in small circles and making me moan loudly into him. Without even thinking, I spread my thighs wider apart to allow him easier access, and felt the low rumble in his throat as he pushed two fingers inside me. I wasn't quite ready for him and I felt the burn as he pumped them in and out of me, reaching deeper inside with each thrust until he was pressing against that sweet spot inside.

'Alex!' I gasped into his mouth, but he didn't let up, devouring my mouth with his own and claiming my pussy with his skilled hands. He brought me to the edge quickly, rubbing against my walls until my cream was spilling over his fingers. When he brushed the knuckle of his thumb over my clit, I came apart around him, my legs trembling violently and my head spinning as the orgasm ripped through me. He kept a tight hold on my hair, and his mouth over mine, swallowing my scream with his kiss.

He rubbed the last of my climax from me, allowing my heart rate to return to normal before he broke our kiss. When he did, he glared at me, his eyes full of fire. 'Who does this belong to?' he growled as he palmed my pussy and squeezed possessively.

I stared into his eyes and realized how foolish I had been to run away from him. 'You,' I panted as I blinked back tears.

'And who do you belong to, princess?'

I swallowed as my pulse started to race again. 'You.'

He pulled his hand free from my panties and lifted it to my face, cupping my chin with his fingers. I sucked in a breath as I felt how wet with my own arousal they were.

'Ciertamente! So, don't you ever fucking run from me again.'

'Okay,' I whispered as a single tear rolled down my cheek.

He pressed his forehead against mine, our bodies molded together, hearts hammering in perfect sync and our breathing ragged.

'What the hell were you thinking? Do you have any idea how worried I've been, Alana? How worried Lucia has been?'

I swallowed. At the time, I hadn't thought about that. I had just wanted away from LA - to be with someone who had always loved me just as I am. 'I'm sorry,' I whispered. 'But I did say I'd be back in a couple days. I just needed some space.'

His eyes searched mine. I felt the anger still radiating from him, but there was something else in his eyes too. 'We had some bad news yesterday, princess. I know that. But you don't just run away when things get hard. We face our problems together. You said you wanted a real marriage. That is what a real marriage is about.'

I shook my head. 'The only reason you married me was so I could give you an heir and now I can't even do that. You should find someone who can.'

He let go of my hair and took a step back from me, his face so full of anger that I wondered if he was about to explode. 'What did you just fucking say?' he growled, his voice low and menacing.

I swallowed. That had been unfair, but I was still hurting. 'I heard you and your father talking. I heard what he said about me and he's right. I am useless to you now.'

'You really think I believe that?' he snarled.

'Well, you didn't correct him. You let him say those awful things about me and you didn't disagree,' I said, my voice trembling as much as my knees.

'If you're going to eavesdrop, princess, you should make sure to listen to the whole conversation. My father has always had my unwavering respect. He is a man who isn't used to being disagreed with and so I let him have his say. But if you'd have hung around, you'd have heard me call him an asshole and throw him out of my office. But instead you ran away. You really think that your only worth to me is to give me a kid?'

'But that is why you married me,' I challenged him.

'But that's not why we're still married, is it? I don't give a fuck about kids, Alana, if I don't have you by my side. You are everything to me and I don't understand how you could think otherwise.'

I zipped up my jeans and walked across the room to sit on Kelsey's bed. 'I heard your dad saying those awful things, and I was upset and scared. The fact that I might never get to have a baby, Alejandro, it's...' I shook my head and started to cry.

He sat beside me on the bed with a sigh. 'There are plenty of ways to have kids, princess. You need to stop putting so much pressure on yourself to be perfect.'

I looked up at him and he reached out and tucked a strand of hair behind my ear. 'I want to be perfect for you though. I want to be everything you need.'

'You already are, princess. I swear I will die a happy man as long as you are by my side. Now, can we go home?'

I chewed on my lip and he sighed again, running a hand through his hair before shaking his head and frowning at me. 'The fact that you think I would allow someone to talk about you like that, and not defend you, kills me. How could you think I would do that? Especially about something like this?'

'Well, it wasn't just anyone, was it? It was your father. And I know how much you love and respect him. I know how loyal you are to your family, Alejandro.'

He closed his eyes and took a breath. When he opened them again, they were full of fire and emotion. 'What you say is true. And I would kill for my father, but I would die for you, Alana,' he breathed and then he leaned closer to me, brushing his lips over mine.

My heart swelled in my chest. I felt like all of the air was being sucked from the room and I took shallow breaths to calm my racing heart. I had been such an idiot.

'Te quiero, princess. You are everything to me,' he said softly.

'I love you too,' I whispered.

'I have a plane waiting at JFK, but if I need to, I will stick you in the trunk of the car and drive us all the way back to LA. It's your call, princess.'

'The plane will do just fine,' I said with a smile.

'Good,' he said as he wrapped his arms around me and kissed my forehead.

'Are you going to punish me for running away?' I whispered.

'I should,' he breathed into my hair. 'I should take my belt to your ass and scar it for life. But no, I'm not going to punish you, as long as you promise never to take off like this again, and never assume that you are anything less to me than my whole fucking world. Can you do that?'

'Yes,' I whispered.

'Do you think your friend would mind if I fucked you on her bed?' he growled.

'Yes. I think she'd mind a lot,' I laughed.

'Damn!' he said with a grin.

A FEW MOMENTS LATER, we walked out of the bedroom and back toward the others in the lounge.

'We may as well eat this food, Kelsey. Those two will be fucking like rabbits,' I heard Jax saying as we entered the room.

'Oy!' Alejandro said as we walked into the room and gave Jax a friendly punch on the arm. 'Come on. Let's go.'

'Hang on a minute,' Kelsey said as she stood up. 'You can't just walk in here and take my best friend like that. It's the middle of the night. Our food has just arrived. I haven't seen her for months and I've missed her.'

Alejandro checked his watch. 'We have a delinquent seventeen year old at home who we need to get back to. And we only have two hours before we miss our slot for take-off.'

'Sorry, Kels,' I said.

'You sure you want to go back with him?' she asked me. 'Because I know you guys might be tough and all that but I am not against kicking some ass or calling the cops if you're taking my friend here against her will.'

I felt Alejandro tense beside me, unused to Kelsey's particular brand of humor.

'Yes, I'm sure,' I said. 'I'm sorry I'm running out on you, though. I've missed you, too.'

Alejandro looked between the two of us and rolled his eyes. 'Why not come with us then, Kelsey?' he offered.

'What?' Kelsey and I said at the same time.

'We have plenty of room if you want to come stay with us for a couple days?' he replied.

'But she has a job,' I said.

'Actually, I have some vacation time owing. And they owe me a huge favor anyway after I helped them out of a tight spot today,' Kelsey said with a shrug.

'Why, what did you do?' I asked.

'Can you tell her on the plane?' Jax said with a roll of his eyes. 'I've got a hot date tonight.'

'Please come then?' I said to her.

'Okay. I'll come stay,' Kelsey squealed as she ran off to her bedroom to grab some things.

'Thank you,' I said to Alejandro.

'My pleasure, princess,' he growled as he wrapped an arm around my shoulder.

TWENTY MINUTES LATER, we stepped into the street and the driver, Michael, held open the doors of the car for us. Jax bypassed him and climbed into the front while Hugo and Kelsey got into the back seat, followed by Alejandro.

He held out his hand to me and patted his lap, as it was the only place left for me to sit. I climbed in. 'So I don't even get my own seat?' I said with a flash of my eyebrows.

'Well, I wasn't expecting we'd be bringing a guest home with us,' Alejandro said with a smile. 'So, either you sit on my lap or Kelsey will have to sit on Hugo's.'

'I can certainly live with that,' Kelsey said with a grin. 'I'm all about teamwork.' She winked at Hugo and he stifled a laugh.

'I think Hugo has got himself into enough trouble for one day,' Alejandro replied.

I looked up at him. I hadn't even considered that Hugo would get into trouble for me giving him the slip at the hotel. 'Sorry,' I mouthed and he winked at me in response.

'ALANA, I had no idea you guys had a plane,' Kelsey said as she took her seat and looked around.

'Neither did I,' I flashed my eyebrows at her.

'Actually, we have two,' Alejandro said in my ear as he wrapped an arm around me.

'Two? Why on earth would anyone need two planes?' I said.

He shrugged. 'In case one breaks down.'

'Well, now that I know this piece of information, you can fly me to LA any time I have a few days off, can't you?' Kelsey said with a grin.

'If that's what you ladies want,' Alejandro replied smoothly as he leaned back in his seat and closed his eyes.

WE'D BEEN in the air for half an hour when Alejandro took my hand and signaled his head to the back of the plane. I looked around and noticed that Jax had fallen asleep, and Hugo and Kelsey were deep in conversation.

I stood up and walked to the back with him. He opened a door to reveal a small, but fully functional bedroom.

'You have a bedroom on your plane?' I laughed as I stepped inside and he closed the door behind us.

'Of course, princess,' he said as he took a step toward me, causing me to step back so my legs bumped against the bed. 'Can you think of any better way to spend the next few hours than to get naked under those covers with me?'

I bit my lip and tilted my head as though deep in thought.

He slipped his hands around my waist and onto my ass. 'Well?'

'What about everyone outside? They'll know what we're doing in here.'

'Seems like Kelsey and Hugo might appreciate some time alone themselves,' he grinned. 'And Jax will sleep the whole way home. He always does. And even if they do know... So what? You're my wife and that means I get to fuck you wherever and whenever I want, princess.'

'Then no. I can't think of anything better than getting naked with you,' I said as I snaked my arms around his neck.

He pulled my tank top over my head and tossed it onto the floor before dropping to his knees and pulling off my skinny jeans. I helped him by kicking them off my feet. Then his hands moved to my panties.

'Don't...' I started to say but he'd already torn them off me. He tossed them over his shoulder with a wicked glint in his eye.

'You have a very perverse aversion to panties,' I told him.

He moved his head to my neck and began nuzzling my tender skin. 'No. I have an aversion to you wearing panties, Alana,' he mumbled against me. I wrapped my hands back around him and then I heard him unbuckling his belt. I shivered in anticipation and he looked at me, his forehead furrowed into a frown. 'You want to feel my belt on your ass, princess?' he growled.

'Maybe,' I sucked in a breath. 'I don't know.'

'Why maybe? Are you worried about the noise? Because no-one will hear over the sound of the engines.'

'Not just the noise.'

'Oh?' he said softly as he ran a hand over my ass. 'You're worried I'm going to punish you?'

'Yes,' I panted as his hand slipped between my thighs and through my wet folds.

'But you know my bed isn't for punishment, Alana. And I already told you I'm not going to punish you for running away, didn't I?'

'Yes. But why?'

'Why what?' he breathed against my ear as he slipped a finger inside me.

I shivered at the combination of his breath skittering softly over the delicate skin of my neck as his finger pressed against my walls. 'Why aren't you going to punish me?' I panted.

He lifted his head and looked into my eyes. 'Because we've both been through a lot in these past twenty-four hours. I don't want any more distance between us, princess.'

I bit on my lip and nodded.

'Do you want to be punished?' he asked as he added a second finger to my channel. I held onto his forearm, feeling the muscles flexing as he worked me and I groaned out loud.

'I just want us to be okay,' I breathed.

He brushed his lips over mine while he continued slowly finger fucking me. 'We are okay, princess. I don't want to punish you, but I'm not sure you won't think that I am anyway, so we'll save the belt for another time. Okay?'

'Okay.'

'Now, get your ass onto that bed,' he growled in my ear as he slid his fingers out of my slick channel.

I sat down and crawled back on the bed on my elbows as I watched him undress, sliding his shirt over his muscular shoulders and forearms and letting it drop to the floor. I watched as all of his finely toned muscles flexed with every movement and felt a rush of wetness as I pictured him holding himself over me in a few moments' time. Licking my lips, I thought about how those muscles in his body would completely overpower me, and how easily I would let them, because I craved him being in control.

He slid his suit pants and boxer shorts down his thick thighs and kicked them off. When he stood back up, I couldn't keep my eyes off his huge stiff cock as it glistened with his arousal.

'You are so damn hot,' I said as I bit on my lip.

He laughed softly as he crawled over me. 'If I'm hot, princess, then you are fire.'

He bent his head and sucked one of my pebbled nipples into his mouth as he gently kneaded my other breast and I moaned out loud. Then his head was moving southwards as he kissed and nibbled his way down my stomach until he reached my thighs. He kissed each of my inner thighs in turn, right by where I wanted his mouth. I pushed my hips upwards and he smiled against my skin.

'I can smell how much you're creaming for me already, princess, and it's making me so fucking hard I could come right now,' he growled.

'Alex, please?' I begged him.

'Tell me what you want, Alana,' he said softly as he continued planting soft kisses all around my pussy but deliberately avoiding the spots where I wanted him most.

'I want you to make me come,' I gasped.

'What with, princess?'

'I want mouth and your fingers.'

'Both? I'm not sure you've earned both, Alana,' he growled.

'Please?'

'Hmm,' he hummed against my skin and the vibration rocketed around my body. 'I always take care of you, don't I?'

He pushed my thighs flat against the bed before he licked all the way from my hot opening to my clit. He settled his mouth there and started to suck gently before moving the fingers of his right hand to my hot entrance and sliding two fingers inside, curling them until he was hitting my G-Spot and my whole body was trembling with the impending orgasm. But he didn't let me have one, he kept me there on the edge and every time I was about to fall over the cliff, he pulled back slightly before starting again.

'Alex, please?' I panted as I ran my fingers through his hair.

He stopped and looked up at me, his eyes full of fire and his face wet with my juices. My legs shook violently as my release ebbed away again and I threw my head back against the pillow in frustration. But he didn't go back to eating my pussy. He slid his fingers out of me and then he moved up the bed, nestling himself between my thighs until he was pressing at my opening.

'You are dripping all over this bed, princesa. Your cream is fucking delicious. But it's not enough,' he growled as he pushed himself inside me and my eyes almost rolled into the back of my head. 'Because I want every last drop from you.'

He lifted my legs and wrapped them around his waist as he fucked me slowly. 'I want you to soak these bedsheets with your cum. I want you to scream my name because I need you to remember how good we are together. I want to remind you how much our bodies were made for each other.'

'Alex,' I gasped as I opened my eyes and looked at him. God, he was so damn beautiful. And he made me feel beautiful too. 'I love you so much.'

'Te quiero,' he breathed before sealing his mouth over mine. Then he fucked me so slowly and perfectly that I felt like I might have died and gone to heaven. When I finally climaxed, a rush of wet heat gushed out of me and soaked the sheets just like he'd wanted.

It was only then that he broke our kiss and smiled at me. 'Jesus, Alana! You are fucking perfect, mi reina.'

CHAPTER 19

ALANA

*A*s soon as the plane touched down on the runway, Alejandro and Jax turned on their cell phones. Both of their devices pinged to life with message alerts and missed calls. They frowned at each other and before either of them could say another word, Alejandro's cell phone started ringing in his hand.

'Hola?' he said as he lifted it to his ear.

I couldn't hear the conversation or even tell who was on the phone, but my heart sank as I watched his face turn an unusual shade of pale.

'We'll be there as soon as we can, Mama,' he said quietly. 'Si. Te quiero,' he said before ending the call. He took a deep breath and looked at me. I felt my pulse start to quicken as I waited for whatever terrible news he was about to give me.

'Papa has been shot. He's in ICU,' he said matter of factly.

'What?' I gasped, my hand flying to my mouth. 'Shot?'

'What the fuck?' Jax hissed as his own cell started ringing. 'By who?'

Kelsey looked at me wide eyed from beside Jax, her hand reaching for Hugo's.

Alejandro shook his head and I took hold of his hand and

squeezed. 'I don't know. But find out everything you can and then...' He looked around the small plane, seeming to remember that Kelsey was with us, and stopped himself from saying anything further.

'I'm on it, amigo,' Jax replied, not needing any further clarification.

'Hugo, can you take Kelsey to the house please?' Alejandro said as he squeezed my hand. 'You're coming to the hospital with me?' he said as he turned to me. As if he even needed to ask.

'Of course I am.'

'Good,' he nodded before turning back to Kelsey. 'I'm sorry that this has been your introduction to LA, but Hugo will look after you.'

'You don't have to apologize. I hope your father is okay,' Kelsey replied quietly before drawing in a shaky breath.

I squeezed Alejandro's hand again and he responded in kind.

As SOON AS we got outside LAX, there were three cars waiting, one to take Alejandro and me to the hospital, one for Jax who'd had his cell phone glued to his ear since we'd touched down and was heading to the hotel, and one to take Kelsey and Hugo to the house.

Alejandro and I sat in the back seat of Jacob's car as he drove us to the hospital. Alejandro was quiet and understandably distracted and I wished there was something I could say to make him feel better. All his mom had told him was that his father had been shot in the chest earlier that morning while he'd been on his way to see Alejandro at the hotel, and we were on our way back from New York. He had been rushed into the ER and they were doing all they could to save him.

I held on tightly to Alejandro's hand, threading my fingers through his. He continued staring out of the window, but he lifted my hand to his mouth and brushed my knuckles across his lips, and despite the awful situation we were heading into, I still felt a spark of electricity from his touch.

WE WERE GREETED by Alejandro's mom, Maria, and his two uncles, Phillipe and Carlos as soon as we reached the ER. Maria looked at us as we walked through the doors and at the sight of her son, her face crumbled.

'Mama,' Alejandro said as we reached her, letting go of my hand and pulling her into an embrace.

'Oh, hijo,' she sobbed into his arms.

Alejandro kissed the top of her head. 'He'll be okay, Mama. Papa is the strongest man I know.'

She nodded, her face pressed against his chest. Alejandro glanced up at his two uncles, who looked at him gravely, their faces full of fury and anguish. Then the three of them shared a look which had Alejandro untangling his mom from his arms. 'I'm just going to talk the doctors, Mama. Alana will sit with you,' he said.

She nodded and stepped back from him. I put my arm around her shoulder and she leaned her head against me. 'Come on, let's have a seat,' I said as I guided her to the nearby seating area.

Then I watched as Alejandro and his uncles walked down the corridor, and I knew that they were doing much more than talking to any doctor. I may have been new to this life, but even I knew that the attempted murder of Mateo Montoya was about to start an all-out war and my husband and his generals were already planning their next move.

CHAPTER 20

ALEJANDRO

I hated hospitals. I hated everything about them. The smell. The bright lights. The weight of all of the grief in the place, as though the walls held onto the memories of all of the pain and suffering endured here.

'So, what the fuck happened?' I asked my uncles as we walked down the corridor.

It was my Uncle Phillipe who answered me. My mother and father lived in Vegas, and were only visiting LA for a few days, where they were staying with him and my aunt, Rachel. 'He left the house in a rush this morning. Wouldn't even wait for his bodyguards to go with him and insisted on driving himself. He was at a stop sign when someone pulled up alongside him and shot him. We got all of the local CCTV and there's not much on it. But the shooter was on a motorcycle which was dumped further down the road.'

'Fuck! Do we have any leads?' I snapped.

'Do *we* have leads?' Carlos hissed. 'Where the fuck were you this morning, Alejandro? And why was your father so desperate to get to your hotel to see you that he took off without any of his men for protection?'

I glared at Carlos. 'I was in New York.'

'New York?' he snarled. 'What the fuck were you doing in New York when we have all of this *mierda* going on here in LA?'

'I was looking for Alana,' I said with a sigh.

'You were chasing some puta!' Carlos snorted.

'Don't you ever call my wife a whore!' I snarled at him through clenched teeth. He was my uncle and I had never laid a hand on him, but he was pushing every single one of my buttons.

'Carlos!' Phillipe said, quietly. 'Now is not the time for fighting amongst ourselves.'

'Then when is the time, Phillipe? Because our brother is fighting for his life, and his idiot of a son was halfway across the country when he needed him.'

Carlos was right. If I had been here, maybe my father and I would have spoken last night and settled our differences. Maybe he'd gone to my house to see me and I wasn't there? If I had been, maybe he wouldn't be here in this goddamn hospital, but I couldn't admit that to them, or even to myself right now.

I felt anger surging through me like a geyser as I grabbed the collar of Carlos' jacket and pushed him against the nearest wall. 'What the fuck did you just say, cabrón?' I snarled, my face pressed against his.

'You should put that wife of yours on a leash!' he spat.

I pulled my fist back without even thinking about it, but Phillipe's hand was on my arm before I could land the punch. 'Alejandro,' he said quietly in my ear. 'Now is not the time.'

His calm voice seemed to snap me out of the rage I was in and I released Carlos from my grip. He straightened his jacket and flexed his shoulders while he glared at me.

'To answer your question. We have no leads yet. But, given your recent troubles with the Ortegas, they are our primary targets,' Phillipe said.

I nodded. 'I thought that too, although this isn't exactly the Ortegas' style.'

'I know,' Phillipe nodded his agreement.

'Jax is at the hotel now doing what he does best. We'll find out who is responsible for this,' I told them.

Phillipe put his hand on my shoulder. 'I know. You're a good son, Alejandro,' he said while Carlos didn't even attempt to hide his disdain as he snorted and shook his head in disbelief. I couldn't help but worry that he was right. What if my father died? What if the last words I said to him were to call him a jackass and tell him to get out of my office?

Fuck! I needed my Papa to pull through for so many reasons, not least of all that I would never be able to forgive myself if he didn't.

CHAPTER 21

ALEJANDRO

Two hours later, I was sitting in the small hospital waiting room with Alana, my mama and my uncles when a surgeon in scrubs walked in. I stood up to greet him and my mama gasped out loud behind me, preparing herself for the worst.

'Mr Montoya,' the surgeon addressed me.

I stared at him, wondering whether he was about to blow our whole world apart.

'Your father made it through the surgery and is stable,' he said and I heard the collective sigh of relief reverberating around the small room. Then my mom was beside me, taking the surgeon's hands in hers. 'Thank you so much, Doctor,' she sobbed and I put my arm around her shoulder.

'He's in recovery now. You can see him for a few moments, but he's going to be out for at least the next twelve hours and he needs his rest.'

'Thank you, Doc,' I said to him.

'Your father is a fighter,' he said with a nod before turning and walking out of the room.

. . .

TWENTY MINUTES LATER, I was standing at my father's bedside. My mom and my uncles had come in to see him first, and then Alana and me. She had left me a few moments earlier to allow me some time alone. I looked at him lying there, helpless and hooked up to a dozen machines and felt the weight of guilt on my shoulders. If only I had been here. Could I have stopped this? The doctors said he was stable, but he would need weeks, maybe months to fully recover, and that was if he would ever return to the man he once was.

I knew that my time to step up and try to fill his shoes was here, and I wasn't sure that I would ever measure up to this man lying in front of me. Our relationship hadn't always been an easy one. He had kept me at a distance for a lot of my life. He had taught me well and he was always there when I truly needed him, but the day to day stuff was often lacking. He'd always told me that me and my mom were his biggest weaknesses and as a kid I'd always kind of resented that. But now I completely understood what he meant. Loving someone was like walking around with your heart outside of your body, with that most precious part of you exposed for the whole world to see. Now that I had Alana, I understood that so much better than I ever had. And it was that which I was sure had brought my father and me closer together in these past few months.

I sat beside him and took hold of his hand. It was warm to the touch, but it didn't look quite as big as it once had and I wondered at the last time I had held my father's hand. I must have been a small child, and he would have been big to me then. In fact, he had seemed like a giant. Not now though. Now he was just a man.

'Lo siento, Papa,' I said as I kissed his knuckles. 'But I will find whoever did this to you and I will make them pay in ways they can't even imagine.' I felt the fire surging in my belly. This was what I needed. There was no more time for remorse or regret.

The anger would be my fuel. It would be that which I'd need to get me through the next few weeks.

CHAPTER 22

ALANA

*A*lejandro had hardly said two words to me since we'd left the hospital. The doctors had told us all to go home and get some rest and go back the following morning to see Mateo. Despite Alejandro's insistence that she stay with us, his mom had gone back to his Uncle Phillipe's house. She and Phillipe's wife, Rachel, were as close as sisters, and it was where Maria wanted to be. I got the sense she didn't want to worry Alejandro any further, or have him feel like he needed to look after her too.

The tension between us was palpable. His Uncle Carlos had barely been able to hide his disdain every time he looked at me and I wondered if they knew that Alejandro and his father had fought about me. Or if they knew I had run away to New York. Worst of all, I worried that they blamed me somehow for Mateo being shot. Maybe they thought it wouldn't have happened if Alejandro hadn't been chasing me across the country?

Was Alejandro was regretting his last contact with his father too? The things he'd told me he had said can't have been easy for him, and until Mateo was awake and Alejandro could speak to him, was he worried that the last words they had ever spoken had been in anger?

I looked at my husband, his face full of turmoil and my heart almost broke for him. I wanted to make it better for him, but I didn't know how. I felt so guilty for running away to New York like a child. I hadn't considered the possible consequences at all and now our whole world felt like it was tumbling in on us.

BY THE TIME we reached the house, I could feel Alejandro's rage radiating from him like heat from a furnace. Jacob opened the car door for me and I stepped out. Lucia, Kelsey and Hugo were waiting on the doorstep for us. I'd almost forgotten about Kelsey. My poor best friend had come for a break and she was now stuck right in the middle of all this.

Lucia wrapped her arms around Alejandro's waist as he reached the doorway. 'I'm glad Mateo is okay,' she said.

'Thanks, kid,' he replied as he gave her a soft kiss on the top of her head.

Then she stepped back from him and looked up at me, and the anger in her face almost took my breath away. The next thing I knew, she had turned on her heel and was storming back into the house.

I looked between Kelsey and Hugo. 'What the hell?'

It was Alejandro who answered me. 'What the fuck did you expect, Alana?' he snapped. 'She's pissed at you, and she has every right to be. You are the closest thing to family that kid has. Every single person she has ever known has either let her down, used her or abandoned her, and the minute things got a bit tough for you, you fucked off out of here without a thought for anyone but yourself.'

Then he turned and walked into the house toward his office, leaving me standing there, blinking like an idiot as I realized he was right. Poor Lucia.

I felt tears running down my cheeks and the next thing I knew, Kelsey had her arm around my shoulders. 'Come on, honey. Let's get you inside,' she said softly. 'Leave that asshole to calm down.'

I smiled at her as I wiped the tears away. There was no point in crying, I had to fix this mess with Lucia and try and get through to Alejandro somehow. 'Thanks, Kels, but I need to go and talk to Lucia.'

'Okay. I'll be in the grounds with Hugo then,' she said as she linked her arm through his. He coughed awkwardly and I couldn't help but smile as he looked at me like a deer trapped in the headlights. Kelsey would eat him alive if he wasn't careful.

'Actually, I'm sure the boss will need to speak with me,' he said. 'Sorry, Kelsey.'

She sighed dramatically. 'Fine. I'll be outside on my own then,' she smiled and then walked off in the direction of the French doors.

'Are you okay?' Hugo asked as we walked down the hallway together.

'Yes. Thanks. I'm worried about Alejandro though.'

Hugo nodded. 'He's had a rough couple days. But then so have you. And Lucia has been desperate to have you home, you know.'

'I know. But, Alejandro was right. I shouldn't have left her like that.'

'Hey, we do what we need to do. Don't be so hard on yourself,' he said with a smile.

'Thanks, Hugo.'

'Any time. Now, I'd better go and find the boss.'

I nodded. 'Sure. And I'll go find Lucia.'

AFTER CHECKING her two favorite places, the den and the kitchen, I eventually found Lucia in her bedroom. Her door was open but I knocked lightly before popping my head inside. She was sitting up on her bed flicking through a magazine.

'Hey, sweetheart. Can we talk?'

'Whatever,' she said with a roll of her eyes.

I walked into the room and sat on the bed beside her. 'I'm really sorry I took off like that. It was wrong of me.'

'Nothing to apologize to me for. Like I care, anyway. You don't owe me anything,' she snorted.

I swallowed. She wasn't going to make this easy on me, was she? 'Well, I think I owe you an apology, even if you don't, and an explanation if you'll hear me out?'

She looked up from her magazine and shrugged her shoulders. 'Whatever,' she said but she kept her eyes fixed on me.

'You know I was having those tests at the doctor's?'

'Yeah?'

'Well, yesterday, Dr. Kelly told me that I'll find it very difficult to have children naturally.'

'Oh,' she said, her face softening slightly.

I took a deep breath. 'So I kind of got a bit upset and then I started overthinking things and questioning what kind of woman I was if I couldn't have a baby-'

'A woman is not defined by her ability to have a baby, Alana!' Lucia snapped.

'I know that,' I smiled at her. 'And I'm glad that you do too. But like I said, I kind of got lost in my own head. Sometimes, I don't think straight when I'm upset,' I said with a shrug. 'I also overheard part of a private conversation that I shouldn't have. What I heard was out of context, but I didn't know that at the time, and so that suddenly compounded all of those thoughts I've ever had about not being good enough. About not being worthy.'

'I get that,' Lucia said sadly.

'It's crap, isn't it? We women are more powerful and stronger than half the world gives us credit for and the sad thing is we struggle to remember it ourselves sometimes.'

Lucia nodded as she stared at me.

'Don't you ever forget that, my little warrior!' I said to her as I reached out and touched her hand. 'You are one of the strongest and bravest people I have ever met.'

She squeezed back. 'So are you.'

I smiled at her. 'You really think so?'

'You've got the King of LA whipped, haven't you?' she giggled.

I laughed too. 'Don't let him hear you say that. He'd probably toss you out on the street.'

She nodded as she started laughing harder. 'Can you imagine his face if I told him he was whipped?'

'Yes, I can,' I nodded, imagining that very thing.

When she had stopped laughing, I spoke again. 'I really am sorry, Lucia. I shouldn't have left without talking to you first and telling you what was going on. And, I know it might take time to win back your trust, but I promise you I will never do it again. You can count on me every single second of every single day. You got that?'

'Yeah,' she smiled.

'Good,' I let out a long breath, thankful that we were on good terms again. If only Alejandro would be so easy to win over. Then without warning, she launched herself forward and wrapped me in a massive hug. 'You're going to be a great mom one day,' she said softly.

I hugged her back. 'Thank you, sweetheart,' I said as I choked back a sob.

CHAPTER 23

ALANA

fter my chat with Lucia, she and Kelsey and I sat outdoors for a few hours catching up and regaling Lucia with tales of our time in college — although most of the funny stories involved Kelsey rather than me.

It had been nice to feel normal again for a few hours. But even as I sat with the two of them, I couldn't stop thinking about Alejandro sitting alone in his office. I wondered if I should go in there and speak to him, but I sensed he needed some time alone.

As it grew dark out, Kelsey started yawning and I realized we'd hardly slept in the past forty-eight hours. I noticed the light in Alejandro's office switch off and suddenly I was feeling tired too. 'Shall we call it a night?' I suggested.

'Sounds good to me,' Kelsey replied. 'That king-sized bed in your guest room has been calling to me for hours.'

'The school sent me some reading to do before I start next week, so I'm going to catch up on a bit of that,' Lucia said as she bounced up out of her seat.

'Sounds like a good idea,' I said to her. One of the conditions of her staying with us was that she had to enroll in the local high school and attend all of her classes until she had the baby. She had agreed to our request and seemed happy to be going back to school and being able to act at least a little like a normal teenager again.

I WALKED into the bedroom to find Alejandro in there. He had his back to me and was standing beside the bed pulling off his shirt. I felt a fluttering in my stomach as he slipped the crisp, white cotton over his shoulders and his strong forearms and tossed it into the laundry hamper. The muscles in his back flexed as he moved his hands to his belt and I drew in a shaky breath as I watched him.

I walked further into the room and he turned his head slightly as he heard me, but he didn't acknowledge my presence in any other way. So, it seemed he was definitely not speaking to me then, and I feared I knew the reason why. I also knew that bringing it up would start an argument, but anything was better than this silence between us. It was hellish and I couldn't spend the rest of the night in this limbo, without knowing for sure what was going on in his head.

'Are you okay?' I asked him.

He snorted in response as he pulled his belt off and tossed it onto the bed. Despite the atmosphere between us, I shivered as I recalled the promise he had made me about that belt just a few hours earlier.

'Are you thinking about the last conversation you had with your father?' I asked as my heart started to hammer in my chest.

'Alana! Don't!' he growled.

'Don't what?'

'Don't push me.'

'I'm not pushing you. I'm asking you a question. If you don't like that one, here's another. Do you blame me for what you said to your father?'

He turned around, his face full of fire and fury. 'No!' he snarled. 'I will never forgive myself if they are the last words I ever say to him, but that's not your fault. He should never have said those things about you.'

I blinked at him. 'Then why does it feel like you're so angry with me?'

'I'm not,' he barked as he continued undressing.

'It certainly feels like you are.'

He stepped out of his suit pants and threw them onto the bed too. 'Seriously? You really want to do this right now?'

'Yes.'

He scowled at me and then he took a few steps toward me. 'Okay. If you really want to do this, yes I am pissed at you. If I hadn't been chasing you across the fucking country, I would have been here in LA and my father would have been with me,' he snarled as the vein in his temple throbbed.

I swallowed as he towered over me, shaking with fury.

'And then he wouldn't have been shot and he wouldn't be lying in a hospital bed with half a dozen machines keeping him alive!' he shouted at me, and I took a step back from him.

'I never asked you to come after me,' I snapped. 'I told you I needed a few days.'

'No,' he shook his head. 'No, you fucking didn't. You ran off like a spoiled child and you sent a vague fucking text message to Lucia. You didn't tell me anything at all, Alana. You left me to go fucking crazy wondering where the hell you were and if something had happened to you.'

I blinked at him as I felt the tears stinging my eyes.

'Don't start with the tears, Alana,' he said with a shake of his head. 'I'm not in the goddamn mood for them.'

He pulled off his boxer shorts and climbed into bed. I looked at him, wondering whether to climb in there with him, but decided against it. It was clear he didn't even want to look at me right now. I got that he was pissed at me for going to

New York, but how could he blame me for his father being shot?

He turned away from me and I knew for certain then that he didn't want me there.

Asshole!

I walked out of the room and down the hall to find Kelsey.

CHAPTER 24

ALANA

*a*n hour later, Kelsey and I lay on her bed eating peanut M&Ms. The TV flickered in the background but we weren't watching it, we were still too busy catching up on all we'd missed over the past few months. She was the perfect distraction from my fight with Alejandro.

We were giggling about the time she had abandoned a date in the middle of Central Park Zoo when we heard the knock on the door. We froze, looking at each other with our eyes wide and our mouths hanging open. I picked up the remote and turned off the TV, hoping that if that was Alejandro outside, he would think we were asleep and go away.

'Alana,' he said in his low growling voice as he knocked again.

My heart started to hammer in my chest and the two of us remained quiet, staring at each other.

'Don't make me come in there, princess,' he said, the edge to his voice clearly audible.

I swallowed and sat up.

'You don't have to go out there,' Kelsey said with a flash of her eyebrows. 'I will totally kick his ass if you want me to.'

I stood up and smiled at her. 'No. I'd better go.'

'Well, remember, I'm only down the hall. Scream twice if you want me to come rescue you.'

'Twice?'

'Well, if you only scream once, it's probably because you're hate-fucking, or make-up fucking,' she said with a grin.

I picked up the pillow and hit her over the head with it, making her squeal.

I could sense Alejandro's impatience from the other side of the door as I walked to it. Pulling it open, I blinked as I saw him standing there – six feet of solid muscle, anger and fire. He didn't need to say anything for me to know what he was thinking. I was his wife and I slept in his bed. Period. Even if he had acted like a complete jerk.

'Night, Kels,' I said softly.

'Night sweets. Night Alejandro,' she said with a huge grin.

'Goodnight, Kelsey,' he said as he stepped back, allowing me to walk out of the room. I closed the door behind me and followed him silently to our bedroom and I couldn't help feeling like I was walking to meet my fate. With each step we took, my pulse raced faster and the churning in the pit of my stomach grew more insistent.

What if he had changed his mind about punishing me for going to New York? When he'd promised that he wouldn't, things had been very different. Was he going to punish me because he blamed me for the last conversation he'd had with his father or because he believed it was my fault his father almost died?

I swallowed as we reached the door to our room and stepped inside. Alejandro closed it behind us and walked to the bed. He slipped his black sweatpants off over his legs and tossed them onto the floor so he was standing naked, his semi-hard cock hanging heavy between his thighs.

I remained still, unsure of what he wanted from me. 'Are you planning on coming to bed fully clothed?' he snapped.

'No,' I whispered as I unzipped my jeans and slid them over

my legs, kicking them into the laundry hamper. I pulled my tank top over my head and threw that in too. Then I stood there in my underwear and his eyes roamed over my body, his cock hardening further as he looked at me.

Reaching behind me, I unclipped my bra and let it fall to the floor. My nipples were hard and I saw his eyes were drawn to them. I'd like to have said it was due to the cool air conditioning hitting my warm skin, but it was because being anywhere near this man made me wet and needy.

I walked over to where he was standing, so close that I could smell his incredible scent and it made my insides contract.

He glared at me, his tongue running over his lower lip as his eyes roamed over my body. Shit! He was going to punish me. And while his punishments usually left me a hot, trembling mess, I didn't want that tonight. I was still reeling from the news I'd been given by the doctors. I still felt guilty about upsetting Lucia and making her feel abandoned all over again. Most of all, I was still upset about our fight. I didn't think I could handle any more hurt, even if it was only the physical kind.

But he didn't touch me. Instead he turned away and climbed into bed until he was lying with his hands behind his head. I slipped in beside him and put my hand on his chest and he stiffened.

'Why did you ask me to come back here if you're just going to ignore me?' I asked.

'Because I can't sleep when you're not here,' he growled.

'I'm sorry,' I whispered.

'What for?'

'For running away.'

He didn't reply.

'I know you don't believe me, but I truly am.'

'I do believe you,' he said quietly, taking me by surprise.

'Then why won't you touch me?' I asked, surprised at the emotion that question stirred in me. I blinked back tears, remembering what he'd said about me crying earlier. 'Don't you want me?'

He turned, his face pulled into a deep scowl. 'You think I don't want you? My cock is weeping for you, princess. God help me, I always want you.'

'So, what are you waiting for? I'm right here.'

'Because I'm so fucking angry and I don't want to hurt you,' he growled.

'That's never stopped you before,' I reminded him.

'Oh, but it has, princess. You think you've seen me angry? You have never seen the real me. He's a devil and he will fucking devour you.'

I ran my hand down his chest and heard a low growl in his throat vibrating through his body. 'Then show me.'

He moved before I'd even finished my sentence, flipping me over and pinning me to the mattress with the weight of his body. 'Don't tempt me, princess,' he snarled.

'I'm not. You could never hurt me,' I said as I stared into his eyes. 'Not like that.'

He sealed his mouth over mine, kissing me so fiercely that I struggled for breath. He pushed his tongue deep inside, claiming me. I responded as greedily for him. We were both angry, both in need of some release.

He grabbed hold of my wrists and pinned them above my head with one of his giant hands as the other ran down my body, tugging at my panties until they were halfway down my legs. He shifted between my thighs, nestling between them as much as he could, given that my ability to spread them wide was restricted by my underwear.

He reached for his cock, gripping it firmly as he guided the tip into my hot entrance. I gasped into his mouth and he responded by pushing himself inside me — as far as he could go. I wasn't quite ready and I winced at the burning sensation as he stretched me wide open. I tried to wrench my mouth away, but he wouldn't let me and he bit down on my lip as he pounded into me. After a few thrusts, he threw his head back and let out a loud growl of frustration.

'Goddamn fucking panties,' he roared as he pushed himself up onto his knees and using both of his hands, he tore them straight down the middle before throwing the material over his shoulder. 'What have I told you about wearing panties when you're in this house with me?' Then he grabbed my thighs and pushed them apart, almost pressing them flat to the bed.

I looked up at him, his fierce, hard body vibrating with tension and anger, and his face full of rage. My pulse quickened. Why the hell was this so freaking hot? I wanted him as much as I ever had. He leaned back down, taking one of my wrists in each hand and pinning them to either side of my head.

He nudged at my opening again, his breathing hard and ragged. A fine sheen of sweat coated his forehead. 'You don't have to hold back,' I whispered.

He glared at me. 'Don't worry, I won't,' he growled as he thrust himself inside me, impaling me with his cock. Then he buried his face in my neck as he nailed me to the bed. He growled and cursed in Spanish in between biting and sucking on my tender flesh. I felt a rush of wet heat as he increased his pace, driving against that one spot inside of me. Over and over. Until I was coming apart around him.

My own groans of pleasure seemed to tip him over the edge and he climaxed with a roar. For a few brief moments, everything that had happened in the past few days was forgotten and all that existed in the world was the two of us. I wrapped my legs around him and we lay together for a few moments, him breathing heavily against my neck and me panting under the weight of him.

'Fuck!' I heard him mumble before he pushed himself up and walked to the bathroom without another word. I watched after him and swallowed the sob in my throat.

Asshole!

I heard the sound of running water and then a few seconds later, he walked back into the room with a damp washcloth. I blinked at him as he sat beside me on the bed.

'I think I bit you a little too hard, princess,' he said as he brushed my hair away and held the cloth to my neck. 'I might have broken the skin.'

'What?' My hand flew instinctively to my neck and he moved the cloth so I could feel. 'It didn't hurt. I hardly even felt it.'

I brushed over the area he'd been tending to and my fingers rubbed over the small indents his teeth had left. Pulling my hand away, I checked for blood but there wasn't any. He placed the cloth back against my neck.

'Lo siento,' he said, apologizing in Spanish.

'It's okay. Your spankings hurt much more,' I said with a half grin.

'Not for your neck. Well, maybe a little for your neck. I didn't mean to bite you so hard. But I'm mostly sorry about what I said earlier.'

I nodded at him. 'I know how worried you must be.'

'I am,' he sighed, 'but that doesn't excuse what I said to you, princess. What happened to my father — none of that is your fault.'

'You were upset...' I started to say.

'So were you,' he interrupted me. 'And you are always my priority, Alana. I need you to know that.'

'I do,' I said, placing my hand on his face. 'And you are mine. But you need to let me in, Alejandro. I don't need protecting from the truth. I understand that you don't need to give me the details of your day to day life, and I don't want them. But the big stuff... I want to know that. If I had known you were in the middle of this thing with the Ortegas, I would never have gone to New York.'

'I understand, but I want to keep you out of all that, princess. I don't want you worrying about who we're at war with. That's my job.'

'You think it's your job to protect me? To look after me? Well, it's my job to do the same for you, too. And how can I do that when I don't know what's going on with you?'

He placed the washcloth on the nightstand and lay down beside me, pulling me into his arms until I was lying with my head on his chest. 'Are you sure you want to know about my world, Alana?'

'Yes.'

He kissed the top of my head and then he told me all about what had been going on for the past few weeks. When he'd finished, he tilted my chin up so he could look at my face, searching for my reaction.

'Thank you for trusting me,' I said with a smile.

'It was never about me not trusting you, princess. I thought keeping you out of it would keep you safe. But you're right, how can you protect yourself if you don't know what to look out for? If you are ever taken from me, Alana, then know that I will be moving heaven and earth to find you, so do anything you can to stay alive.'

I shuddered involuntarily. I knew what his business was. I knew what had happened to his father was deliberate and was because of who he was. And I had asked to know more, but hearing him say that out loud, suddenly made everything all that more real.

'You should listen to everything,' he went on. 'Always be listening. People usually aren't as smart as they think and they will leak something that will be useful to you. You listen first and talk later, understand me? You learn everything you can about your attacker or your kidnapper, and you use it.'

'Okay,' I breathed.

Suddenly, he was rolling on top of me and brushing my hair back from my face. 'Have I frightened you, princess?'

'A little,' I admitted. 'But it's okay. I asked to know. I needed to know.'

'Tomorrow, I'll have Hugo teach you the most effective ways to cause someone pain and some escape techniques.'

'Why can't you teach me instead?'

He narrowed his eyes at me and I felt his cock twitching against my stomach. 'I'm pretty sure that anything involving me restraining you, or generally putting my hands on you, is only going to end one way, princess.'

'Oh? And what way would that be?' I purred.

'You dripping wet and my cock buried inside you,' he growled. 'Besides, Hugo is an expert.'

'Okay. Maybe Kelsey and Lucia could join us? Sounds like it could be useful stuff for any woman to know,' I suggested, thinking that having both of them involved would make it feel less like preparation for a potential kidnapping and more like one of the self-defense classes I took in college.

'I think that's a great idea. Then I won't have to have to think about you and Hugo alone together wrestling in my gym.' He flashed an eyebrow at me and I pushed him in the chest.

'You're kind of possessive, do you know that?'

'Yes, I do. And you love it. You're all mine, Alana,' he growled, pressing his hips into mine so I could feel every inch of him.

'I know,' I groaned as I raised my hips to meet his. 'Just like you're all mine.'

'Fuck, yeah, I am,' he breathed as he shifted his hips lower and pushed his cock into me. 'And you can have every last inch of me, princess.'

CHAPTER 25

ALEJANDRO

*A*lana squeezed my hand as we stood outside my father's hospital room. We'd had a call from the doctor at 6am to say my father was coming around and would be waking shortly. We'd left the house and got over to the hospital as soon as we could. My mama had gone in to see him first and had just walked out of the door with tears in her eyes and a huge smile on her face.

'He wants to see you, hijo,' she said to me.

'Come on,' I tugged Alana's hand.

'No. You go on in and see him first. I'll wait with your mom for now,' she said softly.

I nodded at her. There would be things we'd need to discuss that I didn't want her or my mother hearing about and the fact that she was aware of that only made me love her even more.

'Gracias, princesa,' I said as I kissed her on the forehead and let go of her hand.

I took a deep breath and pushed open the door to my father's room. He was lying on the bed, still surrounded by machinery and with his eyes closed. He looked so peaceful that I didn't want to disturb him. But his eyes snapped open as soon as he heard a footstep on the floor.

He turned his head. 'Mi hijo,' he croaked with a smile.

'Papa.' I walked over to the bed and sat beside him, taking hold of his hand and squeezing. 'It's good to see you awake.'

'It would take more than a couple of bullets to stop me, hijo,' he said with a faint laugh.

'I know.'

We sat in silence for a few moments with all of the unanswered questions and unspoken words hanging in the air between us.

'I haven't found him yet, Papa,' I said eventually as I put my head in my hands.

'I know you will, hijo,' he said as he placed a hand on my head. 'You are your father's son.'

I looked up at him. This man had taught me so much. He was the man I respected more than anyone else in the whole world. The fact that I'd almost lost him felt like a knife twisting in my heart. I realized that I had never once told him how much he meant to me.

'I love you, Papa,' I said quietly. I expected a slap around the head. This man didn't do overt displays of emotion.

'I know,' he croaked. 'I love you too, hijo.'

More silence followed and then he said three words that I had never hear him say to me before in his life. 'Lo siento, Alejandro.'

I frowned at him.

'For what I said about Alana. I was angry about the Ortegas' situation. I see how much you love her. How much she loves you.' He closed his eyes again as the effort from talking was so obviously draining him.

'I'm sorry too, Papa,' I said as I squeezed his hand again. 'Did you see anything at all that might help us find who did this?'

He shook his head. 'But whoever it was knew exactly where I

would be. That means you can't trust anyone, hijo. Only me and your uncles.'

I nodded.

'It's time for you to step up. Phillipe and Carlos will need you more than ever.'

'I know,' I replied, the weight of that knowledge lying heavy on my shoulders. My father had always looked out for his younger brothers, always protected them from any potential dangers.

'You need to keep an eye on Carlos especially. I'm worried about him. You know he can be a loose cannon.'

'Well, he's just pissed that somebody tried to kill his big brother.'

My father opened his eyes again and stared at me. 'No. It's more than that. I think he might be getting sick again.'

'Oh?' I sat back in my chair. Seventeen years earlier, my Uncle Carlos had had some kind of breakdown and had gone on a brutal killing spree. He'd been found sitting naked, covered in the blood of his victims and mumbling incoherently. My father had managed to cover up the killings and Carlos had spent a year in one of the best mental health facilities in California until he was deemed fit to be released. It was a time in our family's history that we never spoke of. 'I'll keep an eye on him,' I promised.

My father squeezed my hand. 'You are a good son, Alejandro.'

He closed his eyes again and I watched as his chest rose and fell and he drifted back to sleep. I don't know how long I sat there with him, holding his hand and watching him sleep. My mind raced with dozens of questions and I was turning over every stone I could think of to find the answers, but I wasn't finding them fast enough.

CHAPTER 26

ALANA

I walked into the small private family room at the hospital carrying two cups of hot coffee. Alejandro's mom was already in there waiting for me.

'Here we are,' I said as I handed her one and placed mine on the small Formica table.

'Thank you, Alana,' she said with a smile before she held the cup to her lips and took a sip. She winced as she tasted the bitter liquid. 'Ostia! This is just about the worst coffee I have ever had,' she said with a laugh as she placed her cup down beside mine.

'I know,' I laughed too. 'The vending machine was all that was available, sorry,' I said with a shrug.

'At least it is hot.' She smiled at me and patted the seat beside her. 'Come, sit. You look tired.'

'A little,' I said as I stifled a yawn and sat down beside her. 'I'm sure you didn't get much sleep yourself?'

'Not a wink,' she smiled at me and her beautiful hazel eyes twinkled. 'But, there will be plenty of time for sleep when I'm dead, cariño,' she laughed.

I smiled at her. I knew that cariño meant sweetheart and it felt nice to hear her call me that. I loved Alejandro's mom. She was so warm and caring — she reminded me a little of my grandma, although I would never tell her that. I wasn't sure she would take being compared to my grandma as the compliment I'd intend it to be. 'I'm so glad Mateo has woken up. Did the doctors say how he's doing?' I suspected it was all good news given her mood this morning, but I had no idea what Mateo's prognosis was.

'They said it will take him a few weeks to get back on his feet and the machines will need to help him breathe until his lung is fully healed. But he is alive and he is going to be just fine.' She smiled again as she squeezed my hand. 'This time yesterday, I thought I was going to lose him, so today, Alana, is a good day!'

'It certainly is,' I agreed.

'I always knew this day was coming. I suppose we have been lucky that Mateo has never really been hurt before now. But, now I see the mantle being passed to Alejandro, and while I know it is what he wants, it breaks my heart. I never want to sit in one of these places wondering whether my son is going to make it,' she said softly.

'I know exactly what you mean,' I said as I squeezed her hand. 'The thought of anything ever happening to Alejandro…' I didn't need to finish my sentence. Maria knew better than anyone else the worry of being married to a Montoya.

I knew this was the life I was signing up for, but it didn't make me worry about him any less. It made me feel even more selfish for running off to New York the way I did. As if sensing the change in my mood, Maria turned her body so she was facing me.

'Alejandro told me about what the doctor said, cariño. I am so sorry.'

I sucked in a shaky breath. In all that had gone on in the past two days, I hadn't thought much about my test results. 'Thank you, Maria.'

149

'Everything will work out just as it should for you and my Alejandro, though. I know it.'

I smiled at her. 'You think so?'

'I know so, cariño.'

'It's just that we wanted children. We had ideas of filling the house with them. I feel like I'm letting him down.'

'You are not!' she gently admonished me. 'And there are plenty of ways to have a family, Alana. You just have to be a little more creative.' She arched one perfectly manicured eyebrow at me.

'I guess you're right.'

'I am right. Never argue with your mother-in-law,' she said firmly but with a twinkle in her eye.

'Okay. Point taken,' I agreed as I reached for my coffee and took a sip before almost spitting it back into the cup. 'Oh, this really is terrible,' I said as I wiped my mouth with the back of my hand.

'Told you!'

We sat in comfortable silence for a few more moments until Maria spoke again. 'I wanted to fill my house full of children too, you know?' she said with a sigh.

'You did?'

'Yes. But it took me two years to fall pregnant with Alejandro. It was a traumatic birth. Both he and I almost died. The doctors warned me it would be risky to have another child, so Mateo expressly forbade us from trying again.'

'And how did you feel about that?'

She looked into the distance. 'I was annoyed with him at first. But then I saw how blessed my life was in so many ways. Alejandro was the most perfect, beautiful little boy I had ever seen. I had never felt such love in my life as I did for him. I realized that he was enough for me. And the thought of leaving him without a mother was unthinkable.'

'I can understand that. So, you and Mateo were on the same page eventually then?'

'Yes. And we always have been ever since. People see him as hard and unyielding, but with me he is different. Soft even,' she said with a smile and a tear in her eye.

'I definitely understand that,' I laughed.

'Hmm,' she gave me a knowing smile. 'I'm sure you do. I see the way my Alejandro looks at you, Alana. You have put a fire in his eyes that I have never seen before. I used to worry about all of those women he dated who had no personality. I wondered if he had closed off his heart to anything coming close to real love, but then he met you. And I have never seen him so happy... so fulfilled as he has been these past few months.'

I felt my heart almost burst out of my chest with happiness and gratitude at her words. 'Thank you, Maria,' I said as I blinked a tear away.

'You are most welcome my cariño,' she patted my hand. 'Now, tell me about this young lady who is staying at your house with you now. Mateo tells me she is from Chicago?'

'Ah, Lucia?' I said, her name bringing a smile to my face and then I told Maria all about our new houseguest and how she was managing to work her way into Alejandro's affections too.

CHAPTER 27

ALANA

I walked onto the patio and placed the bottle of wine and two glasses on the table before taking a seat opposite Kelsey, who had her face tilted toward the sun and a huge smile on her face.

She looked up at me as I sat down. 'This is some amazing place you've got here, Alana. I could get used to this,' she said with a sigh.

'You'd never leave New York,' I laughed as I poured the wine.

She shrugged. 'Maybe I would. For a house like this.' She grinned at me. 'Or the right guy?'

'What?' I smiled at her. 'You'd seriously consider moving to LA?'

'New York isn't as much fun without you. The landlord has put the rent up again on my apartment. I hate my job. I kind of feel like I need a fresh start.'

'But you love the city,' I reminded her.

'So do you. Or at least you did. Would you move back there now?'

'No,' I shook my head. 'I hated it here when I first arrived, but now it feels like home.'

'I can see why you love it. It's beautiful. And Alejandro - well he's hot!' she laughed. 'And he has so many hot bodyguards too,' she flashed an eyebrow at me.

'Hmm. So, you and Hugo? Tell me everything.'

'Oh, he's as hot as hell. And when we were on the plane over here, while you and the panty melter were otherwise engaged, we had a bit of a kiss and well, you know? But since we landed in LA, he's been super professional and as much as I try to tempt him, he's not biting. I suppose he has a lot going on with trying to find out what happened to Alejandro's father?'

'Yeah. I guess they're all kind of busy right now.'

'Does Alejandro have any idea who is responsible yet?'

'No,' I shook my head. 'At least not that he's told me anyway. And I'm sorry that you're practically on house arrest here. I'd love for us to have gone out while you're in LA. Alejandro has an amazing club, but he says it's just too risky right now.'

Kelsey nodded. 'Don't worry, honey. I totally understand. It's no hardship being confined to this house anyway.'

'I know. But you're only here for a few days. I'd have at least liked to have shown you some of the sights.'

Kelsey placed a hand on my knee. 'Will you stop worrying? This isn't your doing. I'm a big girl and if I want to get out of here, I will, but I'd rather spend my last two days here with you, by this beautiful pool. Do you think we could encourage Hugo to come out here and have a swim?' She lifted her sunglasses and gave me a cheeky wink.

'I think he might consider that a dereliction of duty,' I laughed.

'But he's your bodyguard. If you're in the pool too, then isn't he doing exactly what he's paid to? Oh, I wish he'd offer to guard my body,' she sighed.

'Maybe the next time you visit, he won't be so distracted with work,' I suggested.

She smiled at me. 'Oh, do you think? Maybe we could all go

out to Alejandro's club. That would be awesome. Clubbing with my girl and her hot bodyguard,' she giggled.

'You are man crazy,' I said as I swatted her playfully on the arm. 'I'm sure you'll forget all about poor Hugo as soon as you're back in New York.'

'Oh, I don't know honey, those eyes and those biceps are kinda hard to forget.'

'I seem to recall you saying that about Logan Woods not so long ago.'

'Oh, well he turned out to be a complete asshole didn't he? You always had his number though, Alana, You're such a great judge of character when it comes to men. I always pick the crazies or the complete assholes.'

'Well, I'm not sure you're entirely right about that,' I laughed.

She took off her sunglasses and looked at me while she took a sip of her wine. 'Actually,' she frowned. 'You hardly ever dated at all, even in college. Not since Bobby Conroy broke your heart.'

'Exactly, I didn't pick well there, did I?' I flashed my eyebrows at her.

'Jerk!' she snorted.

'Hey, did I tell you I ran into him the other week? He's some tech millionaire now.'

'Really? Bobby the jock a tech geek? No way!'

'Yes way. He was the keynote speaker at some convention at the hotel.'

'I bet Alejandro loved that,' she started to laugh. 'You running into your handsy ex-boyfriend.'

'He is not handsy,' I insisted.

'Whatever! So, did Alejandro like him?'

'No,' I grinned at her. 'Not even a little bit.'

'Good,' she said as she raised her glass in a toast. She read magazines as much as I did and knew all about the legions of women Alejandro had dated before me. I had also told her that we bumped into them frequently.

'You certainly seem to have picked a good one now, though,' she said with a smile. 'He adores you, honey.'

I smiled back. 'You think?'

'Girl, I know! He can hardly keep his eyes or his hands off you. And why wouldn't he? You're a knockout. But it's more than that. The way he looks at you. It's everything,' she sighed dramatically. 'Every woman deserves a man who looks at them the way Alejandro looks at you.'

I smiled at her. 'Sometimes I can't believe he's my husband, Kels. He is just... he is everything I have ever wanted, and everything I didn't even know I wanted, rolled into one hot package of fine ass man!'

'Speaking of a fine ass man,' Kelsey nodded toward the French doors and I looked up to see Hugo walking out into the grounds.

'I'm signing off, Alana. Hank, Ray and Max are here in the house and the patrols are outside as usual. Lucia is studying in her room and Mr Montoya asked me to tell you that he'll be home after dinner so not to wait for him to eat.'

'Thanks, Hugo,' I said.

'You fancy sticking around for a quick drink, Hugo?' Kelsey asked as she lifted the half empty wine bottle.

He cleared his throat. 'I'd better not,' he said but his eyes were drawn to Kelsey's legs as she crossed them, exposing the skin at the top of her thighs in her short sundress.

'I'll see you tomorrow, ladies,' he mumbled as his cheeks flushed a light shade of pink.

Kelsey stared after him as he walked back into the house. 'Oh, I would climb him like a tree,' she said as she fanned herself with her hand.

I laughed at her. Having her here made being confined to the house so much easier to bear. I suddenly remembered that she had to go home in two days and felt a wave of sadness.

'What time is your flight on Monday?' I asked.

'Eight am. I'll be home in time for my shift on Monday night.'

'I'll miss you.'

'I'll miss you too, honey. But now that I know my bestie has her own freaking jet, you can send it for me next time I have some time off work,' she said as she poured us each a fresh glass of wine.

'Sounds like a great plan.'

'Hey, I meant to tell you I saw your mom last week.'

I swallowed. I hadn't spoken to my parents since the morning I had confronted my father and he had admitted that Alejandro had paid him three million dollars to marry me. He had sold his only child and I had told him that I never wanted to see him again. I had no idea if my mother had even found out about my visit that morning, but she hadn't contacted me either way. I was done with the two of them, but it was hard to cut them out of my life, even though I knew it was the right thing to do.

Kelsey had no idea about what had happened with my parents or the fact that my marriage to Alejandro hadn't started out anything like the fairy-tale she believed it to be.

'How was she?'

'She didn't look well, to be honest. She asked how you were. When was the last time you spoke to her?'

'It was a while ago. We kind of had a falling out. Well, me and my dad did.'

'And your mom took his side, like always?' Kelsey asked with a roll of her eyes.

'I'm not even sure she knows about it. But, she must know something as we used to speak a couple times a week. Who knows what my father must have told her? But I'm done with them, Kels.'

She nodded at me. 'You deserve to be happy, Alana, and I don't think you ever really were in New York. Not like you are here. I think your father had a lot to do with that.'

'What do you mean?' I asked her. She had never mentioned anything like this to me before.

'He always had you working for him, covering his ass, or playing some angle so he could score votes. Remember when you had to cancel on our trip to Cabo at the last minute because he had some emergency he needed your help with. Or the time we were supposed to go upstate for Heather Jensen's bachelorette and he asked you to look after your mother because she was sick and he was going out of town? There were so many times just like that, Alana. He never let you live your life.'

I frowned at her. I'd never really thought about how many times I'd had to cancel plans to help out my parents, but it happened a lot. 'I'm sorry, I must have been a crap friend, Kels,' I said as I felt tears pricking my eyes.

'No you weren't,' she said as she placed her hand on my arm and gave me a reassuring squeeze. 'You were always there for me when I really needed you and I know you always will be.'

'Always,' I said as I held up my wine glass. 'I love you, Kels.'

'Love you too, honey,' she smiled as tapped her glass against mine.

CHAPTER 28

ALEJANDRO

I stood at the floor to ceiling windows of my office at my hotel, looking out over LA. Somewhere out there was the man responsible for trying to kill my father. It had been two days since some cabrón had pulled up at a stop sign and put two bullets in his chest. He was lucky to still be alive. But two days later, I was still no closer to finding the shooter or who was behind it.

'Alejandro,' I heard a deep voice behind me. It sounded so much like my father's voice that I shuddered.

'Phillipe,' I said as I turned around and saw my uncle walking through my open office door. Only two years younger than my father, he looked much like him too. The same square jaw and dark hair peppered with silver. He was slightly taller and leaner though, and his temper not so volatile as his older brothers'.

'How are you?' he asked his face full of concern. 'Have you slept at all these past few days?'

I shook my head. 'How can I sleep when that fucker is still out there, Uncle?'

He sucked air in through his teeth, about to reprimand me, I

158

was sure, until we were disturbed by two more figures walking into the room: Jax and my Uncle Carlos.

Carlos was the youngest of my father's brothers, and while he looked like his older siblings, that was where the similarity ended. There was ten years between him and Phillipe, and at forty-eight, he was only fifteen years older than me. As a child, he had always been a hero of mine, but as I got older and started to take on more of a role in the family business, I sensed resentment building between us. He and I had very different ideas about how things should be done.

Carlos was what my father described as a loose cannon. He was unpredictable and impulsive, but he was also a skilled assassin, and he was a feared enemy of any who crossed him. My father and Phillipe had always looked out for him and, for the most part, they kept him in line.

'Have you found out anything useful yet?' Carlos barked as he walked into the room. Jax was directly behind him and rolled his eyes. He wasn't my Uncle Carlos's biggest fan either, largely because Carlos seemed to resent Jax's status as my right-hand man. Jax was from Dallas, the son of a cowboy — he wasn't a Montoya, he wasn't even Spanish, and therefore, in Carlos's eyes, he shouldn't be allowed into the inner circle. But as far as I was concerned, Jax was my brother. We had been through more together in twenty years than most men did in a whole lifetime. I trusted him with my life and we couldn't be any closer even if we had shared the same blood.

'Nothing yet. How about you three?' I asked with a sigh.

'Us?' Carlos sneered. 'I thought you were the brains here, Alejandro?'

I felt anger surging in my chest. Carlos still blamed me for not being here the morning my father was shot. I blamed myself too, but I couldn't let him know that.

I saw my Uncle Phillipe's mouth open as though he was about

to speak, no doubt to intervene the way he usually did whenever Carlos was running his mouth, but I wasn't just their nephew any longer. I was the one in charge now, and it was about time they all remembered that.

I stepped around my desk until I was standing directly in front of Carlos. 'I might have been in New York when my father was shot, Uncle, but *you* took your eye off the ball. *You* are the muscle of this family, are you not? *You* are the one who is supposed to deal with our enemies. *You* are supposed to watch your brothers' backs. This happened on your watch. So, yes, I want to know what the hell you've managed to find out,' I snarled at him.

He scowled at me, no doubt wondering whether to challenge me any further, but he decided against it. He cursed under his breath and sat on one of the chairs opposite my desk. Phillipe sat down too, while Jax stood behind them, near the door. He was chasing leads all over the country, and if he received a call, he could easily step out and take it in the other room.

'What do we know?' I said with a sigh as I sat behind my desk. 'Jax?'

He cleared his throat. 'CCTV from the diner across the street shows a motorcycle pulling up next to your father's car at the intersection. Two shots were fired through the window before the shooter sped off in the direction of downtown. High caliber, armor piercing bullets. Your father was wearing a vest when he was shot. The bike was found abandoned two miles down the road. Whoever was on it must have had someone waiting. The bike was stolen. False plates. No prints. This was a planned and well-executed attack by someone with power and connections.'

I nodded. 'Ruling out the Ortegas?'

'I believe so,' Jax said.

'We can't rule them out entirely,' Phillipe interjected.

'I know, Uncle. Which is why Joey Ortega is currently unconscious in a container at the shipyard. Jax and I are going to pay him a visit shortly. But this doesn't fit with their MO at all. The Ortegas are not this well-organized or sophisticated. They don't use shooters either. Their calling card is to set their enemies on fire and toss them off a building. Besides, they have no beef with my father. It's my clubs and the local drug runners they are interested in.'

'Maybe they are branching out?' Carlos suggested.

'There is always that possibility,' I nodded in agreement. 'But this was so well executed. The shooter had to have known that Papa would be at that intersection at some point that morning. They must have also known that he'd be wearing a vest. Who even knew that he was in LA? He hoped to meet me at the hotel, but nothing was arranged. He told me that he and Mama stopped over unexpectedly.'

Phillipe nodded. 'Yes. Your Mama and Rachel wanted to go over some plans for your cousin's wedding.'

'Anyone could have seen him coming in and out of the hotel, amigo?' Jax offered. 'He is not exactly inconspicuous.'

I couldn't help but smile. 'No. He is not,' I agreed. My father was larger than life. He charmed anyone who met him, until they irked him in some way and then incurred his legendary temper — something which wasn't hard to do. Not to mention he went everywhere with at least two armed bodyguards. Except on the morning he was shot. Why?

I rubbed a hand over my jaw. 'Why did he leave the house that morning? And without his guards?'

'He said that he needed to see you,' Phillipe replied. 'He left in a hurry.'

'Why did he need to see you so bad?' Carlos snapped.

'We'd had an argument,' I replied. That wasn't important right now.

'About what exactly?' Carlos persisted. 'About the business?'

'No. About Alana,' I replied dismissively.

He scowled at me. 'Her again?' he spat and then his mouth started to form another word and I had to stop myself from launching myself over the desk at him.

'Choose your next words carefully, Uncle. Because if you ever call my wife a puta again, I will cut out your fucking tongue,' I snarled at him.

He closed his mouth and I saw Jax smirking from the corner of my eye.

'What do you need us to do?' Phillipe asked.

'Go to Vegas and see what's been going on there. With all of us in LA, maybe there's something he's involved in that we're missing?'

Phillipe nodded his agreement.

I looked at Carlos. 'Look after him while we're gone,' he said with a frown.

'Of course I will,' I replied.

He smiled at me and it was understood that our dispute was dealt with.

'Until we find out who was responsible, trust no-one outside of this room,' I warned the three of them and they all nodded in solemn agreement.

'I'll go call the car around so we can pay Joey Ortega a visit,' Jax said and then he left the room.

Carlos walked out behind him, but Phillipe hung back. 'Carlos is just upset about your father,' he said with a shake of his head.

'I know that. We all are. Tempers are frayed. Things are said. But, we are still family,' I said as I placed a reassuring hand on his shoulder. My Uncle Phillipe was a classic middle child — always the peacemaker, always trying to smooth things over.

'If anything happened to Mateo, it is Carlos I worry most about. He has no-one but us.'

'I know that too, Uncle. But, Papa is going to be fine, and we are going to find whoever is responsible for this.'

'You are a good boy, Alejandro. Your father chose wisely in making you his successor.'

'Thank you, Uncle,' I smiled. It meant a lot to me to have his support. I had a feeling I was going to need it.

CHAPTER 29

ALEJANDRO

*J*ax and I stepped out of the car and walked along the tarmac to the container in the shipyard where my men were holding Joey Ortega. We walked inside and saw Joey strapped to a chair. As per my instructions, he was unharmed.

'Buenos días, Joey,' I said as I approached him.

'Alejandro,' he replied, his voice trembling.

Jax walked to the table nearby and picked up the small pair of long-nosed pliers before passing them to me.

'You can leave now, gentlemen,' I said to the three men who had been holding him for me. They nodded and left the container silently.

I held up the pliers and Joey looked at them before he pissed himself in the chair.

I smiled at Jax who shook his head with silent amusement.

'You've heard what I like to do with these, Joey?' I asked.

He nodded as his whole body started to shake.

'Free one of his hands,' I said to Jax.

Jax walked over to Joey and cut the ties on one of his hands, freeing it from behind his back, before holding it out to me.

'No! Please?' Joey shouted as I leaned down and placed the pliers on the tip of his thumbnail.

'I have some questions, Joey. And if you don't answer me honestly, this will be a very, very long and painful day for you. You understand me, cabrón?'

He nodded as I pulled and tore the nail from his thumb in one swift move.

He shrieked loudly and started to sob.

'That was just a taste of what is to come. I will start with your fingernails and then I will take your teeth. And after your teeth, well...' I looked at Jax.

'Fingers?' Jax suggested.

'Hmm? Or maybe as we're so time-pressed, we go straight for his cock?'

Joey wailed at this. 'I'll answer any questions you have. I swear,' he cried as snot and tears ran down his face.

I pulled up a chair and sat in front of him. 'This is how it will work, Joey. I will ask you a question and every time I think you're lying to me, I will remove something. I will keep going until either your heart gives out because of the pain or I have the answers I want. So how this ends is really all on you, isn't it?'

'Yes,' he sniffed. 'I'll tell you whatever you want to know, Alejandro.'

AN HOUR LATER, Jax and I walked out of the container. I was confident that Joey Ortega knew nothing about my father's shooting. He had lost three fingernails and two teeth proving that to me, but he was lucky he was walking out of that container. The truth was, I didn't have time to keep pursuing dead ends and that made Joey a very lucky man indeed.

What he had given me was lots of very useful information about his crew. He had turned his back on every single one of them to save his own skin. While that information would come in useful in the coming months when I had more time to act on it, it didn't help me right now. I was letting Joey go but I suspected that once his crew found out he had sold them out, he would be a dead man walking anyway. In the meantime, I had his nuts in a vice.

'What next, amigo?' Jax asked me.

'Back to the fucking drawing board,' I said with a sigh.

CHAPTER 30

ALANA

The car pulled up outside the airport and Kelsey turned to me while Hugo climbed out and got her bag from the trunk.

'I'm going to miss you, honey,' she said as she wrapped her arms around me.

I hugged her back tightly. 'I'm going to miss you too, Kels. I'm so sorry you had to spend your weekend with us under house arrest.'

She pulled back and grinned at me. 'Will you stop! I would spend a year under house arrest in that beautiful house. Tell Alejandro to get the pool house into shape and I'll be spending every vacation with you guys,' she said with a flash of her eyebrows.

'I'll get onto it as soon as we get back,' I smiled. The pool house was under renovation, but work had stalled with everything that had been going on. Alejandro didn't want contractors in and out of the house right now.

The car door was pulled open by Hugo and Kelsey gave me a final hug. 'I'll see you soon, honey.'

'Hang on, me and Hugo can walk you to the check in,' I said.

Hank, who was sitting in the front seat, spun around faster than I could even blink. 'Please stay in the car, Mrs Montoya,' he growled.

Kelsey grinned at me and I flashed my eyebrows, feeling like a naughty kid for suggesting such a thing.

'Bye, Jacob. Stay fresh, Hank,' Kelsey chirped as she jumped out of the car and took her bag from Hugo.

'Hey, can you at least walk her to the entrance?' I asked him with a smile.

He cleared his throat. 'Of course, Ma'am,' he replied.

The door closed and the automatic locks clicked. I watched Kelsey and Hugo through the window. He had taken her bag back from her and was carrying it. Then he rested his hand on the small of her back as he escorted her through the crowd. When they reached the entrance, they stopped and turned to face each other. They exchanged a few words and I wished I could hear what they were saying. Then Kelsey's arms snaked around Hugo's neck and she pushed herself up onto her tiptoes and kissed him. I gasped out loud as Hugo stood there motionless.

Oh, for God's sake, kiss her back, Hugo!

As if he had heard me, he dropped her bag to the floor and wrapped his giant arms around her, squashing her body against his as they shared an intense lip-locking session.

Wow! Hugo Fernandez kissed like he meant it.

I sat back in my seat and smiled, feeling like a voyeur. Suddenly I missed Alejandro.

A few moments later, Hugo was climbing back into the car next to me with a slight flush on his cheeks.

'Everything okay?' I asked him as he fastened his seatbelt.

'Please don't tell the boss I was just kissing someone while I was on duty,' he said as he closed his eyes and sucked in a breath.

Jacob chuckled in the front seat as he pulled the car away from the curbside.

'You know I'll have to though, right?' I said, mimicking the same thing he said to me all the time.

Even Hank snorted at that. I supposed it was the closest he ever came to laughing.

'Don't worry. Your secret is safe with me.' I winked at him and he leaned back against the seat with a sigh.

'Is Alejandro at the hotel?' I asked. 'Can we swing by on the way home?'

'Yes, but he said he's not to be disturbed,' Hank replied.

I looked out of the window and sighed. I wanted to see him so much. He had left for work early that morning. I had a vague recollection of him kissing my cheek but by the time I'd fully woken up, he had gone.

'I'm sure Mr. Montoya wouldn't mind being disturbed by Mrs. Montoya,' Hugo offered. 'We could stop by for a few minutes.'

'On your head be it, kid,' Hank growled.

'I'm sure he won't mind at all,' Jacob agreed. 'I'll make a detour.'

AN HOUR LATER, Hugo was escorting me past the armed guards posted at the door to Alejandro's suite.

'I'll be right outside this time,' he said with a flash of his eyebrows.

'I promise not to run away,' I whispered, recalling the last time he had brought me here and I'd disappeared to New York.

'Is anybody in with him?' I asked Lorenzo, one of his guards.

'Not currently, Ma'am. He has another meeting in fifteen minutes.'

'Thanks,' I said as I walked into the room and closed the door behind me.

The door to Alejandro's office was open. I heard him talking and assumed he was on the phone. Walking to his doorway, I saw him with his back to me, facing the window, his cell phone pressed to his ear. I watched him for a moment. He was so damn beautiful. He exuded power and raw sexual energy.

His free hand was in his trouser pocket, so the material was stretched taut across his strong thighs and his perfect ass. He had on a crisp white shirt which was perfectly fitted to his muscular torso, stretching across his broad shoulders every time he moved.

I felt a rush of warmth and wetness between my thighs at the sight of him.

I cleared my throat to let him know I was there. I had learned my lesson about eavesdropping.

He spun around. There was a scowl on his face and I wondered if that was for me, but then he started to smile. 'I have to go, Anton. Something just came up. Keep me posted,' he barked as he ended the call.

'Princesa?' he said as he walked toward me. 'What are you doing here?'

'I missed you,' I said with a smile as I walked toward him too. 'I know you're busy, but I just wanted to see you. You didn't kiss me goodbye this morning.'

He pulled me to him as he reached me, sliding his hands over my hips and onto my ass. 'I kissed you before I left. I promise.'

'Not a proper kiss though,' I purred.

'You came all this way just for a kiss?' he said as his lips brushed lightly over mine, teasing me.

'Yes,' I breathed as I lifted my hands to the back of his head and pressed him closer to me until our lips were sealed together.

He slipped his tongue inside my mouth and swirled it against mine. My heart started to hammer in my chest as the energy thrumming between my thighs ratcheted up to dangerous levels. He grabbed my ass possessively and pressed his hips further into me. I groaned into his mouth as I felt how hard he was already. Then he kept on kissing me until my head started to spin.

When he pulled back, he smiled at me. 'Just a kiss?' he growled.

'Well, I always want more from you,' I purred. 'But I know you're busy.'

He glanced at his watch and groaned. 'I have to meet with someone in ten minutes, princess, or I would spread you open on my desk and eat your delicious pussy until you come all over my face.'

'And then what?' I breathed as my hands slid to the zipper of his suit pants.

'Then I'd bend you over it and fuck you until you were coming on my cock, too.'

I groaned as my walls tightened at the thought. Reaching my hand inside his boxers, I pulled out his cock. He was stiff and hot and smooth. I squeezed him tightly and he groaned against my lips. 'I told you, I don't have time, Alana.'

'Not for what you just said, but I'm sure we have time for something else,' I purred before I dropped to my knees.

'Alana,' he growled as I wrapped my lips around his thick shaft, keeping my hand wrapped tightly around his base.

I swirled my tongue around the tip, licking off the delicious beads of pre-cum that had already formed as I continued fisting him at the root. His hands were in my hair as he pushed further into my mouth. I sucked on him, pressing my tongue flat against the underside of his cock.

'Fuck, Alana! How did you get so good at this so quick, princess?' he growled. 'You make me feel like a fucking teenage boy when you're giving me head.'

His hands fisted in my hair, pulling gently as he pushed himself deeper into my mouth. I removed my hand so I could take him all the way to the back of my throat and he cursed loudly in Spanish.

Placing my hand flat on his powerful thighs, I snaked the other one around to his ass in an effort to steady myself as he took complete control and started to fuck my mouth. I felt the tremors in his thigh muscles as his release approached. A few seconds later, his hot seed spurted down my throat. I swallowed it all, sucking every last drop and reveling in the way I was able to make him lose control so completely.

He pulled me up to a standing position, wiping the sides of my mouth with his thumb. 'I don't know what I did to deserve that, but thank you for making this shit-show of a day a whole lot better, princess,' he said as he tucked himself back into his suit pants. 'I'm sorry, I can't return the favor.'

'That's okay,' I smiled. 'I'll take care of myself when I get home.'

His eyes almost rolled into the back of his head. 'Oh, princess, now all I'll be able to think about is you at home in our bed, making yourself come, while I'm stuck here.'

He wrapped his arms back around me.

'Well, I would much rather it was you making me come,' I whispered. 'So I can wait for tonight if that will make you less distracted in work.'

'I will make you come plenty tonight. But you don't have to wait,' he mumbled against my skin. Then he looked up at me with a wicked glint in his eyes. 'Are your panties wet?'

'Of course.'

'Give them to me,' he ordered as he held out his hand.

'What? And go home with no panties on?'

He looked down at my legs. 'Your dress is long enough. No-one will see. Now hand them over.'

'You are a serious panty fiend,' I said with a laugh. 'But I wanted to stop by the shelter too, and I can't go to work with no panties on.'

He frowned at me. 'No, Alana. It's too dangerous. You said you could work from home?'

'I can. But there are some things I need to go into the shelter for. I have to speak to some of the women.'

He shook his head. 'I'm sorry, princess. It's still not safe. I can't do what I need to do here if I'm worrying about you. You're safe at the house. You shouldn't have even come here today.'

I felt a pang of disappointment and instinctively took a step back from him. He grabbed me by the hips and pulled me back to him. 'I'm glad that you did. I needed that more than you know. But now I need you to go straight home, and stay there, Alana. Please?'

'Okay,' I said softly.

'Buena chica,' he said as he brushed my hair back from my face.

'I should go and leave you to your meeting then?' I said. 'Do you still want my panties?'

He laughed. 'No, it's okay. On second thoughts, you keep them on while you're dripping with your sweet cum and sitting in a car full of my men.' He flashed an eyebrow at me. 'I don't want to torture them.'

'Probably for the best,' I agreed, although a part of me was stupidly disappointed that he wasn't going to sit through his meetings with my damp panties in his pocket.

He held my jaw with his hand. 'I'll see you tonight.'

'Okay.'

We were interrupted by a knock at the door and Alejandro's mask of cool, calm confidence was firmly back in place.

'Come in,' he shouted.

CHAPTER 31

ALANA

*A*fter five days of pleading, and promising that I wouldn't do anything reckless, Alejandro had finally relented and allowed me to leave the house to go to work at the shelter for a few hours, under the watchful eyes of Hugo and Hank. Whilst I completely understood why he didn't want me to leave the house with everything that was going on, I was going stir crazy being stuck indoors. Alejandro was working long hours. Lucia was back at school. I could do some work from home, but I missed being at the shelter and working kept me feeling sane.

I'd arrived at my office ten minutes earlier. Hank wasn't allowed in because he was so serious and grumpy he scared some of the women and children, so he waited outside, but Hugo was like my shadow and I imagined he would be for the rest of the afternoon. I was just about to make a fresh pot of coffee for us both when I got a message that Kristen was looking for me.

I walked down the hallway and popped my head into her office. 'You wanted to see me?'

'Alana! Yes, come on in,' she said as a smile spread across her face. 'An old friend of yours called by, and he's presented us with an offer we can't refuse.' Then she looked at whoever must have been sitting across the desk from her, but was obscured from my view by the door.

I stepped into the room and her visitor turned and gave me a huge smile too, showing off his perfect white teeth.

'Bobby?' I stammered. 'What are you doing here?'

'Hey, Alana. I found out you worked at this place and I thought I'd stop by. I got chatting to Kristen here and I think we can do some business together.'

I stared at him. I had so many questions, but Kristen was my boss and I didn't want to look completely unprofessional in front of her.

I forced a smile and walked further into the room, leaving Hugo standing in the hallway. 'What kind of business?' I asked.

'Well, first and foremost, I'd like to make a sizable donation to the shelter,' he said as he leaned back in his chair and flashed his eyebrows at me.

I wondered if I was supposed to be impressed by that. Probably.

'Well, that's very generous of you,' I said with all the charm I could muster.

'I've spoken to the board and my corporation would also like to fund your post for the next five years.'

Jackass!

'I work for free,' I said with a smile. 'But that money will come in handy, I'm sure. There are so many things we could do with it.'

Kristen sucked the air through her teeth. 'Actually, Alana, having a full-time fundraising co-ordinator post puts the shelter in a much stronger position. The money will be ring-fenced anyway, it doesn't detract from the sizable donation Mr Conroy is already prepared to make. Obviously, it goes without saying that the job is yours for as long as you want it. You know that. But if something happened to you, or you found another job, or decided not to work here anymore, I'd be stuck. This way, the post would still be funded and you would also be under contract and that offers me certain protections.'

I sat down in the chair and blinked. 'Seems like you two have this all worked out?'

'Alana, I know that you have given your all to this place and I know that you will keep on doing so, but none of us knows what the future holds, and I always have to have the center's best interests at heart.'

'I know that,' I said. 'It's just...'

'Just what?' Bobby asked, his eyes burning into mine and the hint of a grin on his lips. He knew exactly what the problem was. When Alejandro found out that my ex-boyfriend was essentially paying my salary, he would go loco. I had a suspicion that was exactly what Bobby wanted.

'Never mind. Whatever you think is best for the center, Kristen,' I said with a smile as I stood up.

'That's not all though,' Kristen said.

'Oh?' I frowned. What else did Saint Bobby have up his sleeve?

'We're working on an app that will assist abuse victims to record and report any assaults. It's discreet and undetectable. It could be a game changer,' Bobby said, puffing his chest out with pride.

'And what does that have to do with us?' I asked.

'Bobby wants to trial it here for some of the women at the shelter or in the outreach programs.'

'I'd love for you to work on it with me, Alana,' he said with a smile.

'I'm not tech savvy at all,' I replied.

'You don't have to be,' he fired back. 'I've got that side covered.'

'You have a connection with the women here though, Alana, and a way of making people see things from a different perspective. I think you and Bobby would make a great team,' Kristen said.

'So, what do you say?' he asked.

I swallowed. 'I'll have to think about it.'

'What's stopping you? This could be huge. It's the perfect challenge for someone as smart as you,' Bobby said, his face almost a sneer.

Jackass!

'I'm busy is all, with Lucia, and Alejandro's father is in hospital. Developing an app with you might be a little too much to take on right now, that's all.'

'Well, think about it, won't you?' Kristen said. 'Please?'

'Yes, of course. Now, if you'll both excuse me, I have some calls to make.'

I walked out of the office and took a deep breath. What the hell was Bobby playing at?

'Everything okay?' Hugo asked as he stepped across the hallway toward me.

'For now,' I replied.

'Who was that?' he asked as we walked back toward my office. 'Did Kristen say he was an old friend of yours?'

'Yes,' I said with a sigh as I rubbed the back of my neck. 'He's also an old boyfriend.'

'Oh,' Hugo replied.

'I'll tell him myself,' I said with a sigh, knowing exactly what would be on his mind.

'I know...'

'But you'll have to tell him anyway. I get it.'

'More than my job's worth not to, Alana. You know that. I'm sure he'll be fine with you working with your ex-boyfriend,' he said with a flash of his eyebrows.

'Yeah, right. Besides, I don't know if I am going to work with him yet. I'm trying to work out what his angle is.'

'Well, how about I make us that fresh coffee while you think on it,' he said as we reached my office.

'That would be great. Thanks, Hugo.'

FIFTEEN MINUTES LATER, I was setting up some new spreadsheets and Hugo was looking out of the window when there was a knock on my office door. I looked up to see Bobby standing there.

'Hey, Alana, can we talk?' he asked.

Hugo turned around and glared at him.

'Hugo, can you give us a few minutes please?' I asked with a sigh.

'I don't think that's a good idea, Alana,' he said, his eyes narrowed.

'It's just a few minutes. You can wait right outside.'

'Fine,' he snapped as he stalked toward the door.

'Don't worry, I'll take good care of her,' Bobby said with a grin.

'You lay one finger on her and I will break every bone in your body, cabrón,' he snarled as he walked out of the room and closed the door.

'What the hell are you doing here, Bobby?'

He sat down in the chair opposite me. 'I wanted to see you. And when I found out you worked here, I wanted to help.'

'How did you even find out where I work?' I snapped.

'You'd be surprised at the type of information I can get my hands on, Alana,' he chuckled.

'But why? Why did you want to see me?'

'I was worried about you. That husband of yours seemed like a bit of a jealous asshole. Then I looked into him. Do you have any idea who he is?'

I frowned at him. 'Of course I know who he is, Bobby. I married him, didn't I?'

'He's bad news. The guy is a stone cold killer.'

'You know nothing about him.'

'I know enough. And you can't even come to work without one of his goons following you around.'

'Hugo is my bodyguard. He's only here for my protection.'

'Exactly, Alana. You married a guy so fucking dangerous that you need a bodyguard. If you need an out, then I can help you. I can get us both out of here and take you somewhere he'll never find you. You don't have to put up with his shit if you don't want to.'

I placed my hands on the desk. 'Enough!' I snapped. 'How dare you come in here and criticize my life choices. Alejandro is my husband. He makes me happy. I love him. That is all you need to know. So, if that is all, please get out of my office. We won't be working on any app together, Bobby, because I don't trust you. If you still want to donate money to the shelter, then that would be great, but do not think for one second that puts me in your debt in any way.'

He stood up and planting his hands on my desk, he leaned forward. 'Seems I had you pegged all wrong, Alana. All this time I had you down as the sweet little girl next door, but you like the bad guys really, don't you? Is that what gets you off? The danger? Maybe if I'd killed someone you'd have let me fuck you too?' he snarled.

'Get out!' I snarled back. 'Before I have Hugo come in here, rip your arms off and shove them up your ass!'

He smiled at me as he straightened up. 'Feisty now, too. I'll be seeing you, Alana.'

'No you won't,' I hissed.

Then he walked out of the door and I leaned back in my chair as blood thundered in my ears.

'Are you okay?' Hugo asked as he walked back into the room.

'I am now,' I nodded. 'What a jerk!'

'Want me to go kick his ass?' he offered.

'As tempting as that is, no thanks. Let me finish up here real quick and then we can go home.'

'Good,' he nodded in agreement. 'I'll feel much better when you're safe at the house.'

CHAPTER 32

ALANA

*L*ucia and I were sitting at the breakfast bar in the kitchen. She was eating a bowl of ice-cream and I was flicking through a magazine. We both looked up when Alejandro walked into the room. He threw his car keys onto the counter and stood leaning against it, glaring at me.

'I'm going to take this to my room and have a look at my history homework,' Lucia said as she slipped off the stool and gave me a sideways eye roll.

'Goodnight, Lucia,' Alejandro said, his voice low and smooth.

'Night guys,' she replied and then she left the kitchen, closing the door behind her.

'Do you have something to tell me, princess?' he growled.

'Well, by the look on your face, I assume Hugo has already told you that Bobby Conroy paid a visit to the shelter today.'

'Yes, he did,' he said as he crossed the kitchen in two large strides until he was standing directly in front of me. 'What he couldn't tell me is what went on between you and Bobby when you asked him to leave the room.'

'We talked,' I started to say before he interrupted me.

'If all you did was talk, why the fuck did you send Hugo out of the room?'

'Because I wanted a private conversation, Alejandro. You know what one of those is, don't you? You get to have them all of the time.'

He leaned his face close to mine. 'Don't push me, Alana. This is not about me.'

I slipped off my stool. 'No? What is it about then? Because it feels very much about you.'

'What did the two of you talk about then?' he growled. 'What was so private that you couldn't have Hugo in the room?'

I couldn't help it. I rolled my eyes. Shit!

He wrapped his hand around my throat before I could even blink. 'Did you just roll your eyes at me?'

'Yes,' I said. I felt a slight pressure on my windpipe and a flash of heat between my thighs. What the hell was wrong with me?

He pushed me backwards until I was pressed against the breakfast bar as he ran his thumb along my jawline. 'Answer the fucking question, Alana.'

Crap! This was not going to go well. 'He has offered to donate money to the shelter. His corporation is going to fund my post for the next five years.'

He dropped his hand to his side and frowned at me. 'You're a volunteer. Your post isn't funded.'

'I know. But it should be. And having a properly funded post gives Kristen some protection in case I stop working there for some reason.'

'Good, because you won't be working there any longer,' he snapped.

'The hell I won't,' I scowled at him. 'I love that job.'

'This is not up for negotiation, Alana,' he snarled.

'I know it's not. Because I am not giving up my job.'

He pressed his face closer to mine and I felt the breath catch in my throat. 'You are my wife and I will not have your ex-boyfriend paying your salary.'

'But, Alejandro...'

He slammed his fist onto the breakfast bar. 'Alana! Can you ever just do as you're told! You are not to have anything more to do with that prick and if I find out he has come anywhere near you ever again, I will break every bone in his body.'

I tilted my head up to look directly into his eyes. Anger coursed through my body. It didn't matter that I didn't actually want anything to do with Bobby myself anyway; it was the principle of the matter. 'I get that you're a possessive asshole. In fact, most of the time, I think it's really hot. But this is a step too far. I have never given you any reason to doubt me. How dare you try and tell me who I can and can't work with? *If* Bobby donates money to the shelter to fund my post, then that is all it will be. There is nothing between me and him and there never will be.'

'So why couldn't you talk to him in front of Hugo then?' he shouted.

'Because I didn't want to, Alex. I didn't know what he was going to say and how Hugo would react to it. The shelter is where I work. The women and kids there have already been through enough; the last thing they need there is any more drama.'

He narrowed his eyes as he stared at me and I felt anger vibrating through his body. I was angry too. I wanted to shout at him. To rage at him for being so pig-headed, but I knew that wouldn't get me anywhere.

'What is this really about, Alex?' I asked as I placed a hand on his cheek. 'Bobby is in my past. Way in my past. He means nothing to me.'

'You say that now, but if you start spending time with him again...' He shook his head. 'I forbid you to see him again, Alana.'

'I am a grown woman. You don't get to forbid me to do anything.'

'Yes, I fucking do,' he snarled at me. 'You are my wife.'

I nodded. 'Yes, I am. So why can't you believe in that? Why don't you trust me?'

He glared at me. 'You wouldn't understand,' he hissed.

'Try me!'

'Because...'

'Because what?'

His nostrils flared as he stared at me. 'Because he is the man you should be with,' he shouted.

'What?' I blinked at him.

I saw a look of anguish flicker across his face. 'He is a better man for you than I am, Alana. You wouldn't be in so much danger if you were his wife. You can't deny that.'

Shit! He was insecure. The King of LA was worried that he wasn't good enough for me. What the hell!

I placed my other hand on his face, my fingers brushing against the dark stubble on his jaw. 'But I can deny it, and I do. Bobby Conroy is *not* the man for me. I could spend one thousand years in his company and there would still only ever be you, Alex. I am yours — body, heart and soul, remember?'

He pressed his forehead against mine. 'When Hugo told me he'd come to see you, and you were alone with him...' He closed his eyes.

'What? You thought something happened between us? We were alone for like two minutes. You really think I'd do that?'

'No,' he shook his head. 'But I couldn't stop picturing him with his hands on you. I trust you, but I don't trust him. Why the fuck would he bother to find out where you work?'

I swallowed and he placed his hand beneath my chin and tilted my head up to look at him. 'What?' he frowned. 'Did something happen?'

'Promise you won't get mad.'

'I'm already mad, princess.'

'He asked me if I knew who you really were when I'd married you, and whether I needed him to help me get away from you.'

'Hijo de puta!' he snarled. 'I will fucking destroy him.'

'Hey, I handled it. I told him to get lost. Believe me, I'd be happy never to see him again.'

He frowned. 'And what did he say when you told him that?'

I didn't answer, because I couldn't lie to him, but I knew that the truth was likely to set him off again.

'Well?'

'He said he'll see me around,' I replied.

'He said what?'

'It's just a saying, Alex.' I wrapped my arms around his neck. 'Please can we forget about Bobby?'

'It sounds more like a threat to me. There is no way you are working with that guy, Alana. I don't care if I have to keep you locked up in this house.'

'I know. I'm going to tell Kristen I won't be working on the app with him,' I said with a sigh.

'What app?'

'He's developing some app for abuse victims. He wanted me to work on it with him.' I felt Alejandro's grip on me tighten. 'I'm not going to. I don't want anything to do with him.' I shuddered and he stared down at me.

'Did he do something to you?'

'No,' I shook my head. 'He just said something, that's all.'

'What? What the hell did he say?'

I took a deep breath. 'He asked me if I would have let him fuck me if he had killed someone too,' I whispered.

The vein in his forehead throbbed as he glared at me. 'He is a fucking dead man!'

I pressed my face against his chest. 'He is really not worth it, Alejandro. He's probably already halfway back to New York by now. Please, just forget about him.'

He grabbed hold of my ponytail and wrapped it around his fist, tilting my head up to look at him. 'For your sake, princess, I won't hunt him down like a dog and put a bullet in his head. But if I ever see him anywhere near you again, I will break his goddamn neck.'

'I'm still going to work at the shelter though,' I said. 'I'll explain to Kristen that I don't want to work with him, but I'm not giving up my job, Alex.'

He frowned at me and I wondered if he was going to keep on pushing to get his own way, or whether he would relent.

'Fine,' he eventually agreed before slipping his hands down to my ass cheeks and lifting me onto the breakfast bar. He pushed my dress up to my waist and tugged my panties to one side.

'Lucia might come back in,' I breathed.

'She's not stupid. She knows we're in here. She'll knock.'

'Shouldn't we go upstairs though? Or to your office?' I panted, even as I pulled him closer to me.

'No. I want you right here. Right now,' he growled, pushing two of his thick fingers into my opening as he unzipped his suit pants with his free hand, making me groan out loud. 'I want you to remember that I own you, princess, and I will fuck you anywhere and any way I want to. And you will moan my name. Every. Single. Time.'

Dear God!

'Care to tell me why you're already soaking wet, princess?' he said against my ear as he pressed his fingers in deeper and curled them against my G-spot. The low vibration of his voice sent shivers down my spine and I ground my hips onto him.

'Because you are so freaking hot when you're angry,' I purred against his neck.

'Oh, princess, you know how dangerous it is to make me angry, don't you?'

'Yes,' I breathed.

'Coz I'm gonna fuck you so hard you won't be able to get out of bed to go to work for the rest of the week.'

CHAPTER 33

ALEJANDRO

I saw the call coming through as I drove along the interstate. I frowned as I pressed the button to answer.

'Hey, amigo. Where are you?' Jax asked, his voice coming through the speakers of my car.

'Just dealing with something. I'll be back later.'

'Something I should know about?'

'It's personal,' I snapped.

I heard his soft chuckle. 'Just don't kill him, amigo! We've got enough to deal with without me having to hide another body.'

'If you know where I am, why did you ask me?' I snapped.

'I suspected, but I wasn't sure. I could have dealt with this for you.'

'Not a chance!' I growled.

'Well, like I said, don't kill him.'

'I'm just going to talk to him.'

'Okay. I'll see you later,' Jax laughed again.

'Later, amigo.'

. . .

I PULLED up outside the hotel and turned off the car engine. The valet was waiting for me when I stepped out.

'Good afternoon, Mr Montoya,' he said with a slight bow of his head.

'Buenas tardes. Did you get me what I asked you for?' I asked him as I handed him my keys.

'Of course,' he replied as he slipped the key card into my hand. 'Room five one two.'

'Gracias,' I nodded as I placed the key in my pocket. 'Give my regards to your mama.'

'I will, Mr Montoya. And thank you.'

'Look after that car, Henry. I only just bought it.'

'You betcha,' he nodded eagerly as he opened the car door.

Henry was a good kid who had ended up getting into a lot of trouble with some very nasty people a few months earlier. He was a talented thief, but he was also stupid enough to steal something he shouldn't have. Fortunately for him, his mama and mine came from the same neighborhood. So, I helped him out, and recommended him for a job in this hotel. It was the second best hotel in LA, and now that Bobby Conroy was no longer welcome in any of mine, he had no choice but to stay here.

I WALKED along the hallway until I came to Bobby's room. Taking the key card from my pocket, I swiped it into the lock and smiled when I heard a satisfying click. A few seconds later, I was stepping into the room, closing the door behind me.

Bobby strolled out of the bathroom and his eyes almost popped out of his head when he saw me standing there.

'What the fuck! How the hell did you get in here?' he snapped.

'I think you'll find there is nowhere in this city where I can't go, Bobby.'

'This is my fucking hotel room. I'm calling security,' he

snorted as he looked at the phone on the nightstand, the one he would have to walk through me to get to.

'Be my guest,' I said as I held my arms open in invitation. I would like nothing better than for him to put his hands on me, because then I would be entirely justified in breaking every one of his fingers.

He stared at the phone and then back at me. 'What the hell are you doing here in my hotel?' He straightened up, puffing his chest out, as though that would somehow intimidate me.

'I came to tell you politely to stay the hell away from my wife.'

He started to laugh and I frowned at him. Did this guy have a death wish?

'Are you really so insecure that you can't handle a little competition?' he challenged me.

I ran a hand across my jaw, remembering the promise I had made to Alana the night before, and just a few minutes earlier to Jax.

'Or are you worried that once she starts working with me, spending time with me again, she'll realize it's me she really wants after all?' he grinned at me, one eyebrow arched and his arms crossed over his chest.

Cocky cabrón!

The vein in my neck throbbed with the effort of not strangling him or throwing him off the hotel balcony.

'Just stay away from her!' I warned him.

'Hmm. Maybe you should be telling her to stay away from me,' he laughed.

I felt the anger that was bubbling beneath my skin bursting to get out. 'What?' I snarled at him.

'You heard me. What are you going to do? Kill me? There must be a dozen witnesses that saw you walk in here to threaten me today. There is CCTV all over this hotel. My father is a district judge. I'm not some lowlife scum you can just make disappear!'

I flexed my neck and the sound of my muscles cracking reverberated around the room. I stepped toward him and was pleased to see him flinch, but he stood his ground.

Maybe Bobby had some balls after all?

I stood in front of him, so close that I could hear his breathing coming fast and shallow now. Fight or flight mode.

'I know all about your father, Bobby, the district judge with a particular taste for high class hookers. I also know about your married lady friend from the Upper East Side. And about that little misdemeanor you think you got away with in college,' I said quietly.

I watched in satisfaction as his face turned a strange shade of grey.

'I don't know what you're talking about,' he stammered.

I smiled at him. 'Oh yes you do, Bobby. You see, I know you think I'm a thug. A stone-cold killer, is that what you called me? But I am also a very resourceful man. There are very few skeletons that stay buried when I am looking for them. I generally find there are much cleaner and easier ways to control my enemies than to simply kill them.'

His nostrils flared as he stared at me, trying to control his anger and his fear that I might expose him. I guessed that Bobby liked to think he was a top dog and people generally spoke to him with nothing but reverence.

'That being said,' I snarled as I pressed my face closer to his. 'If you ever go anywhere near my wife again without my express permission, you will learn the depths of my viciousness like no-one ever has before. You think that witnesses and security cameras can keep you safe from me, cabrón? For every rumor you have ever heard about me, I can guarantee the truth is far more terrifying. I have done things that you couldn't even imagine in your wildest dreams. I know many wonderful ways to inflict the maximum pain on a man's body while still keeping him alive. I could take you from this room right now and make sure that no trace of you was ever found. And I would get away with it too.'

He blinked at me, his pupils dilated in fear and his breathing becoming even more labored.

'And to answer your earlier questions, no, I have no doubts about my wife. She is not a liar or a cheat. Am I a possessive demon when it comes to her? Yes, I fucking am, because she is mine and I would never be stupid enough to let her go. I have no worries at all that she will realize it's you she wants. She didn't want to fuck you when you dated and she doesn't want to fuck you now. You're goddamn lucky she is such a good influence on me, because I should cut out your tongue for what you said to her. I will not be so merciful a second time! Do you understand me?'

'Yes.' His lip quivered as he spoke and I suppressed a smile.

I looked down at his suit pants, noting the large wet stain on his crotch and smiled.

'Good! I'm glad we understand each other.'

CHAPTER 34

ALANA

*A*fter the incident with Bobby a few days earlier, I restricted my time at the shelter to just two afternoons a week. That was enough for me to keep feeling sane and it helped stop Alejandro worrying about me.

I was in the break-room chatting to one of the other volunteers when Kristen popped her head in. 'Alana, can I have a quick word?' she asked.

'Sure,' I replied as I picked up my mug of tea and followed her to her office.

She closed the door behind us and I sat down and looked around. I loved her office. She always had the sweetest smelling diffusers dotted around, and statues of the Egyptian Goddess, Isis, and Buddha, as well as dozens of bright green plants.

'I wanted to catch up with you today anyway, Kristen. I need to talk to you about Bobby and the app.'

'That was why I wanted to talk to you, too,' she said with a frown. 'Mr Conroy's organization have pulled out and withdrawn their funding offer.'

'What?' I snapped. Was this because of our conversation a few days earlier? I hoped I hadn't unintentionally lost the shelter a lot of money. 'Why would they do that?'

'I have no idea. Someone from their HR department called me and simply said we weren't the right fit,' Kristen said as she rubbed a hand over her chin.

'Wow! How infuriating!' I snapped as I shook my head and sat back in my seat.

'Well, yes, except we have a new, mysterious benefactor in their place. They have doubled Mr Conroy's pledged donation and also agreed to fund your post indefinitely.'

'Indefinitely?'

'Yes, and at a much higher salary too.'

'Oh,' I said. Suddenly, I realized exactly who our mysterious benefactor was.

'You know something about this?' she asked.

'Probably,' I said with a sigh. 'I'm pretty sure our new mystery donation is coming from the Montoya Corporation.'

'Your husband's company?'

'Yes.'

'But they already donated a sizable amount this year.'

'I know. But… I don't know how to tell you this, so I'll just lay it all out for you. Bobby was my ex-boyfriend from high school. I'm not sure that his offer to fund my post and donate to the shelter was entirely altruistic.'

'Oh, really?' Kristen replied. 'And he seemed so nice.'

'And he is. Well, he used to be. But I saw a different side to him last week, too. He was nasty.' I shook my head. 'That doesn't detract from the fact that my husband is an egomaniac though,' I said with a grin. 'And he didn't want my ex-boyfriend paying my salary. He would rather I worked for the hotel, but he understands that I want to work here. I had never thought about the post being funded before and how that would make the whole charity more secure, but if I had I know he would have offered to fund it, and I think he was kind of hurt by that, too.'

Kristen nodded. 'Well, as long as you're happy with the arrangement, Alana, it works out well for the shelter.'

'It's all fine by me,' I agreed, even as I was thinking about exactly what I was going to say to Alejandro when I called him in a few minutes' time.

He was a possessive asshole sometimes, but who was I kidding? I loved it. And I loved him.

I closed the door to my office and took my cell phone out of my purse. I'd asked Hugo to wait outside for me a few minutes while I spoke to Alejandro.

I dialed his number and waited for him to pick up. It rang out a few times before he finally answered.

'Hola, princesa,' he said breathlessly when he did.

'Hi. Is this a bad time?'

'Kind of. But I always have time for you. What is it?'

'Did you warn Bobby off donating to the shelter?'

'Hang on,' I heard him sigh, and then he barked some orders in Spanish. A few seconds later, he spoke to me again. 'What were you saying?' he asked, with clear exasperation in his tone now.

'I asked you if you are responsible for Bobby's company withdrawing their donation to the shelter?'

'Yes,' he snapped. 'I told you I don't trust him.'

I wasn't sure what to say next. I hadn't expected that to be so easy.

'Is there anything else, princess? I'm kind of busy.'

'Yes. Did you offer to fund my post instead?'

'Yes,' he replied.

'Oh,' I said softly. I knew that he had. And I was kind of mad at him for it. But what could I say? He had made his feelings clear about Bobby. He had made sure that the shelter wouldn't lose out because he had matched the donation and then some. What the hell did I have to argue with him about really? I knew the kind of man he was, and it was one of the many things I loved about him.

'I'll let you get back to your work then,' I said.

'Good.'

'Alejandro! Wait. There is one more thing.'

'And what's that?' he asked, the irritation in his voice clearly audible now.

'Te quiero.'

I heard a soft sigh this time, not one of exasperation, but perhaps of relief. 'I love you too, princess.'

CHAPTER 35

ALANA

I walked through the house to the kitchen, repeating the phrase I'd heard over and over in my head. I had never so much as seen Hank crack a smile before, so whatever the joke was it must have been incredibly funny. I could ask Alejandro what they had said, but I had hardly seen him this past week. He was doing everything he could to find the person responsible for shooting his father and that meant he was spending most of his time at the hotel. He still came home every night, but sometimes it was after midnight before he finally got back. I missed him, but I couldn't tell him that because he had more important things to deal with.

I sensed some distance between us and I didn't know if he was still angry with me because he'd had to follow me to New York or over the Bobby situation, or whether it was simply because we hadn't spent much time together.

Lucia had made herself a girlfriend who lived nearby. Alejandro knew the family, and they had good security at their house, so she often went there after school, still in the company of one of Alejandro's guards of course.

I walked into the kitchen to find our housekeeper, Magda, preparing dinner.

'Evening, Alana,' she said with a smile.

'Hi, Magda. Need any help?' I replied as I walked over to the counter to stand beside her.

'No thank you, dulce niña. I'm almost done.'

I leaned back against the counter and popped a piece of bell pepper into my mouth. Magda was putting some dishes into the sink by the time I'd finished eating it. 'Magda, what does la llevamos por las dos puertas mean?' I asked with a smile.

Magda almost dropped the plate she was carrying onto the floor. She fumbled and managed to prevent it from slipping from her hands but her face turned a bright shade of red and she stared at me with her mouth gaping open.

'Alana!' I heard a voice behind me and realized Alejandro had just walked through the door. I smiled at the sight of him. I hadn't expected him home so early. He was dressed in one of his impeccably tailored suits and, as usual, he looked good enough to lick from head to toe.

Although his reaction did make me wonder what the hell I had just said. 'What?' I said with a shrug. 'I was just asking.'

Magda cleared her throat and carried on clearing the dishes as Alejandro crossed the room to me. 'You almost gave Magda a heart attack,' he said half scowling, half grinning. 'Come with me.' Placing his hand on the small of my back, he guided me out of the kitchen.

'What?' I whispered as soon as we were in the hallway.

'Tell me again what you just said. I need to make sure I heard you right.'

I blushed. Whatever it was, was obviously either very offensive or very inappropriate. 'La llevamos por las dos puertas?' I said quietly. 'Maybe I'm pronouncing it wrong?'

'Oh, you're pronouncing it fine, princess. But where did you hear that?'

I swallowed. 'A couple of the guards said it to Hank just now and he burst out laughing. Like tears coming out of his eyes, laughing. I've never even seen him smile before. I thought it must have been something really funny.'

He rubbed a hand across his jaw. 'Hmm. It's not exactly funny, but I'll deal with those canallas later. Where is Lucia?'

'She's at the Neilsons' again. Why? Do you need to speak to her?'

He shook his head. 'No. Just checking we're alone,' he said as he started walking toward the stairs.

'So, what does it mean?' I asked for the third time.

He stopped in his tracks and grinned at me, before bending his head and brushing his lips across my ear. 'Come with me and I'll show you,' he growled before grabbing hold of my hand and leading me to the bedroom.

As soon as the bedroom door was closed, Alejandro walked me to the bed and silently undressed me, running his hands over my body and planting soft kisses as he exposed my skin to the cool air. When he took off my panties, he held them to his face, inhaling deeply.

'Fuck, princess, you smell delicious, do you know that?' he said and then he gave me a quick kiss on the lips before pushing me back onto the bed.

'I'm glad you're home early,' I whispered.

'So am I, princess. I've missed you, and I'm sorry I haven't been around much,' he said as he started to undress. 'But I'll make it up to you.'

I watched him intently, enjoying watching his deft fingers removing his clothes until he was naked too. He licked his lips as he looked down at me, as though he wanted to devour me and I felt a thrill coursing through my body. What the hell had I asked Magda in the kitchen?

Alejandro walked to the nightstand and took out a bottle of lube and the vibrator he'd bought me a few months earlier when I'd complained about missing him on his trip to Chicago. He placed them down on the bed beside me and I swallowed.

'So are you going to tell me what it means now?' I breathed.

He crawled onto the bed, holding himself over me. 'Well, the literal translation is *we took her by the two doors*. Do you know what that means, princess?' he growled before he sucked one of my nipples into his hot mouth.

I remembered now the looks on their faces and the way Hank doubled over with laughter, and it made sense that Magda almost dropped the dishes when I asked her to translate. 'I think I have an idea,' I groaned as one of his hands slipped between my thighs.

'Tell me what you think it means,' he said as he moved his head southwards, planting deliciously soft kisses over my stomach.

'That those two guys had sex with a woman at the same time?' I panted.

'Yes. One fucked her pussy, while the other one fucked her ass,' he said as he moved his head between my thighs and planted a soft kiss on my clit.

'Oh?' I groaned as he slipped two fingers inside me.

'And obviously, there is not a chance in hell that I would let anyone fuck you, princess, but I can show you how it would feel to have both of your beautiful holes filled at the same time. So, I need you really relaxed for me,' he said and then he sucked my clit into his mouth and I felt the endorphins coursing through my body as he sucked and rubbed on my most sensitive spots.

'Alex,' I groaned as he brought me to the edge of ecstasy and kept me teetering on the brink until I could hardly stand it any longer and I started begging him to let me come.

He chuckled against my skin as he finally gave me my release. As the orgasm washed over me in long rolling waves, he crawled back up the bed until he was lying beside me.

'Turn onto your side, princess,' he said softly in my ear.

I did as he told me, so I was facing away from him, my legs still trembling. He reached over and grabbed hold of the lube and the vibrator. I heard the cap of the lube snapping open and then the sound of liquid being squirted into Alejandro's hand. My legs trembled as I felt him behind me coating his cock ready to slide into me.

He pressed his lips against my ear. 'Open those legs wide for me princess. Let's put all that yoga you do to good use,' he growled.

I raised my right leg into the air and he pressed closer to me. I heard the vibrator buzzing to life before he slid it inside my pussy. I groaned out loud and he kissed my neck at the same time. He slid the toy in and out of me until I felt the familiar pressure building in my abdomen and my legs began trembling again.

'You ready for me too now, princess?' he asked as he stilled his hand.

'Yes,' I panted. The vibrator felt good but there was nothing better than the feeling of him inside me. He pressed his cock against my ass and pushed the tip in a fraction.

'Alex,' I moaned at the stretch. Having my pussy full of the vibrating toy while he pushed his cock inside me felt over-whelming and I had to take a deep breath.

'That's it, princess, breathe. You can take me too,' he growled in my ear. 'Keep those legs spread until I'm all the way in.'

'Okay,' I nodded and he pushed in further. Then he started to thrust the vibrator slowly in and out of me again. As he pulled it out for the third time, he took the opportunity to push his cock all the way into my ass and I cried out in pleasure.

'You okay, princess?' he whispered as he planted soft kisses on my neck.

'Uh-huh,' was all I could reply.

'I want to make you squirt while I'm fucking your ass. You think you can do that for me?'

'Yes.'

'Good girl. You can put your leg down now. Rest it on mine,' he said softly.

I lowered my leg, resting it on his and hooking my foot over his calf, so that we were spooning comfortably. Then he started to fuck me slowly. Each time he pushed the vibrator back inside me, he pulled out slightly and pleasure rolled through me in wave after wave. He continued like that, over and over, until I felt like my insides were going to explode.

'Reach down and rub your clit, princess,' he growled

'I can't,' I breathed. 'It's too much.'

'Alana!' He warned. 'Do as you're told.'

With trembling fingers, I reached down and started to rub my swollen clit gently while Alejandro fucked my ass and pussy to a slow, steady rhythm.

'Alex,' I gasped as the tears started rolling down my cheeks. 'Please?'

'Come whenever you want to, princess,' he chuckled. 'I'm not stopping you.'

'You are,' I groaned. He was slowing his pace to keep me teetering on the edge.

'Next time will you think twice about asking my housekeeper to translate for you?' he chuckled softly in my ear.

'No. Not if it leads to something like this,' I breathed.

'Joder! I love how much you enjoy being fucked, princess. Because there is nowhere I'd rather be than buried inside you.'

He thrust deeper into me, pushing the vibrator deep inside at the same time and I felt the torrent of wet heat rushing from me.

'Alex,' I shouted as tears ran down my face.

'That's it, princess, come for me,' he growled as he came too, hot and fierce, pumping every last drop into me.

My body trembled as he pulled the vibrator out of me and tossed it onto the floor. Then he slowly slid out of me and I moaned at the loss of fullness. He rolled me over and pulled me to him until I was lying on his chest with his strong arms wrapped around me. I took deep breaths as I tried to slow my heart rate and recover from the complete sensory overload.

'You understand what la llevamos por las dos puertas means now, princess?' he chuckled.

'Yes,' I panted.

'Good. And I hope you don't ask Magda to translate all of the filthy things I say to you when I'm fucking you,' he laughed again.

'Of course I don't. I think I'm going to have to find a class and learn Spanish.'

'Hmm, I would love that,' he said as he placed his hand under my chin, tilting my head up so he could look at my face. 'But until then, I can think of a few phrases I can teach you.'

I raised an eyebrow at him. 'Let me guess, they all involve fucking?'

'No,' he said with a grin. 'I'll also teach you how to tell me you'd like to suck my cock too.'

I shook my head. 'You're a sex maniac.'

'Me? You're the one who's soaked the bedsheets with your cum, princess.'

I blushed and he bent his head to kiss me.

'Hey, I do know some Spanish,' I said as I broke our kiss.

'Do you?'

I nodded. 'Lo eres todo para mi.'

He blinked at me in surprise. It was something he said to me often 'And what does that mean, princess?'

'You are everything to me.'

He smiled at me. 'Te quiero.'

I knew what that meant too. 'I love you too,' I replied and then he kissed me again and I thought that I had never felt as happy in my whole life as I was right now. When we were alone together, it felt like nothing else in the world existed, and I had started to live for moments like these when we could just be us. But, with everything going on around us, I wondered how long before we were facing our next obstacle.

CHAPTER 36

ALANA

I wandered down the hallway to Alejandro's office. I'd seen his car pulling into the drive half an hour earlier but he still hadn't come to bed. It had been two days since he'd come home early and we'd spent our incredible evening in bed together, and since that time I had hardly seen him.

His office door was ajar and I pushed it open. He was sitting at his desk with a half empty bottle of Scotch in front of him and a glass of amber liquid in his hand, staring into space.

'Alejandro. Are you okay?' I asked quietly as I slipped inside the room and closed the door behind me.

My voice seemed to snap him from his trance and he blinked at me.

He looked completely exhausted and my heart wanted to break for him. I wished there was something I could do to help. He still hadn't discovered who was behind his father's shooting, and while Mateo got stronger and healthier every day, Alejandro seemed to be deteriorating. I knew that the guilt and responsibility weighed heavy on him.

'Why don't you come to bed and try to get some sleep?' I suggested as I stepped toward his desk.

'Sleep?' he snorted before knocking back the remaining whisky in his glass. 'And just how the hell am I supposed to sleep, Alana, with everything that I have to deal with?'

'You'll make yourself ill, and then...'

He interrupted me before I could finish my sentence. 'And you think anyone cares about that? Do you think my enemies give a shit if I don't sleep? Because they don't sleep, princess, and that means neither do I. You have no idea the pressure I'm under... The responsibility to protect everyone!' he snarled.

'You don't have to protect everyone,' I said softly. 'That's not on you.'

He looked at me like I'd grown two heads. 'What?' he growled. 'You saw what happened when I wasn't here. My father was almost killed. I have you running around LA and refusing to stay in the house. What else am I supposed to do, Alana, but work twenty-four hours a day to try and keep a handle on it all?'

I swallowed. I hadn't thought about what it meant for him to have to worry about me whenever I left the house, but he didn't need to carry that all himself.

'Let me help then.'

'Help?' he scoffed. 'How can you help when you are part of the problem?' he slurred and it was only then that I realized he was drunk. 'I'm starting to think my father was right all along. Love is far too much trouble for a man like me. It makes me vulnerable. Weak!' He spat out the last word.

'Are you saying you regret marrying me?' I asked, feeling the sob catch in my throat.

He didn't answer. He stared at me instead, unblinking, his face devoid of emotion and I felt my sadness turn to anger.

'If either of us have regrets, don't you think that should be me?' I snapped, unable to contain my emotion. 'I was the one ripped from my life. I have done everything I can to make a life and a home here. I have done everything I could to make a life with you. My whole world has changed. I can't even leave the goddamn house without an armed escort. And you're the one with regrets?'

He stood up so fast that I flinched, pushing his chair back before striding right past me, opening the door.

'Where are you going?' I asked.

'To the hotel,' he barked.

I watched him leave and sat down on the chair. I blinked away the tears, determined not to cry. He hadn't stayed at the hotel alone in over seven months, not since the night we'd consummated our marriage. That was the place where he'd taken all of his other women before me.

The thought that he might seek comfort in the arms of one of those women tonight forced itself into my brain. I didn't believe he was capable of that, did I?

He was angry and drunk. But maybe it was more than that? Maybe he really did regret marrying me? Maybe our honeymoon period was officially over? Had I been a complete fool to think that I could hold the attention of a man like Alejandro before some other woman caught his eye again?

I wandered back to bed and lay awake in the dark. My stomach churned and all I wanted was for him to climb into bed beside me the way he usually did and wrap me in his arms. That was the place I felt most myself. It was the place I felt safe. It was home.

CHAPTER 37

ALEJANDRO

I lay in the dark listening to the sound of my own heartbeat pounding in my ears. I saw her face every time I closed my eyes.

'Do you regret marrying me?' she'd asked.

No. Not even for a heartbeat. So why hadn't I told her that? Why had I just sat there and let her believe that wasn't the truth?

Because I was a selfish cabrón. Because loving her made me feel exposed. I worried about her every second of every day. That someone might hurt her because of me made me feel like someone constantly had a knife to my heart. And so I wanted her to have some idea of how that felt.

I still had no idea who was behind my father's attempted murder and the fact that some madman was out there with a desire to hurt my family terrified me. Guilt, shame and anger ate me up day and night and I had taken it all out on the one person I loved more than anything else in the world. The one person I was most terrified of losing.

I should have followed her up to bed. I should have pulled off her clothes, pinned her to the bed and buried myself in her. That was the way we resolved our issues. That was what grounded me.

I needed her. So why the hell was I lying alone in bed halfway across the city?

Even my cock was weeping for her. I reached down and wrapped my fist around my shaft, squeezing tightly for some relief. Wishing it was her hands on me. Wishing that it was her tight, hot pussy squeezing me instead of my own hand.

I closed my eyes and pictured her lying in bed. Was she thinking about me too? Touching herself in those places that belonged to me? I moved my hand up and down, stroking my length as I remembered how sweet she tasted. How she was always willing to let me do anything I wanted to her. No matter how hard or rough, or often I fucked her, she always took it all. My chest burned with anger, shame and arousal as I kept pumping my shaft, imagining it was her.

When I finally found my release, I shouted her name into the darkness.

CHAPTER 38

ALANA

I smiled at Lucia as the sonographer rolled the small machine over her stomach and showed us the images of her unborn child on the screen.

'Oh look, Alana,' she said with tears in her eyes. 'He's perfect.'

I took hold of her hand and squeezed tightly. 'He certainly is, sweetheart,' I said with a smile. Seeing her baby on the screen was the perfect antidote to the completely crappy start I'd had to my day.

Alejandro had been true to his word and had stayed at his hotel all night. I had hardly slept, foolishly hoping that he would come home and slip into bed beside me. When he hadn't, I had wondered again if someone else had slipped into his bed — our bed – at the hotel instead.

Sex was his favorite way to unwind and deal with stress, and if he wasn't doing it with me, then was he looking elsewhere?

'Would you like some photographs?' the sonographer asked, breaking my train of thought.

'Yes, please. We'll need three, won't we?' Lucia replied. 'One each for me and Alana, and one for Alejandro.'

I nodded at her. 'Yes, that would be nice,' I said as my mind drifted back to our argument the previous night. I had outright asked if Alejandro regretted marrying me and he had just sat there staring at me, as though he didn't want to admit the truth. And then I had only gone and made the whole situation worse by suggesting that I regretted our marriage, when that couldn't be further from the truth.

I had checked my phone a dozen times that morning, hoping for a text or a call, but I had heard nothing from him.

I contemplated calling him, but I didn't know what I would have done if he'd ignored me. While we weren't in communication, I could pretend that this was just a silly argument. A blip that we would get over in no time at all.

A SHORT TIME LATER, Lucia and I were climbing into the armored SUV with Hugo and Hank, as well as our new driver, George. Alejandro insisted that if we must leave the house, we do so with armed guards and in the safest vehicle.

We were just pulling out of the parking lot and toward the intersection when I heard Hugo shout to George in Spanish. I couldn't understand what he said and before I had time to ask, or react, the whole car shook and shuddered and I was thrown forward, my seatbelt cutting into my neck as the sound of crunching metal and smashed glass filled my ears.

I grabbed hold of Lucia's hand as the car skidded along the road. My ears were ringing and my head spun. I heard shouting and gunshots and then nothing.

CHAPTER 39

ALEJANDRO

I looked at my watch. It was a little after eleven am. I'd been woken by Jax at six because he had a lead for me to chase.

Five hours later, we were at yet another dead end. I couldn't understand how nobody seemed to know who was responsible for my father's shooting. It didn't make any sense that at least one person hadn't cracked by now.

I had intended to go home as soon as I'd woken up and apologize to Alana. I hadn't even had a chance to call her yet. I knew she was accompanying Lucia to her doctor's appointment this morning. If I left for home now, I could be waiting for her as soon as she got back. Fuck the dead end leads I kept chasing, I was going take her to bed for the rest of the day and show her how much I needed her.

I was walking to my car when I felt a hand on my shoulder. 'Alejandro,' I heard Jax's familiar voice in my ear. 'Something's happened.'

I spun on my heel. 'Whatever it is, it can wait,' I frowned.

He shook his head and I knew instinctively that he was about to blow my world apart.

'Alana and Lucia have been taken,' he said.

I stared at him as my heart threatened to explode out of my chest. 'No.' I shook my head. 'It's a mistake.'

'I'm sorry, amigo. Another SUV plowed into theirs while they were on their way back from the doctor's office. Hank and George are dead. Hugo has been taken to County General. They're not sure if he'll pull through. But the girls were taken alive. Our friends in the LAPD are keeping a lid on it for us for now, but it was a well-planned and orchestrated hit, Alejandro.'

He continued talking but his words were drowned out by blood thundering in my ears. I had felt fear many times in my life but this was nothing like I had ever experienced before. I was paralyzed. My future flashed before my eyes — a future without her.

It was incomprehensible.

I had to get a grip on myself. I had to focus on the only emotion that would get me through this. The only emotion I could control.

My anger.

'Speak to our friends in LAPD again and get me everything on the incident, and I mean everything, Jax. Pull every man off every single job we have and get them on this. I don't care how many people we have to step on to get information, just find out whoever has them.' I swallowed the emotion down and concentrated on the rage inside me.

'I'm already on it, amigo,' he said as he placed a reassuring hand on my shoulder. 'We'll get them back. I promise.'

'We'd better, Jax. Because if we don't, I will burn this city and everyone in it to the ground!'

CHAPTER 40

ALANA

I opened my eyes and tried to swallow but my mouth was completely devoid of any saliva. I blinked in the bright light of the room and looked around me. It looked like we were in a basement of a house. Lucia was sitting across from me. She was unconscious but she was breathing and she was tied to a chair. Instinctively, I pulled my arms and legs and realized I was bound too.

I couldn't see Hugo, or George or Hank and my heart sank in my chest. What had happened to them? Were they still alive? God, what I wouldn't give to see them right now, even Hank's grumpy face would be a welcome sight.

'Good afternoon, sleeping beauty,' I heard a low, raspy voice beside me.

I turned my head to see two large men dressed entirely in black. One of them was sitting on a sofa and the other stood near a small table.

'I've been waiting for you to wake up,' he leered at me as he crossed the room until he was standing right in front of me. He reached out and ran a calloused fingertip down my cheekbone. 'So fucking sweet,' he hissed. 'I'm looking forward to making you scream.' He started to laugh and his accomplice on the sofa joined in.

I felt bile burning the back of my throat, but I swallowed it back down. I remembered what Alejandro had told me. Don't ask questions. Be silent for as long as you can — and listen.

'Remember, you can't play with her yet,' the one on the sofa warned when he'd stopped laughing, and I heard the Spanish accent. See, I'd learned something already. Alejandro would be proud.

Alejandro. Thank God for him and his over-protective streak. He would already know we were gone and would be looking for us. He would find us soon, I was sure of it. That was what I told myself anyhow.

'The boss said we need to keep her intact. For now. Until we have Alejandro exactly where we need him.'

That was three things I'd learned now. These two goons worked for someone else and they wanted to exploit my husband in some way.

The one in front of me cupped my chin with his hand and tilted my head upwards. 'I'm going to have so much fun with you, chica!' he sneered and I couldn't hold back the bile any longer as I vomited all over him.

He cursed in Spanish and the guy on the sofa started laughing again as the one in front of me brought his hand back and slapped me across the face with the back of it.

My head snapped back as I coughed and spluttered, trying to clear my throat of bile.

'Fucking puta!' he snarled and then he turned away from me. 'I'm going upstairs to clean up,' he snapped to his associate.

THE ROOM WAS quiet again when he left. I looked at the man on the sofa. I guessed he was in his late thirties. He had a tattoo of a crucifix on his neck and I winced at the irony. He stared back at me for what felt like an eternity, neither of us flinching.

'Alejandro has taught you well, little puta,' he eventually said with a grin. 'Soon, you will know exactly why you're here, and who took you. But it will make no difference. Because you will still be leaving here in pieces. And me and my buddy upstairs will take great pleasure in breaking you before you do. We will make sure Alejandro knows every single filthy way we're going to violate you.' He started to laugh again. 'Then he will have to live with that for the rest of his life.'

'Alejandro will find you and he will peel your skin from your body while you're still alive, hijo de puta!' I spat at him.

He shook his head. 'Oh, puta, you have no idea,' he continued laughing and I closed my eyes.

Please, Alejandro, hurry.

CHAPTER 41

ALEJANDRO

Twenty-one hours. That was how long it had been since Alana and Lucia had been taken and I was still no closer to finding out who took them. I had watched the CCTV over and over again, looking for clues. Four armed men had rammed into their car, shot all three of my men and pulled the girls out. Both of them had fought like crazy too until they'd been knocked unconscious.

Hugo was still in critical care in the hospital and I prayed that he woke up. Not only because I had already lost two good men in Hank and George, or the fact that he was a good and loyal soldier, but also because he might have some more information on who was responsible. The hit had been meticulously planned and executed. We were most definitely dealing with professionals here. And not only that, someone who knew about Lucia's doctor's appointment.

That meant I could trust no-one.

That security footage had been the hardest thing I'd ever had to watch. Seeing Alana and Lucia being taken and not being able to do a damn thing about it had felt like someone was reaching inside my chest and tearing out my heart. I had to keep my mind constantly occupied because as soon as it wasn't, all I could think about was what they might be going through. The thought that someone had their hands on them made me physically sick.

The only way to manage my anger was to hurt people, and that was exactly what I planned to do until I had some answers.

I walked into the middle of the warehouse where Joey Ortega was being held. I took off my suit jacket and handed it to Jax who stood waiting for me.

'Has this piece of shit told us anything?' I snarled.

'Nothing, at all, amigo. Alana – your father, he still says it was nothing to do with him.'

I picked up the power drill from the table beside me. 'Well, we'll see how much longer he can hold out on me for,' I snarled.

Joey looked up at me. He was naked and tied to a chair. One of his eyes was swollen closed and a trickle of blood ran down the length of his face from his head.

'Please, Alejandro, I have already told you everything. I know nothing about any of this. Please,' he wailed. But, I felt nothing as I listened to him beg for his life. All I could think about was what Alana and Lucia might be suffering through with each second that passed.

'Do you really think I give a single shit about you crying and pissing yourself, cabrón? Someone has taken my fucking wife!' I roared, the sound reverberating around the empty warehouse.

ONE HOUR LATER, I was walking out of the warehouse covered in Joey Ortega's blood. Jax walked quietly beside me.

'Don't look at me like that, amigo,' I warned him.

He held his hands up in surrender.

'I can fucking see the cogs turning in your brain,' I hissed.

'I just haven't seen you like that for a long time, that's all,' he replied.

I hadn't been that man for a long time, that was why. I had

just tortured Joey Ortega to death, and I had taken perverse comfort in hearing his screams filling the air, but I was still no closer to finding Alana and Lucia. I had known Joey knew nothing, but I had kept on anyway.

'I don't know what else to do, Jax? Why haven't the kidnappers made contact yet? It doesn't make sense. There should have been something by now. A ransom demand or something!'

'I know, amigo. It doesn't make sense. So what do we do now? You have worked your way through every enemy we have. You have killed more people in the past twenty-four hours than the Spanish flu.'

I frowned at him. 'They all deserved it,' I snapped. Even if they hadn't taken Alana, they were our enemies for a reason.

'I don't doubt it. But what now?'

'We haven't spoken to all of our enemies,' I reminded him. 'Have someone prepare the jet. We're going to New York.'

Jax nodded and then he slipped off to make a phone call as I climbed into the waiting car.

CHAPTER 42

ALEJANDRO

I waited on the steps of the old brownstone with Jax by my side. I had no idea what I hoped to gain from this meeting, but I knew that I had to explore every possible avenue. We had still received no word from Alana and Lucia's kidnappers and as time ticked away, I knew that the chances of finding them both alive were diminishing.

A few moments later, the door was opened by a woman I assumed to be the housekeeper. 'I'm here to see Foster Carmichael,' I said.

She looked both Jax and me over. 'I'm sorry, he's not in.'

'That's okay. We'll wait,' I said with a smile. 'This is concerning his daughter, Alana.'

At the mention of Alana's name, she hesitated. 'Hold on for a moment,' she said and then she closed the door before returning a moment later.

'Mr Carmichael will see you now,' she said curtly as she allowed us inside.

'Thought he wasn't home?' Jax muttered under his breath.

We were shown into the sitting room where Foster Carmichael was sitting with his wife, Alana's mother, Audrey. I had only met her once before, at our wedding. She had sobbed through the whole thing. Alana had told me afterwards that they were tears of happiness as her mother had had no idea about our original business arrangement, most notably that her father had sold her to me for three million dollars. As far I was aware, she still had no clue.

'Alejandro. Jackson,' Foster said as he looked up at the two of us walking into the room. 'Please have a seat.'

We sat on the sofa and I glared at him, trying to read him and determine if he had any idea of the reason we were there. I had managed to keep Alana and Lucia's kidnapping from the news. It was better to work in secret than have the whole media circus surrounding us. I already had the best of the LAPD's resources at my disposal anyway.

'What brings you here, gentlemen?' Foster asked as he leaned back in his wingback chair, his hands steepled under his chin.

'I came to ask you a question, Carmichael. And if you lie to me...' I didn't need to finish that sentence. He was well aware of what would happen to him if I ever wanted him to disappear.

'And what is that?' he frowned as Audrey shifted in her seat and looked between me and her husband.

'Do you know where Alana is right now?'

He frowned at me in bewilderment. If he wasn't lying then he was a good actor — but I already knew that.

'I don't know the answer to that, Alejandro. Because as you know, she has disowned me and her mother. But I think the more pressing question here, is why don't you know where she is?' he snarled, but there was a clear tremor in his voice.

I stared at him and then at his wife.

'What the hell is going on, Montoya? Where is my daughter?' he shouted.

'I don't know,' I said as I leaned back against the sofa.

Audrey's hand flew to her face and she gasped out loud as

Foster's face turned a strange shade of pale while his cheeks remained red with anger.

'You don't know? Has she had enough of you and just taken off? Or...'

'She has been kidnapped,' I said, trying to keep my voice calm and steady while my heart hammered so hard against my ribcage I wondered how everyone in the room couldn't hear it.

Audrey slumped against her chair, while Foster jumped up out of his. 'What? How do I not know about this? When? Who?' he stammered as he started to pace up and down the room.

'Just over a day ago.'

'A day!' he raged at me. 'Over a whole day and you're only just telling me. Why isn't it all over the news? Why isn't my daughter's face all over the television?'

'Because, in my experience, it is much better to handle these things quietly and discreetly,' I hissed. 'And not turn them into a media circus or an opportunity to draw attention to ourselves.'

'You think I want to use her disappearance to help my career?' he snapped.

'Well, it wouldn't be the worst thing you've ever done, would it, Carmichael?' I reminded him.

He lunged for me, but I was quicker than he was and was off my feet before he could reach me. I grabbed him by the throat, pushing him back into his chair. 'This isn't helping anyone. So, sit down, and think long and hard about anyone you may have upset enough that they would take your daughter.'

'You think it was something to do with Foster?' a small voice from beside me piped up and I realized that Alana's mother was still in the room.

I turned to her. She was impossibly thin. She looked frail and half vacant. It made me wonder who Alana got her fire and her assertiveness from. 'It's a possibility. And I need to explore every avenue we have.'

'I trusted you to look after her,' Foster sniped. 'I can't believe you let her slip away from under your nose.'

'Listen to me, you selfish son of a bitch!' I hissed as I pressed my face close to his. 'I did not *let* her slip away. She was taken from me! And I will kill every single person who has ever even looked at her if I have to, but I need her back with me. And so I need you to fucking think!' I heard my voice crack and it was only then that Carmichael stopped glaring at me.

'I can't think of anyone off the top of my head. No-one who would do that. But I will give you a list of the people I may have... upset... in recent years,' he agreed. 'And you have all of my resources at your disposal.'

'I have resources,' I snapped. 'Send the list to me as soon as you have it. And let me know if you think of anything helpful. Do not go to the press with this, Carmichael. I am warning you.'

'I'll give you another forty-eight hours, Montoya. But after that, I am contacting the FBI.'

I glared at him.

'She is my daughter!'

'She was. Until you fucking sold her to me, you narcissistic prick!' I spat. 'Get me the names.'

He sat back in his chair again, but I had no doubt he would go to the Feds if I didn't find Alana soon. If I didn't find her soon, I doubted I would find her alive. My legs almost buckled beneath me at the thought of never seeing her again. Of never telling her how much I loved her.

I pushed the thoughts out of my head. They served me no purpose right now. 'Come on. We've got a plane to catch,' I said to Jax.

A few moments later, the two of us were in our car being driven to the airport.

'Do you think he will come up with anything useful?' Jax asked.

'No,' I shook my head. 'I don't think it has anything to do with him. But I had to be sure. Had to look that fucker in the eye myself and make sure this was nothing to do with him.'

'I understand, amigo,' he replied.

'Did you believe him, too?'

'Yup,' Jax nodded. 'I don't think he has a clue where Alana and Lucia are either.'

CHAPTER 43

ALANA

I looked across the room at Lucia. She had come around shortly after I had, during what I assumed was the day before. It was hard to keep track of time in this goddamn basement. There was no natural light and we remained bound — all except for when we needed to use the bathroom – which was no more than a bucket in the corner. Lucia had at least been taken from the chair and allowed to sit on an old sofa bed on the other side of the room. She was still shackled to the floor.

She was pale and shaking now.

'Are you okay, sweetheart?' I asked her.

She nodded at me. 'I just feel a little lightheaded.'

'Hey, tattoos,' I said to the man who seemed to be the one in charge out of the two men.

'My name is Rafe,' he replied with a grin and I swallowed. I didn't want to know his name.

'Can you let her get some fresh air? She's six months pregnant.'

'I can see that,' he growled at me. 'Not my problem.'

I sucked in a breath. 'Whatever my husband has done, Rafe, this girl and her baby are entirely innocent.'

'We won't be hurting her or her baby, don't worry,' he snapped.

'She's just a kid, Rafe. Just let her outside for some air. She's hardly going to escape with you two watching her, is she?'

He shook his head. 'Boss says she's to stay down here. But don't worry, we're not allowed to harm a hair on her pretty little head. You, on the other hand...' He licked his lips and my stomach turned. 'You're fair game. Just as soon as we have your husband where we want him.'

I swallowed a rush of bile.

'My husband will cut off your balls,' I snarled.

He scowled at me and stepped toward me with his hand raised, but he was disturbed by the ringing of his cell phone. He pulled it out of his pocket and held it to his ear. I listened to the one-sided conversation.

'Yes, Boss?'

'They're fine. His puta is a mouthy bitch though. I can't wait to teach her a few manners.'

Laughter.

'Well, of course he is. He's a fool.'

'No. He'll never find them. Because he'll never suspect you. Arrogant prick!'

'We can do a few more days, yes.'

'He'll be on his knees. He'll be ready to sell his soul by then.'

More laughter.

'Adiós.'

Rafe turned to me with a grin on his face as he pocketed his cell phone. 'Seems your husband is creating quite the stir looking for you, puta! He is causing World War Three out there. But he isn't even close to finding you or discovering who is double-crossing him.'

So, it was someone who Alejandro trusted behind this? Or Rafe wouldn't have mentioned being double-crossed. Because your enemies didn't stab you in the back — they looked you right in the eye as they twisted the knife.

'He'll find out soon enough and then no-one will be able to protect you, Rafe. And if you know my husband at all, you know that what I'm saying is true.'

I bit back a smile as I saw him wince.

'Fuck you, puta!' he hissed.

CHAPTER 44

ALANA

I had no idea how long we had been in this dark and filthy basement. In that time, goons one and two had started to call each other by name - Enzo and Rafe. I knew instinctively that it was a bad thing they didn't care that we knew their names. They had fed us and kept us hydrated. And apart from having to endure their lewd comments about me, and Enzo's wandering hands, they hadn't followed through on any of their threats yet.

Mercifully, they hadn't laid a finger on Lucia and I was eternally grateful. She had been incredible. So brave and strong. I kept on telling her that Alejandro would find us soon and take us home. Enzo and Rafe laughed every time I said it, or occasionally Enzo slapped me for being so annoying, but it didn't deter me. It was the only hope we had.

Lucia and I were still tied up. I had scoured the room to look for something to use as a weapon or to cut our ties and while there was a knife nearby, the two men never left us alone. And they watched us constantly.

'What time did he say he'd be here?' Enzo said impatiently and I sensed the tension seeping into the room.

'He'll be here soon. Chill,' Rafe replied.

I watched the two of them. They were edgy. Nervous. Their boss must be making an appearance. Maybe I would finally get some answers.

I DON'T KNOW how much longer we waited until the door at the top of the stairs opened, letting natural light flood the basement. I saw the outline of a figure stepping into the shadows.

I heard a familiar voice breaking through the silence. 'I hope my men have been treating you both well.'

My heart felt like it stopped beating in my chest and suddenly it felt as though all of the air was being sucked from the room. Surely my eyes and ears were deceiving me, because this couldn't be true?

'You?' I stammered.

'Yes. Me,' he replied with a wide smile.

'But why? I don't...' I shook my head. This made no sense at all. 'How could you do this?'

'Quite easily actually, *princess*,' he sneered.

CHAPTER 45

ALEJANDRO

I looked up as my office door opened and Jax walked inside. He had a look in his eyes that I hadn't seen for days.

'Please tell me you have some good news for me,' I pleaded.

'Hugo is awake,' he said with a smile.

AN HOUR LATER, I was walking into yet another hospital room. Hugo was sitting up in bed and a nurse was dressing his bandages. She turned to me as though she was about to ask me to leave, and then she must have recognized me. There were few people in this city who didn't know my face or my name.

'I'll just be a few minutes, Mr Montoya,' she said.

I nodded and watched her work, chewing my lip and willing her to hurry the fuck up. After what felt like five hours rather than five minutes, she finally walked out of the room.

'I'm sorry, Boss,' Hugo said before I could speak. 'I...' He shook his head as tears filled his eyes.

'I know you are,' I nodded. 'But can you tell me anything? Anything at all that might help me find them?'

He closed his eyes for a few seconds. 'They came out of nowhere. A huge black SUV. They knew we'd been at that clinic. They didn't follow us. I always check, Boss. They knew we would be turning into that junction on Seventh and they were waiting for us.'

'How many of them?' I snapped.

He frowned as if trying desperately to remember. 'I saw three, I think, but there could have been more. There probably were. But as soon as they hit us, well, I was in and out. I heard three gunshots. And I heard them talking to each other. At least one of them was Spanish.'

I swallowed as my heart hammered in my chest imagining what Alana and Lucia had been through, what they were still going through.

'What did they say? Think, Hugo. Anything is important.'

'I heard snippets mostly. They referred to *the boss*,' and then he looked up at me and opened his mouth as if to speak but for some reason he was hesitating.

'What is it? What else did they say?'

He swallowed. 'One of them said *the boss said do what you want with his puta, but don't touch the girl.*'

I felt like someone had hit me in the solar plexus with a base-ball bat. My knees buckled. All I could see was Alana's beautiful face. Imagine what those animals might be doing to her. Jax put a hand on my shoulder and squeezed, grounding me back to the present.

'We're going to find them, amigo. I promise you,' he growled.

I turned to him and nodded before taking a deep lungful of air. Now was not the time to think about these things. Now wasn't the time for fear or worry. Only my rage and anger were of any use to me right now, and that was all I could focus on, because to think about anything else would have made me completely useless to both her and Lucia.

'If Lucia is important then I want you to redouble your efforts in Chicago, Jax. Find out who the fuck has got my wife!' I snarled.

'I'm on it,' he said and then he walked out of the room.

I turned back to Hugo. 'Get yourself back on your feet as soon as you can. And if you remember anything else, you call me right away.'

He nodded. 'I will, Boss.'

CHAPTER 46

ALEJANDRO

*M*y cell vibrated on the desk in front of me. I saw Jax's name on the screen and put him on speaker. 'Please tell me you have some fucking leads for me, amigo.'

'Maybe. I'm not sure.'

'Go on,' I said as I leaned forward in my chair.

'I still got nothing on who might want Lucia dead. I think we've dealt with that threat effectively, amigo. So that got me thinking, who would want her alive?'

'And?'

'I didn't even know where to start, but I spoke to a few people from her old neighborhood. The ones I'd spoken with when you first had me look into her.'

'Yeah?'

'You remember that hooker I mentioned. Crystal? The one who made me buy her four cheeseburgers and kept me talking in her apartment for three hours?'

'Yes,' I snapped, wishing he would get to the fucking point.

'Well, she was stoned off her ass, and she talked a lot of shit. At least I thought she did. But, something stood out among her ramblings. She mentioned something about Lucia not being a real Ramos. I thought she was referring to her being different to her brothers, but, fuck, amigo, I had no other leads to follow. So, I went back to speak to her just now. It took me a hell of a lot more than four cheeseburgers, but she admitted that Lucia was not Miguel Ramos's kid.'

'How the fuck would she know that?'

'Seemed she was friends with Lucia's mom. That was why Ramos hated the girl so much. He always suspected but it was never proven. He never wanted it to get out that his wife had fucked someone else behind his back. Imagine what that would have done to an ego like his? So, he made his wife's life a misery and punished her daughter for her mother's sins.'

'And you believe this Crystal?'

'I'm not sure why she'd lie about it now. I gave her the money upfront so she had no reason to lie to me. She never told anyone while Ramos was alive because she knew he would kill her. And then Lucia disappeared and she had no-one left to tell. Seemed like she was telling the truth to me anyway, amigo.'

I sat back in my chair. I didn't know who or what to believe any more. Jax stayed silent while the cogs in my brain ticked over as I tried to slot this new piece of the puzzle into place.

'Did Crystal say anything about who Lucia's father was?' I asked.

'Lucia's mom told her he was Spanish. Handsome. And even more powerful than her husband.'

Lucia was born seventeen years ago. In September 2004. It was a summer that my family never spoke of. I swallowed the bile as it rose in my throat.

'Fuck, Jax!' I hissed.

'What?'

'Get your ass on a fucking plane right now because if I'm right, I'm going to need you by my side.'

'The jet is at O'Hare. I'll be back by tonight, amigo.'

'Good. You'd better be ready for a fucking bloodbath, amigo.'

CHAPTER 47

ALANA

My eyelids fluttered open as I felt a warm hand on my throat. My head snapped up and I realized Enzo was standing behind me. I recognized the smell of cigarette smoke on his clothes. He pressed his body against my back until I could feel his erection pressing between my shoulder blades and I flinched. He wrapped his large hand around my neck and tipped my head back so I could see his face.

'I wonder if Alejandro would ever look at you the same way again if he knew about all of the things I'm going to do to you, little puta,' he said, licking his lips.

'I thought you were planning on killing me?' I hissed at him. 'So he'll never have to look at me again in any case, will he?'

He squeezed my throat harder as fury flashed in his eyes. His other hand slid down my body and he squeezed my breast hard. It hurt like hell but I continued to glare at him. I wouldn't give him the satisfaction of seeing that he'd caused me pain.

'You like that, huh? Puta!' he spat as his hand moved lower until it was between my thighs. He grabbed my crotch possessively, pushing his fingers into my folds through the fabric of my jeans. 'I'm going to fuck you raw, little chica. And I'm going to make you enjoy it too. You'll scream my fucking name!'

'I'd rather die!' I snarled.

He scowled at me and then he looked around the room. Rafe was nowhere to be seen. Lucia was asleep. Suddenly, he looked down at me with an evil grin on his face.

He leaned down to my ear. 'If you scream and wake the girl, I'll hurt her too,' he whispered.

I swallowed. What the hell was he going to do? Rafe seemed to be able to keep Enzo in check. Where the hell was he now?

Enzo walked around to the front of my chair. He held my face with one hand, squeezing my cheeks until my mouth opened, as he undid his zipper with the other. I watched in disgust and horror as he pulled his dick out. It was hard and purple and looked as angry as he was.

'Suck it, puta!' he hissed.

I felt tears stinging my eyes. I remembered what Alejandro had told me. Do anything you need to, to survive. But I couldn't do this.

I felt bile burning my throat again and I tried to swallow it down. I glanced at Lucia. She wasn't to be touched. That was what their boss had said. I doubted that Enzo would risk the wrath of his employer.

He edged closer to me, his dick nudging at my lips. 'I said suck it,' he growled. 'Make me come and maybe I'll go a bit easier on you.'

I shook my head but he held me firm with his strong hand.

'Now! Hurry the fuck up, puta,' he hissed.

I suspected that Rafe or his boss would be back soon and he didn't want to be caught forcing me to suck his dick. He squeezed harder, causing my mouth to open wider.

'Good girl. Take it all,' he crooned as he pushed the tip into my mouth. I balked at the invasion, and the taste of him. All that did was make him laugh.

Bastard!

I bit down hard until I tasted blood and Enzo let out a blood-curdling scream. Lucia woke with a start and I watched as Enzo stumbled backwards, his hands clutching his dick, which was trickling with blood.

'You put that thing near me again and I'll bite it clean off,' I snarled.

The noise must have alerted Rafe because he came bursting through the door and running down the stairs.

'What the fuck is going on?' he shouted.

'She bit me,' Enzo howled as he kept hold of his junk with two hands.

'You were told not to touch her yet,' Rafe warned him and then he walked over to me, his face full of anger. Raising his fist, he brought it down against my temple.

I felt a searing pain. Heard ringing in my ears. And then everything went black.

CHAPTER 48

ALEJANDRO

I walked into my father's hospital room. He was sitting up in bed and looked much better than when I'd seen him three days earlier. There was color in his cheeks now and he wasn't attached to so many machines. The doctors had said he may be able to go home in a few days.

My mother sat beside him in the large wingback chair. She was holding onto his hand and smiling at him. I wished that the scene could bring me some comfort. A few days earlier, to see the two of them like this and my father almost back to full health, was what I had wanted most in the world, but I could take no comfort in anything while Alana was still missing.

'Alejandro?' they both said in unison as they looked up and saw me.

'Hola, Mama. Papa,' I nodded.

'What is wrong, hijo? Have you found Alana and the girl?' my father asked, his face suddenly full of concern.

'No. Not yet. But I'm close,' I said as I stared at him.

My mom was well accustomed to the lives my father and I led, and she could read a room like nobody else I knew — except maybe for Alana. The sudden thought of her made my heart constrict in my chest, as though someone had thrust their hand inside and was squeezing it with their fist.

'I'll leave you two alone for a while,' she said as she stood. 'I'll fetch us all some fresh coffee.'

She walked toward me and wrapped her arms around my neck. 'She will be home with you soon, hijo. I feel it,' she said softly.

'Gracias, Mama,' I said as I gave her a soft kiss on the cheek.

I waited for her to leave and then I sat on the seat she had just vacated. It was still warm and I wondered how long she had been sitting there and felt a pang of guilt. 'I'm sorry I haven't visited much, Papa.'

He shook his head and frowned. 'You have more pressing matters to attend to. I don't expect you here visiting an old man when you should be out there finding your wife.'

I sucked in a deep lungful of air.

'What is it, hijo?' my father asked.

Fuck! What I was about to tell him was unthinkable, but I had gone over and over the information in my head dozens of times and it was the only explanation that made sense. Perhaps my desperation to find Alana and Lucia had clouded my judgment? But I had nothing else.

'I think I know who ordered the hit on you, Papa. And I think he is responsible for taking Alana and Lucia too.'

He frowned at me as he sat up straighter in his bed, shuffling his body and wincing at the effort and the obvious pain in his chest. I realized in that moment that he would never be the man he once was ever again.

'Who?' he demanded, snapping me from my thoughts.

TEN MINUTES LATER, I had told my father all I knew about Lucia and Chicago, and all I had learned and pieced together in the last twenty-four hours since I had spoken with Hugo.

He stared at me, with tears in his eyes and a look of shock and horror on his face. But there was something else there too. He believed me.

I leaned forward, placing my hands on his bed and resting my forehead on them. I felt his rough hand on the back of my head as he stroked my hair.

'I wish this wasn't true, mi hijo, but I fear that it is. You are a smart boy, Alejandro,' he said with a sigh. 'This is why I chose you to take over instead of one of your uncles. You know what must be done.'

I looked up at him and for the first time in my life I saw my father crying. 'I do, Papa.'

CHAPTER 49

ALEJANDRO

I looked out of the window as the car sped along the highway. Jax sat next to me in the back seat while Jacob was our driver for the evening. My stomach churned as I thought about what we were about to do. It was unthinkable, but every instinct in my body told me I was right.

I felt Jax shifting in his seat beside me. He had looked at me like I'd grown an extra head when I'd told him my suspicions. He'd told me I was loco, especially when I'd told him that it was just me and him who were going to end this. I didn't trust anyone else with the information. I couldn't afford for anyone else to know; it could cost Alana her life if I did. And possibly Lucia too.

I trusted Jacob; he had been my driver since I was a little kid, but he was little more than a chauffeur these days. He hadn't been in the thick of the action for over a decade. Besides, I needed him outside for Alana and Lucia, ready to drive them to safety in case Jax and I didn't make it.

'I appreciate you doing this with me,' I said to Jax.

He turned to me and grinned. 'Where else would I be but by your side, amigo? Until the end. Remember?' He held out his fist and I touched it with mine.

'Until the end.'

HALF AN HOUR LATER, the car rolled to a stop a few hundred yards from the house where I prayed Alana and Lucia were being held. Jacob had switched off the headlights a quarter of a mile up the road so they wouldn't see us coming.

Jax and I slipped out of the car, sticking close to the tree line for cover as we made our way toward the building. 'Remember the plan?' I whispered.

He nodded. 'Kill anyone who moves who isn't a Montoya,' he said with a flash of his eyebrows as he took one of his guns from his holster and connected the silencer to the end.

I looked toward the house. There were two men patrolling the perimeter. Jogging closer to them, we each took one out with a clean shot to the neck.

I indicated my head to the back of the house and Jax nodded his understanding as he edged past me. If I was going into this house, then I'd walk in like I always did. Through the front door.

Walking to the front porch, I looked inside and couldn't see anyone. I took a breath to calm my racing heart. Maybe I was wrong about this? But, if I was, then where the hell were Alana and Lucia?

I pulled open the screen door and as I knew it would, it creaked, alerting the guard who was in the hallway to my presence. He ran to the door, but he didn't even have a chance to draw his weapon before I shot him between the eyes. I looked down at his body. He had worked for my family for twenty years.

Traitor.

I walked further into the house, the floor creaking softly under my feet. Another man walked out of the kitchen. He looked up at me and blinked as I shot him in the face.

I heard the sound of two more muffled gunshots near the back of the house before Jax walked into the hallway to meet me.

He simply nodded at me and I pointed toward the basement.
Something about this felt far too easy.

CHAPTER 50

ALANA

I heard the noise above us, like the sound of something heavy being dropped to the floor and I looked across at Lucia. Her eyes met mine and we shared a look of half fear and half hope. This was either someone coming to rescue us, or someone finally coming to kill us all.

I prayed to God that it was Alejandro.

Alejandro's Uncle Carlos heard it too because he walked over to me and pushed his face against mine. He started to laugh maniacally and I wondered if he had finally become completely unhinged.

'Here's your hero, puta!' he spat in my face. 'Let's see just how much he's willing to sacrifice for his little whore!'

Carlos had brought two more of his men into the basement with us a few hours earlier, no doubt sensing that Alejandro was getting closer to finding out who had betrayed him. The four other men in the room stood in the shadows, with their guns trained on the door. I wanted to scream to whoever was about to come through it that they were walking into a trap but Rafe had stuffed a rag in my mouth earlier and it muffled the sound.

Carlos walked behind me, pressing the blade of his knife

against my throat. The blade was cold and I felt the biting scratch against my skin. My heartbeat thrummed against it, aware that a simple slip would have me spilling my lifeblood all over the floor.

Lucia let out a muffled scream and Carlos laughed again.

A few seconds later, the door to the basement opened.

'I know you're down there, Uncle,' Alejandro called and my heart almost burst out of my chest at the sound of his voice. Dear God, please let him and Lucia get out of this. But please just let me tell him how much I love him first. I screamed again into the rag in my mouth and Carlos pressed the blade closer against my skin until I felt the sting of the steel and a trickle of blood running down my neck.

'Alana!' he called then. 'I'm here, princess. I'm going to take you home.'

Then he stepped out of the shadows as he walked down the basement steps. I almost passed out at the sight of him through fear and panic and hope that there was a chance he could save us from his lunatic uncle.

Enzo, Rafe and the two newer men stood behind me, their guns raised and trained on my husband. My heart hammered so hard in my ears I could barely hear anything else.

'You came alone, Alejandro?' Carlos asked in surprise.

'Not quite,' Jax said from behind him as he stepped out of the shadows, too.

'Ah, of course. Your loyal little puppy dog,' he snarled.

'I wanted to keep this between family, Uncle. That's what we all are, aren't we? Why don't you send these men out and we can talk? Just me, you and the girls? Just family?'

'You found out my little secret then?' Carlos snickered behind me.

I blinked in shock. What secret?

'Sure did. But what I can't figure out is what the hell any of this has to do with my fucking wife?' Alejandro snarled, unable to keep a lid on his anger any longer.

Carlos reached down, pushing his hand beneath the collar of my t-shirt and squeezing my breast painfully, making me wince.

Alejandro took a step closer. 'Take your fucking hands off her!' he barked.

The four men with guns edged further into the room. 'Careful, or they'll take you out before you take another step, Nephew,' Carlos hissed as he righted himself again, keeping the blade at my throat.

Alejandro held up his hands in surrender. 'Okay. I'm all yours. But please, Uncle, let my wife go. Let your daughter go,' he said as he looked across at Lucia.

Lucia blinked at me, her eyes wide in shock and I almost choked on the rag in my mouth. His daughter? What? Lucia was Carlos's daughter?

'Why would I do that, when they are the key to your downfall, Alejandro?'

I saw the expression on Alejandro's face change to one of pain and anguish. 'Why do you want my downfall, Uncle?' he asked.

'Why?' Carlos half laughed, half snarled. 'Thirty years I have worked for your father. Doing his bidding. Cleaning up his messes. Waiting for my time,' he hissed. 'Waiting for it to finally be about me. Even when I did find happiness, I had to let it go. I had to leave the woman I loved with that monster because I didn't have the time to have a family. Always being the good worker bee. Always doing what your father asked of me. Even when she had my child, I couldn't go to her.'

Alejandro took a step closer. 'My father would never have stopped you having a family. He would have wanted that for you. Uncle Phillipe has Rachel and the girls. Why would he stop you from having that too?'

I felt Carlos's grip loosen slightly. 'It was different with me. He was different with me. Always watching me. Always wondering if I was going to have another breakdown. Did he ever tell you that I killed his dog?' he scoffed.

'No,' Alejandro frowned.

'I was eight. It was an accident. I only wanted to see if the dog was tough like us. We couldn't get the blood out of the carpet. Mama had to throw it away and Papa was so mad. None of them ever looked at me the same way again! Especially Mateo. He thought I was broken.'

Alejandro continued to edge closer while his uncle raged.

'And now, after all these years, after I gave up everything, he just hands it all over to you, and I am supposed to accept that? And not only do you have everything I've worked for, you want my daughter too? You are a greedy, selfish hijo de puta!' he snarled. 'Did you know that it was my idea to start this business in the first place?'

'No,' Alejandro shook his head.

'It was. I was the one who was always prepared to do whatever it took. Did you know that I once killed a woman because she wouldn't let me fuck her?' he snarled as his grip tightened again and the blade dug in further. 'I fucked her anyway and then I slit her throat. Your father got pretty mad about that too!'

'No, I didn't know that,' Alejandro said softly as he looked at me for the briefest moment. He gave a subtle nod of his head as though to tell me this was all going to be okay.

'Did you think that you could walk in here and just take her back?' Carlos snarled. 'Although I'm not sure you'd want her now. She screamed for more when my men fucked her like the puta that she is!'

I winced at Carlos's lie, and watched as Alejandro's fists clenched at his sides. Then he looked up at his uncle; his body vibrated with anger but his face remained calm. 'Did you know that Jax is ambidextrous?' he asked calmly.

'What?' Carlos snapped.

'Ambidextrous,' he repeated as bullets whizzed past my ears. 'As skilled with his right hand as he is his left.'

In a matter of seconds the four armed men were on the floor with blood pooling from their heads.

'You know he's from Dallas, right?' Alejandro said.

'Quickest draw in the West,' Jax smiled as he walked down the stairs of the basement. With everyone's attention on Alejandro, nobody had noticed Jax slipping back into the shadows and drawing his weapons.

Alejandro looked between the knife at my throat and his uncle. 'Please let her go, Carlos. You can have everything. I don't want any of it without her.'

'Fuck you, hijo de puta!' he snarled. 'I would die before I give her back to you.'

Alejandro took a deep breath before he spoke. 'Ahora.' *Now.*

I heard another whizz of a gunshot as Alejandro lunged forward, grabbing the blade of the knife before it sliced through my throat as Carlos dropped to the floor.

'Jax, get Lucia,' he shouted and Jax started jogging down the stairs and over to Lucia.

Alejandro dropped to his knees in front of me. He pulled the rag from my mouth with his bleeding hand and I gasped for air. Then he worked quickly, cutting the ties at my ankles before moving behind me and cutting my wrists free. My arms burned with the pain of a thousand needles as I pulled them toward my body. Then he was on his knees before me again. Brushing my hair from my face as the blood from the wound on his hand dripped down his arm.

'Alana. Princess. I'm so sorry.'

I wrapped my arms around his neck, clinging to him as though I would never let him go as I sobbed against his shirt. He ran his hands over my hair and pressed his mouth to my ear. 'I love you so much,' he breathed. 'I need you to know that I have never regretted marrying you. Not even for a single breath. I would give up everything I have ever known if it meant not losing you.'

My heart swelled in my chest and my sobs grew even more persistent. Then he was standing, lifting me into his arms. 'I've got you, princess. You're safe now,' he soothed in my ear.

We both looked over at Lucia. She was in Jax's arms and had her head buried against his chest. 'You okay, kid?' Alejandro asked.

She looked up at him. 'Yes,' she sniffed as tears rolled down her face.

'Come on. Let's get home,' he said as he started to walk toward the stairs.

I nestled my head against his neck, breathing in his incredible scent and feeling the relief at being close to him again settling over me like a warm blanket. I already was home.

CHAPTER 51

ALEJANDRO

y blood thundered around my body as I walked out of my uncle's house with Alana in my arms. Adrenaline was still coursing through me and it would continue to do so until we were safely in Jacob's car. I glanced behind me to see Jax carrying Lucia into safety. She looked unharmed and I felt a rush of relief. That kid had already been through enough in her young life.

Alana, on the other hand, was covered in blood and had cuts and bruising to her face and body. I'd given her a cursory check over and they all appeared to be superficial, but I'd have a doctor check her out as soon as we got home.

It was the psychological scars that would take the longest to heal though. I knew that. I felt bile rise in my throat as I recalled what Carlos had said about his men violating her. I wished that I had been able to make them pay the way they deserved to, but there hadn't been time. I planted a kiss on her head and made a silent promise that I would never let anyone touch her ever again.

Jacob was pulling the car up when another car approached from the distance. I looked across at Jax. I held onto Alana awkwardly with one hand for a moment while I took my gun from its holster. As the car approached, I recognized it as my Uncle Phillipe's. He was either here to help, or to kill me.

Phillipe jumped out of his car. 'Alejandro!' he shouted to me.

'How did you know we were here?' I snapped.

He held his hands up in a gesture of surrender. 'Your father told me. I came to help.'

'Well, everything is taken care of.'

'Everything?' he asked solemnly.

I nodded. 'What needed to be done, is done.'

He nodded but tears filled his eyes. 'Maybe now he will find some peace.'

'I hope so,' I said.

'I'm happy to see you all safe,' Phillipe said as he started to walk back to his car. 'I'll send someone to clean up inside and I'll meet with you tomorrow.'

'Tomorrow,' I agreed.

Then Jacob was opening the car doors. Jax placed Lucia in the back seat and slid in beside her. I climbed in through the other door, holding Alana close to me. 'Do I not get my own seat again?' she said with a faint smile.

'No,' I said as I wrapped an arm around her waist. 'I'm not letting you go, princess.'

'Here you go, Boss. For your hand,' Jacob said as he slid into the driver's seat and tossed me a bandage.

'Allow me,' Alana said as she lifted my hand and gently dressed it with the bandage.

'You still okay, kid?' I nudged Lucia beside me, who hadn't said a word since we'd left the house.

'Um, yeah. I suppose,' she said as she rubbed a hand over her belly.

'And your little guy?'

'I think so. He's wriggling around now,' she murmured.

'As soon as we're home, I'll have a doctor check you and the baby over.'

'Home?' she mumbled with a faint smile.

Alana finished wrapping my bandage and then she leaned back against my chest, wrapping her arms around my neck. I kept one arm around her waist and I reached for Lucia's hand with my bandaged one. Her fingers curled around mine and I saw a faint smile on her lips.

'Yeah, home.' I said with a sigh as I leaned back against the seat and closed my eyes.

CHAPTER 52

ALANA

I lay back against the pillows and let out a long, slow breath. The balcony doors were open and a beautiful breeze was dancing over my skin. The doctor had been waiting for us when we got home. He checked both Lucia and the baby over first. Luckily they were both fine — physically at least. I, on the other hand, had a concussion, a broken rib and two fractured fingers which were currently strapped up, as well as plenty of superficial cuts and bruises.

Alejandro had watched me like a hawk from the moment we'd got back into the house and I wondered if he was waiting for me to have some kind of breakdown.

I wasn't going to, though. At least not that I was aware of. I felt deliriously happy to be home. I had been heartbroken that Hank and George had been killed. George had been new, and I hadn't known him that well, and although Hank had been a grumpy ass at times, he had been in my life for seven months and he had always protected me. The fact that it had ultimately cost both men their lives had been difficult to think about, but I had to remind myself that it was Carlos and his men who had killed them.

I had been so relieved to find out that Hugo was alive and recovering in hospital. Alejandro had promised we could visit him as soon as I was back on my feet. So, despite the heartache of the past few days and weeks, my overriding emotion was still happiness that we were all safe.

I was strong. I knew that already but I had proven it in that basement. Whatever the coming days and weeks might bring, I knew that I would cope with it — especially with Alejandro by my side.

He had insisted I stay in bed while he settled Lucia in her room. He had posted a bodyguard outside her door. I guessed it would make him feel better just as much as it might make her feel a little safer.

He walked into the room and I smiled at him. He'd needed fourteen stitches in his hand from where he'd grabbed the knife from Carlos. 'You okay, princess?' he asked for the hundredth time in an hour.

'Yes. I'm fantastic. I told you a million times,' I rolled my eyes.

'Oh, Alana, did you just roll your eyes at me?' he said as he started to unbutton his shirt.

'I certainly did,' I giggled. 'And there's not a thing you can do about it.'

'Hmm, is that so? Seeing as you're high on some heavy duty meds right now, I'll let it slide,' he grinned as he pulled off his suit pants before climbing into bed beside me. He lay on his back and I rested my head against his chest as he wrapped one of his huge arms around me.

'I'm sorry, princess,' he said as he ran his hand up and down my arm, sending goosebumps skittering over my skin.

'I know you are. But you're not responsible for your uncle's craziness, Alex.'

'But still...' he sucked in a breath. 'I'm sorry that I didn't find you sooner.'

I lifted my head, wincing slightly at the pain, and looked into his eyes. 'What your uncle said about his men, that wasn't true. He only said that to hurt you,' I said softly.

'Alana! You don't have to spare my feelings, princess,' he frowned at me.

'I'm not. If I had been raped by those men, do you honestly think I would lie to protect your feelings? They didn't touch me. Well, one tried. I suppose...'

'What did he do to you?' Alejandro scowled.

'He tried to make me suck his... thing. But I bit him. I think that's how I got my concussion when the other one hit me because of it.'

'You bit him?'

'Yes. Like it was a corn dog. I went for it. He screamed like a baby.'

I felt his chest moving rhythmically beneath me and I realized he was laughing. I giggled too. I suppose it was strange to be laughing after everything we'd been through, but maybe because of that, it felt right too.

'That's my chica,' he said as he leaned down and kissed me softly. 'Are you sure you're okay?'

'Yes,' I sighed against his chest. 'I knew you would come for me, Alex. That was how we got through it, Lucia and me. We knew you'd come for us. That was why they gagged us, because we kept telling them so.'

'I would have burned the whole world to the ground to find you, princess,' he growled.

'I know. And even in that horrible basement, I didn't regret for a single second marrying you. I need you to know that.'

He placed his hand under my chin and tilted my head up to look into his eyes. 'I do.'

'You rescued me, Alex, in more ways than you can even imagine.'

'No, princesa,' he said, his voice a low rumble. 'It's you who has rescued me. I think that my father has been wrong all along.

Love isn't a weakness. You are my greatest strength, Alana. I can do anything when I have you by my side.'

I smiled as I snuggled my head against his chest. 'Te quiero, Alex.'

'Te quiero, Alana.'

CHAPTER 53

ALANA

I woke with the sun streaming through the open balcony doors. I stretched my arms and winced at the pain in my shoulders and ribs.

'Morning, princess.' I heard the soft, low rumble of Alejandro's voice beside me and despite the pain I was in, I felt a rush of heat between my thighs.

I groaned as I rolled over to find him sitting up in bed, fully dressed and with his laptop resting on his legs.

'Morning. What time is it?'

'Half past eleven.'

'What? I've slept for over twelve hours straight. I need to get up.' I tried to sit up but winced in pain.

He put his computer on the bed beside him. 'The doc gave you some strong pain meds. They'll make you drowsy. And no, you do not need to get up. You need to stay in bed and rest, just like the doctor told you to,' he ordered as he reached over to the nightstand before handing me a glass of water and three pills.

'What are these?' I asked.

'For the pain,' he said as he dropped them into my hand.

I swallowed the pills with a long gulp of water and handed the glass back to him. I lay back against the pillows with a sigh. Even if I wanted to argue with him about getting out of bed, I didn't have the energy.

'You look so hot when you're being bossy,' I smiled up at him.

'Stop it!' he warned.

'What? The doctor never said no sex, did he? I'm sure we could find a way to work around my injuries.'

'Don't tempt me, princess. Do you know how hard it's been lying next to you all night and not being able to touch you the way I want to?' he growled.

'Well, yes, I felt it pressing against my ass in the night and it was *very* hard,' I said and then started to giggle before the effort hurt my ribs. 'Ooow,' I winced.

He leaned down, brushing my hair back from my face, and kissed me softly before pulling back. 'Rest for a few days, princess. Because you are going to need it. As soon as you're fully healed, I am going to fuck you harder and longer than we have ever fucked before. You won't even be able to tell me what your own name is by the time I'm done with you,' he growled against my ear and I felt a rush of wet heat.

'Your filthy talk really isn't helping matters here,' I grinned at him.

'Are your panties wet?'

'Soaking,' I nodded.

'Fuck!' he hissed as he palmed his cock through his sweatpants.

We were disturbed by a soft knocking at the door and Alejandro jumped up. 'That will be Lucia. She's been checking in every fifteen minutes since she woke up over an hour ago.'

I nodded. 'She must have so many questions.'

'Come in,' Alejandro said and a few seconds later, Lucia's head popped through the doorway.

'You're awake?' she said softly.

'Yes,' I said as I shifted myself up into a seated position. 'Come in, sweetheart.'

She smiled at me and walked across the room before sitting on the bed beside me where Alejandro had been just a moment earlier. So much had happened the night before. So much had been said that neither Lucia nor I had understood. We both had so many questions. But last night had been about getting home, getting checked out by the doctor, and processing the shock of being free from that terrible basement.

Alejandro pulled up the chair from the dresser and placed it beside the bed before sitting down.

'I suppose you have a lot of questions, Lucia?' he asked.

She nodded. 'You said… You said Carlos was my father?' She almost choked on the words.

He nodded. 'Did you have any idea at all that Miguel Ramos might not be your real father?'

She shook her head. 'No. None at all. I mean, I always felt different to them, but I thought that was just because I was a girl, and you know, not a psycho like him and my brothers. But he was my father. He would have told me if he wasn't — wouldn't he?'

Alejandro rubbed a hand across his jaw. 'I don't think so. He wouldn't have lost face. I know that my Uncle Carlos and your mother had an affair. It lasted almost a year and it ended a few months before you were born. It seems that your mother chose Miguel and my uncle didn't take it well. He was always a liability, but after your mother ended things, he completely lost it. He ended up in a mental health facility for over a year.'

'And you really think he was my father?' she asked.

'Yes. And he certainly believed so too. And your mother. At least according to her old friend, Crystal.'

Lucia smiled faintly at the mention of Crystal's name. 'She was always good to me,' she said softly. 'Until the drugs really took hold of her anyway.'

'So is that why Carlos took us?' I asked. 'Because he thought Lucia was his daughter?'

Alejandro cleared his throat. 'No. It was slightly more complicated than that. He knew that my father was getting ready to hand everything over and he wanted to expedite that process, so he tried to kill him. He also resented the fact that it would be me taking over the family business, rather than him.'

I opened my mouth in shock. 'He had your father shot? His own brother?'

Alejandro nodded. 'He wanted to destroy our family. He wanted to ruin me so that he could legitimately take my father's place. He knew that I would burn this city to the ground to find you. He counted on me getting myself killed, or just being so lost without you that I'd self-destruct.'

I nodded my head while Lucia sat beside me in stunned silence. It was all so much to take in.

'Perhaps he would have eventually used your freedom as a bargaining chip? Who knows what was going through his mind. He was loco. But, he knew that the easiest way to get to me was through you, princess. Then when Lucia came into our lives, that just added more fuel to his jealousy. I honestly think he would have never harmed you, Lucia. I think he wanted to try and be a father, at least in the only way he knew how,' Alejandro finished.

'So that was why they treated me okay?' Lucia asked. 'Well, compared to Alana, anyway?'

'Yes, it would seem so,' he nodded, looking at me and frowning slightly, as though he was thinking about what I'd endured at his uncle's hands.

'Do you think it was him who killed Blake?' she asked.

'Probably. My uncle was the kind of man who could make things like that happen, and it would fit with my theory of him wanting to step into the role as your father and protect you.'

'So, I'm not a Ramos after all, then?' Lucia asked.

Alejandro shook his head. 'No. A Montoya through and through,' he smiled at her.

She smiled back.

'What are your plans now, Lucia?' I asked her, wanting to focus on something positive. 'Now that Blake is gone, and you're not running from anyone. What are your dreams, sweetheart?'

'I guess I still need to apply for emancipation,' she shrugged.

'Unless you're happy to stay with us until you're eighteen?' Alejandro suggested. 'It's only one more year.'

'What?' She sat up straighter. 'Really? You'd both be okay with that?'

'Of course,' I replied.

'You're family now, kid,' Alejandro added.

'What about your future, though? What would you see yourself doing in an ideal world?' I asked.

Lucia leaned back against the pillows, her hand resting on her bump, and sighed. 'I always wanted to go to college. I'd have to work my ass off and get a scholarship, but my grades are good even despite the school I've missed. I figured I could put the little man here in day-care, and then I could pick up some shifts at the shelter and he could come with me.'

I lifted my arm, wincing at the pain, and wrapped it around her. 'Sounds perfect,' I said as I felt a wave of tiredness washing over me.

'Mind if I stay in here with you guys for a while?' Lucia asked softly as my eyelids fluttered. Suddenly, they felt very heavy.

'Sure. I've got some calls to make. I'll sit on the balcony. Why don't you watch the TV? Looks like Sleeping Beauty here is about to fall asleep again,' Alejandro chuckled.

I opened one eye sleepily. 'Hey, I heard that.'

He leaned down and kissed my forehead. 'Get some rest, princess,' he said softly.

I nodded feebly. I heard the muffled sound of the TV in the

background, and felt Lucia's warm body curled up next to mine as I drifted off to sleep.

I WOKE WITH A START, my heart thumping in my chest. It was dark and it took me a few seconds to realize that I was at home and not in Carlos's basement. My back was pressed against Alejandro's hard chest and I heard him breathing softly behind me.

I'd spent most of the day drifting in and out of sleep. I'd woken a few times, taken some pain meds and eaten a little food, but I'd barely been able to keep my eyes open. I'd never felt so exhausted in my life. Alejandro said it was a result of the pain meds the doctor had given me and also my body's reaction to the last few days. I supposed I had hardly slept in that basement. It wasn't easy to sleep when you were tied to a chair and in fear for your life, and I had been too worried about what might happen to Lucia to stay asleep for too long.

Now though, I felt fully rested. The heat from Alejandro's body made me feel safe and secure, but it was stirring something else in me too. I missed the feel of his hands and his mouth on me. I rolled over, shifting onto my back, wincing at the pain in my ribs and shoulders.

Alejandro stirred. 'Are you okay, princess?' he murmured.

'Yes,' I replied. 'Except for...'

'Except for what?'

'I want you,' I breathed.

He groaned out loud. 'You're killing me here, princess. I want you too, but I'm not fucking you while you've got a fractured rib. Now, go back to sleep before you make me even harder than I already am.'

'You don't have to fuck me,' I whispered. 'But you could do other things, couldn't you? And one of my hands is working perfectly.'

He sucked in a breath. 'Stop it. Now.'

'Alex,' I pleaded. 'I need you.'

'Alana!' he groaned.

'Please?'

He sighed, his warm breath dancing across my neck and making me shiver. 'If I make you come, will you promise to tell me to stop if anything starts to hurt?'

'Yes,' I panted.

'And then you'll go back to sleep?'

'Yes. After I've reciprocated, obviously.'

'No reciprocation necessary. I'll be just fine,' he growled. 'Now, if we're going to do this, you'll have to lie still.'

'Okay,' I whispered.

His hand slid over my abdomen until he reached the hem of my tank top, then he pulled it up with his fingertips until he had access to my panties. His fingers slipped beneath the band and he pushed his hand inside the soft cotton, palming my pussy before slipping his fingers through my wet folds and over my clit. I groaned loudly and instinctively took a deep breath.

'Oow,' I winced and silently admonished myself. He was going to stop if I wasn't more careful.

'Relax,' he whispered in my ear. 'I know it's hard but try and steady your breathing. Deep breaths will hurt. I'll take it slow.'

I nodded and focused on taking steady, regular breaths.

'You ready?' he growled.

'Yes.'

His fingers started to circle my clit, softly and slowly, with just the right amount of perfect pressure. He nuzzled my neck as he lazily teased me with his fingers and I felt a wet heat searing between my legs.

'This is fucking torturous, princess,' he growled in my ear. 'I can smell your delicious cream from here and I am fucking desperate to bury my face in your pussy right now.'

'Then do it,' I gasped as I felt another rush of heat at his words.

'You honestly think you'd be able to keep still if I get my mouth on you?' he chuckled. 'You'd be grinding that hot little coño on my face and I wouldn't be able to stop you.'

I closed my eyes as I tried not to move. I wanted to arch my back and press my hips into his fingers and it was a huge effort not to.

He must have sensed my frustration. 'You want my fingers inside you?' he breathed, his hips pressing against me lightly, but enough that I could feel his rock hard erection.

'Yes,' I panted.

He slid through my slick folds until he was at my opening. 'Breathe,' he whispered right before he pushed two fingers inside me.

I groaned out loud again but this time my pleasure far outweighed the pain and I managed not to cry out.

He pumped his fingers slowly as he swept the pad of his thumb over my clit. I heard his own breathing becoming faster as he pressed his groin against me and rubbed his cock gently against my hip.

'Is this okay?' he rasped.

'Yes.'

He continued lazily finger fucking me as he ground himself against me with as little pressure as he could manage.

My orgasm built slowly, starting from the tips of my toes and all the way up to my thighs as they started trembling. I felt the tightening deep in my core and I sucked in a deep breath.

'Easy, princess,' he whispered.

I closed my eyes and concentrated on his fingers rubbing at the sweet spot inside of me. I felt my walls tightening around him, pulling him in further and he groaned in my ear. The feelings of euphoria and energy coursed around my body as his fingers worked me expertly, as though he had known my body for a lifetime.

I was on the edge but I couldn't let myself fall, not unless he said so.

He pressed his face against my neck, his stubble scratching the delicate skin. Our short, shallow panting matched each other breath for breath and our bodies were covered in a thin sheen of perspiration. The effort of hardly moving while we were both so close to the edge was ecstasy and torture at the same time.

'Alana,' he hissed, rocking his hips with slightly more force and I knew that he was close too.

'Come for me, princess,' he growled and I had no choice but to obey him. My orgasm rolled over me in one huge, long, delicious wave. I melted into the mattress, feeling completely spent and entirely boneless. I was half aware of a damp patch at my hip and realized Alejandro had finished too.

'You just made me come in my shorts, princess,' he growled before nipping at my earlobe.

I laughed softly. 'That was incredible, Alex. Thank you.'

'You ready for more sleep now?'

'Hmm,' I said, my eyes already closing.

'I love you so fucking much, Alana,' he said, wrapping an arm around my waist.

'I love you too, you sex god,' I mumbled sleepily.

CHAPTER 54

ALANA

I was sitting reading in the den when Alejandro walked into the room. It had been three weeks since he'd rescued me from Carlos's basement, and my injuries were fully healed.

'Hey, princess. Where is Lucia?'

'Your mom took her shopping. She needs some new maternity clothes.'

'You didn't go with them?' he frowned at me. Usually, I enjoyed a shopping trip as much as the next gal.

'No. I was feeling a bit funny earlier.'

'Are you okay?' he sat beside me and I smiled. His overprotective side had kicked into overdrive since the incident with his uncle.

'I'm fine now. I just felt a little lightheaded and tired.'

He placed his cool hand on my forehead. 'You sure you're okay now?'

'I'm better than okay now,' I said as I slipped my arms around his neck and pulled him to me for a kiss.

He kissed me softly at first, his hands fisting in my hair.

'So, we're alone?' he panted as he broke our kiss.

'Apart from your small army. Yes,' I flashed an eyebrow at him.

'Then why are you still wearing panties, princess?' he growled as he pushed me back against the sofa, slipping his hands beneath my dress and pulling my panties off. He stuffed them into his pocket before he leaned back down against me. 'I want you nice and wet when I bury my cock in your pussy. So, do you want to come on my mouth or my fingers before I fuck you?' he growled.

'Both!' I groaned.

'Greedy, princess,' he chuckled softly as his head disappeared between my thighs.

AFTER ALEJANDRO HAD NAILED me to the sofa, I lay in his arms, listening to the sound of his heartbeat against my ear.

'I want to talk to you about something before Lucia comes back,' he said as he brushed my hair back from my face.

'Oh? What is it?' I asked.

'I made an appointment with a lady from the adoption agency,' he said and my heart felt like it stopped beating in my chest.

CHAPTER 55

ALANA

A few days later, Alejandro and I were sitting in his office at home having just received a call from the adoption agency.

'Are you sure you want to do this?' I breathed as the excitement fluttered in my stomach.

He nodded. 'As long as Lucia agrees, obviously.'

'Of course,' I nodded. 'It looks like you might just get your heir after all.'

He reached for my hand and pulled me up from the chair. 'I told you, I don't need an heir,' he frowned.

'I know,' I whispered.

'Shall we go and speak to her then?'

I took a deep breath. 'Yes. Let's do this.'

Together, we walked through the house to find Lucia eating cereal in the kitchen.

'Hey,' she looked up and smiled at us.

'Hi, sweetheart,' I said. 'Alejandro and I have something we want to talk to you about.'

She swallowed her cereal and blinked at us. 'Okay?'

'We were thinking about what you were saying a couple

weeks ago. About wanting to finish high school and go to college one day. You're such a smart kid, Lucia, and you should be able to do anything you want to with your life,' I said.

She nodded. 'Yeah, but that was just talk. It will be pretty hard to do being a single mom to a kid, won't it?' she said with a shrug.

'We know that. That's why we spoke with a lady from the adoption agency,' Alejandro said. 'We want you to be able to go to college, Lucia, and do all of those things that you've dreamed about. And we want to be the ones who help you to do that. We can have the papers drawn up today if that's what you want, too? But, obviously, you're seventeen years old, and the choice is all yours.'

'You'd pay for me to go to college?' she asked.

'Of course,' I replied.

She blinked at us with tears in her eyes and then she looked down at her bump, rubbing her hands over it lovingly. 'I know that it would probably be for the best.' She choked down a sob. 'I mean, you guys have been amazing to me. You could give this baby a much better life than I could. It's just that... I'm not sure I could just...' She started to sob.

I rushed around the breakfast bar to her and wrapped my arm around her shoulder.

'Jesus!' Alejandro said as he ran his hands through his hair in exasperation. 'We don't want to adopt your baby, Lucia.'

Her head snapped up and she looked between the two of us. 'What?'

'We want to adopt you, sweetheart,' I said with a smile. 'If you'll have us. You can stay here anyway, but this just makes it all a little more formal and legal.'

She started to cry again and Alejandro stared at me with a look of bewilderment on his face. 'You don't have to decide right now,' I said as I kissed her on the top of her head.

'Are you kidding me?' she started to laugh then, wiping her tears on her sleeve. 'You guys seriously want to adopt me?'

'Yes,' we said in unison.

'Then, hell yes. I'm in,' she shrieked as she jumped from her stool and pulled me into a hug. 'Get over here, Daddy A,' she said as she beckoned Alejandro to us.

He walked over and wrapped his arms around the two of us. 'Please don't ever call me that again, Lucia,' he said with a laugh.

'Hmm, I'll think of something more appropriate,' she said with a smile as she buried her head against his chest.

He looked over the top of her head at me and smiled. This wasn't the family we had planned, but it was the one we had, and the one we were thankful for.

EPILOGUE

ALANA

I lay back on the sun lounger and closed my eyes as the heat of the late afternoon sun warmed my face. I smiled as I listened to Alejandro and Matthias splashing in the pool.

Our grandson. That had sounded so strange at first, but he was two years old now and I'd got used to being a nana in my twenties. Lucia had blossomed since she'd become a mom and she was a natural. She adored her son. As soon as she got home from college, she played with him, read to him and made his dinner.

I must have drifted off, because I was woken by a warm hand rubbing over my stomach.

'You ready to come inside, princess?' Alejandro said, his voice as smooth as chocolate.

'Sorry. Did I fall asleep again?' I asked as I opened my eyes and sat up with a groan.

He laughed. 'Yep. I'm going to start calling you Sleeping Beauty.'

I swatted his chest lightly with my hand. 'Don't be so cheeky,' I grinned at him.

'I wouldn't dare, princess. But, seeing as you're tired, how about an early night?'

I laughed at him. 'Your early nights are never about sleep, Alex,' I said, even as I felt a thrill of pleasure shoot through me at the thought. 'I seem to remember you promising me plenty of early nights and rest during our recent vacation.'

'Well, I seem to remember us spending plenty of time in bed, or generally in a horizontal position,' he grinned at me as he continued rubbing his warm hand over my swollen belly. 'And as soon as these babies are born, I'm going to take you all back to our beach house so I can fuck you on the sand every single morning.'

I laughed out loud. We had just spent two glorious weeks at our secluded beach house in complete isolation and privacy, and it had been incredible, but I suspected we wouldn't be getting back there for some time. 'I am pretty sure your mom and dad would have something to say about that. They're almost as excited about these babies as we are. Not to mention Lucia and Matthias. You're going to have to put some of your plans on ice, big guy.'

He flashed his eyebrows at me as he ran his hand down my stomach and slipped it between my thighs. 'Is it my fault that I happen to have an incredibly sexy wife,' he growled.

'An incredibly huge wife,' I reminded him.

He leaned down and kissed me softly. 'You're eight and a half months pregnant with two babies, princess. And you have never looked more beautiful.'

'Now I know you're lying,' I smiled at him.

'Does this look like I'm lying?' He looked down at his swim shorts and the outline of his hard cock could clearly be seen. 'Now, come up to bed so I can make you come before I fuck you senseless.'

'You're a sex maniac,' I grinned at him.

'Me? I've hardly been able to keep up with you and your preg-

271

nancy hormones lately. So stop with your smart mouth, or I'll fill it with my cock!'

I took his outstretched hand and allowed him to pull me up. 'I love it when you're bossy,' I said as I sashayed past him.

He smacked me lightly on the ass and then he came up behind me, slipping his hands over my hips and pressing his mouth to my ear. 'I'm going to fuck you so hard for that, princess.'

I felt his words deep in my core. 'I certainly hope so.'

IF YOU ENJOYED this story and want to find out what happens next for the Montoya family, you can read LA Ruthless book 3 and 4 now:

Fierce Betrayal

Fierce Obsession

ALSO BY SADIE KINCAID

Sadie's latest series, Chicago Ruthless is available now. Following the lives of the notoriously ruthless Moretti siblings - this series will take you on a rollercoaster of emotions. Packed with angst, action and plenty of steam — Order yours today

Dante

Joey

Lorenzo

If you haven't read New York the series yet, you can find them on Amazon and Kindle Unlimited

Ryan Rule

Ryan Redemption

Ryan Retribution

Ryan Reign

Ryan Renewed

New York Ruthless short stories can be found here

A Ryan Reckoning

A Ryan Rewind

A Ryan Restraint

A Ryan Halloween

A Ryan Christmas

A Ryan New Year

If you'd like to read about London's hottest couple. Gabriel and Samantha, then check out Sadie's London Ruthless series on Amazon. FREE in Kindle Unlimited.

Dark Angel

Fallen Angel

Dark/ Fallen Angel Duet

If you enjoy super spicy short stories, Sadie also writes the Bound series feat Mack and Jenna, Books 1, 2, 3 and 4 are available now.

Bound and Tamed

Bound and Shared

Bound and Dominated

Bound and Deceived

ACKNOWLEDGMENTS

I'd love to thank all of the wonderful women who have supported me to write this book — my beta readers, ARC reviewers and the wonderful writing community. With a particular mention to TL Swan, Vicki and the rest of the Cygnets who are an amazing and inspiring group of women.

I also need to give a special mention to Sue and Michelle who have championed my writing from the outset, and Rita, Anna, Kristin and Em for giving their time and feedback.

To my incredible boys who inspire me to be better every single day. And last, but no means least, a huge thank you to my husband, who is my rock and my biggest supporter.

I couldn't do this without you!

ABOUT THE AUTHOR

Sadie Kincaid is a steamy romance author who loves to read and write about hot alpha males and strong, feisty females.

Sadie loves to connect with readers so why not get in touch via social media?

Join Sadie's reader group for the latest news, book recommendations and plenty of fun. Sadie's ladies and Sizzling Alphas

Sign up to Sadie's mailing list for exclusive news about future releases, giveaways and content here